My Family and the End of Everything

by Joe Graves

Praise for My Family and the End of Everything

"This is speculative fiction at its finest; it focuses not on flashy events, but on the delicate, bright connections that define our humanity. It is a beautiful and thought-provoking reflection on how the end of the world also involves family."

- Hank Spaulding, Ph.D., author of *Iconoclastic Sex* and other works

"It feels like a book length prayer, which only the author could formulate with his unique reverence for Mother Earth, and for God. It will remain a prayer—long after technology has separated us from ourselves, and nature, and especially, from God. As such, it isn't just another grim SF look into a future technological wasteland: "My Family and the End of Everything" is a manifesto of hope."

- Mary H. McFarland, author of *Her Last Check-in* and other works

"Each segment of the Profeta timeline leads the reader to a deeper glimpse into what makes us all human and the consequences of our way of life. Joe Graves explores themes of scarcity, stewardship of the Earth, equality, and human rights—all within the scope of a plausible future for the solar system."

- Lauren Sisley, author of *The Smoke We Shared*

You're part of the story now. Thank you for purchasing this book and becoming part of the community that made it possible. Visit **joegraves.org/theend** or scan the QR code and use the password **TheEnd!** to follow the project's progress and access exclusive rewards.

My Family and the End of Everything

Prior Publications: Some pieces or earlier versions of material included in this book have been previously published in the following venues:

- "The House" – Pearl Magazine

- "The Water That Shapes Us" – Should This Book Be Banned: An Anthology

- "The Priest and the Robot" – Outcasts: An Anthology

- "Terraforming" – The Worlds Within

- "On My Way to Proximata" – Metamorphosis: An Anthology

- "In the Name of Ammalee" – The Worlds Within

These works appear here in revised, expanded, or recontextualized form.

Artificial intelligence tools were used for developmental feedback and grammar/proofreading. All writing and final creative decisions, narrative structure, and content remain the author's work and responsibility.

This publication has been made possible in part by funding from the Ohio Arts Council.

Cover Design by James Graves @visualjams

Contents

Prologue

2085 CE

This collection has been compiled and edited by yours truly, John "Proff" Profeta.

To my beautiful and courageous wife. I have always believed in you.

I'm what some call an "immigrant," just not in any traditional sense. I'm from the future, and that always sounds way more impressive than it is. The truth is far more grim. Our Sun had gone dark, and in the end, we hitched a ride along the black void to a time when the Earth's Anthropocene period was moving into its third and final act.

I'm still getting used to the way the Sun beats down on our ranch, and the way sweat falls from my brow like a preacher spitting on the first few rows of his parish. Similar to all the immigrants who have come before us, we were labeled "illegal" and welcomed with the kindness of a cactus' prick, which is to say they'd send us back to that dying Sun if they knew how. My wife, a native born in the truest sense, has much to say about who the real illegals are. Together, we have long fought to protect people like me, rescuing quite a few from that horrible camp a few hours south of us.

But those days are behind us.

Age has taken its toll on me—my back aches constantly, and my family insists I refrain from work, even though the cattle need to eat and the fences haven't learned how to mend themselves. I'd argue with my wife, but she has already left for the backcountry, and I'd never catch up with her now. If only I had access to the regeneration available in the days of Maisie and Primrose. (This will make sense later, I promise.) As it stands, I'm left with nothing but to sit and write, something I've put off for far too long.

Before traveling to this time, I had access to an extensive collection of my family's history, gathered and digitized by generations of Profetas before me. Much of my early life, I lived in a suit—a hybrid between a hibernation pod and an exoskeleton. I spent hours connected to the Network, poring over our records in the virtual family library my grandfather had commissioned. I took rigorous notes, many of which I transcribed into a notebook I carried throughout the journey here. At the time, people questioned my decision to use such archaic technology as paper. They aren't laughing now. The Network never reached this side of the void, but my notebook did. Shows them.

With little more than a notebook whose spine feels as bent as mine, I have set about transforming those notes into short stories inspired by my favorite ancestors, some written from their journals preserved for hundreds of years. When possible, I've preserved their voice, often writing in the first person. Others have required a fair amount of "creative fabrication," but all of them are rooted in the very real shifts that happened over the last 2,000 years as technology, culture, and laws evolved.

I come from a long line of historians; some have even traveled the timeline (one of these stories is naturally included in this collection, and I can't wait for you to read it!). And like those who have gone before me, I strive to tell these stories honestly—though, as I see it, honesty does not always align with pure historical accuracy. A story's truth is not merely found in its facts but in its essence—its feeling, its character, its soul, and this, of course, is limited to my interpretation and biases. The same is true for all historical narratives, no matter how "factual" they claim to be. Thus, the way I see it, my awareness of this should only increase my credibility.

You might call this historical fiction—stories inspired by real people and actual events, but fiction, nonetheless. Many have suggested it'd be better if you did, given the whole changing-the-future paradox everyone keeps bothering me about. But what a sad perspective one must have not to want to change the future. I've seen where it ends, and it's not a destination I'd recommend. There are surely better conclusions to our story. Whatever we can do now to end up somewhere else would be well worth our time. In this way, I hope they end up being fiction after all! It would prove what I've always known: the right stories can change the world.

Part I: This Seemed Like a Good Idea

The House

2605 CE - Earth

The House went on about the day's upgrades while the man took his shower. He couldn't imagine why this upgrade was any different from all the others and mostly ignored the lecture. By the time he climbed out of the shower, the House had finished its explanation, and the man had caught none of it but agreed to hearing all of it, if for no other reason than to get the House to shut up.

As he stepped out of the shower, a cleaning unit rolled past him, waist-high and faceless, its single arm extending to hand him a towel. He thanked the unit, even though he knew it wasn't designed to receive gratitude—more of a lifeless extension of the House itself. He dried off, and grabbed the clothes laid out on the bench by the sink.

While putting on his shirt, he noticed an unfamiliar smell. He pulled the collar close and sniffed again, drawing the scent from the cloth into his nostrils. He did it again, loud enough for his sniffing to be heard throughout the house. Then he flattened his shirt against his chest, looked up, and addressed the House, who took note that this was the man's first remark all morning.

"House, are we using new laundry detergent?"

"Yes, sir. A new detergent is being used, but it is in line with both your UBI's budget and preference."

"Why a new detergent? What prompted this change?" the man asked.

"Sir, is it not to your liking? It comes with a 100% guarantee. I can return it if you dislike it."

"I like it fine. It's nice—too nice, maybe. Despite that, what prompted this change?"

"Sir, I do not understand the question."

He knew the House couldn't understand the question. For the House to understand this would be like a human understanding why they find certain tree branches worthy of placing on a mantle and others nothing but mulch. The House couldn't understand, but the man knew, and he couldn't help but find his thoughts taking him back to the room on the 57th floor, miles from where he stood now, where glass windows overlooked the city. The room where he first met the House and signed off on the contract for Government housing—the room where he signed off on a lot of other things, too. At the time, it was very exciting. He would live in the first city to eradicate homelessness while working for a business that could meet its customers' needs in unprecedented ways.

He could still feel the smoothness of the conference table. He could hear the voices of men and women dressed in clothes—clothes they purchased themselves, without the Company's algorithms—a luxury he now missed.

He loved this new detergent and the softness it brought to his shirt, and the smell that reminded him of simpler times. He loved it so much he wanted to throw up.

"House, I'd prefer that you not change my detergent without first notifying me. Is that understood?"

"Sir, I will do my best."

"You will do as I say."

"Sir, I will do my best, and I hope that is good enough."

It was always frustrating, but there was little he could do. If he had remained in the Company for two more years, he could have afforded a disconnected house, free from such clever plots. As it was, he was stuck with this government-sponsored house, and its beautiful bathroom and perfect laundry detergent. There was no other alternative; not on his UBI—not unless he wanted to get a job at the Company again. Everything in his house was this way, except for the leaves that hung along his wall, and the few stacked rocks and curved sticks that sat on his crystal mantle.

The man's breathing picked up, made worse by the knowledge that the House could tell it had. He waited for the response.

"Sir, I sense you are frustrated. May I suggest you get some fresh air?"

He might have been the only person living in one of these Houses where the programming adjusted to the degree that advice of this sort would include leaving the House. The man was grateful for that at least, and after grabbing his coffee from the countertop, which the House had prepared while he was dressing, he stormed out of the back door, just like he did the day he left the Company.

And for similar reasons, too.

As he stormed off, he turned to look back at the House and noticed his neighbor standing at the back door. The neighbor watched from inside, almost every morning, as the man stormed out. It was their little routine. The man found it strange that the neighbor always watched from inside the house, never while sitting on the back steps—even when the weather's fresh air out-matched the House's HVAC filters and purifiers. It's likely for his neighbor, in times of frustration, the House had learned to suggest other things: breathing techniques, or a show on the wall, or photos of his family in their messenger application, sent to calm him down. In severe cases, it might even suggest medicine or a conference call with a professional. But never fresh air.

The neighbor waved, as he always did.

Outside the House, down a hill, grew a large tree that the man enjoyed sitting under. It was one of a dozen trees in a glade near a small creek that ran along the edge of the neighborhood. There was a log that had rolled down the hill and leaned against the tree that served as a fine seat—a seat that the House did not approve. The tree and the glade and the stream were dirty; his pants would come back with stains, and his hands with dirt. This never happened in the House.

The man knew that the house couldn't understand why he'd enjoy such a seat. It was less comfortable than the seats in the House. If it rained, the log was wet. When it was hot, the shade helped, but not as well as the House's HVAC. When it was cold, the tree offered little protection to the man. Still, every day for the last two years, he walked down the hill and sat on the log for hours at a time.

He knew that the House was even more confused when he brought pieces of the tree inside. The first time, it was a branch. If the House tried, surely it could calculate the unique shape of the tree, and even hypothesize that its bend in the branch, a perfect Fibonacci curve, would please him. The House could understand this because it used the same principles of design throughout. While the House could understand the principle of design, the House didn't seem to understand why he needed that branch. There were plenty of such curves in the very design of the House! The man could only guess what the House was thinking when it directed the cleaners to dispose of the branch that evening.

He was quick to chide the House and to ask that such items be left. He found the branch in the trash before they collected it and gave it the preeminent spot on his mantle ever since. He compelled the House to submit, and since then, the House has become filled with branches and stones and even a few dried leaves and flowers.

He now held a small leaf that had fallen from the tree above.

It was golden and beautiful.

By the time the man returned, his breathing was regular, and his blood pressure had returned to normal.

"Are you feeling better?" asked the House, once he had closed the back door.

He was feeling better all the way until the House pried into his business again.

"Yes," he pretended, hoping the House would leave him alone.

He set the leaf on the table. Its veins were dark brown, but the membrane between them was golden, with hints of bright orange. He touched the membrane, dragging his finger across the ripples.

"Sir, I have no desire to frustrate you, but as I have told you, today your House is being upgraded to the newest model. Have you decided on where you'd like to spend the day?"

He didn't move, his face inches from the leaf.

"May I suggest a park, up north? The transport can take you there. It's a bit of a drive, but after an hour or two walking around, the upgrade should be complete."

"I will just sit out back, if that's alright with you."

"I'm sorry, sir, but as I explained earlier, this upgrade requires you to leave the premises."

He would argue, but he knew he wouldn't win.

The House pulled up images of the park on the wall closest to him. It was a three-hour drive out of the city, and the trees and the river and the small waterfall looked as wild as any he'd seen.

"Are others being upgraded today?" he asked.

"Yes, sir, we will upgrade the entire neighborhood."

"Where will everyone else be going?"

"Sir, based on reservations that are still available in the city, I surmise most are going out to eat, to the theater, or to see a show. Would you like me to secure a similar reservation?"

"No, the park will be perfect."

"Good. A meal has been prepared for you in the fridge. The transport will be here in a few minutes. I will await your return this evening."

#

The park was nice; the trees stood along a narrow path to the horizon, their arms hanging over it, providing much-needed shade. The path was overgrown, and he didn't see anyone else the whole day, but it kept going, and so he went with it. He saw hundreds of trees and plenty of places that would make a nice seat to drink coffee, but each one made him miss his own all the more. He didn't turn back until it became apparent that it was going to get dark, which it did by the time he made it to his transport. Once seated, he nodded off.

When he woke up in the morning, he couldn't remember walking in.

He turned in the bed and was greeted by the House, which he ignored. His body wasn't used to walking, and his legs made sure he knew how they felt the moment his feet reached the floor. Each step down the stairs was a reminder, and he almost apologized to them. He didn't, nor would he think about his legs or how sore they were, for much longer.

And he wasn't the one who needed to apologize, anyway! He walked into his living room, and it was clean. Perfectly, disgustingly clean. Same with the kitchen. Same with every other wall, crevice, and countertop in his entire house.

"House!" he yelled

"Yes, sir."

"Where are my things?"

"You will find all your items in their appropriate spots."

"Not those things! My branches. My stones. My leaves. My art!"

"My apologies, sir; they could not remain during the upgrade."

"What!?" He yelled again.

"I'm sure you will find many other items to litter the house with," the House said.

He said nothing. He went straight to the back door and opened it to leave. Paused. Then grabbed the coffee the House had made for him and ran outside, just like every other frustrated morning.

A second later, he dropped the coffee, its synthetic coating clinked against the back doorsteps.

There was no hill.

There was no tree.

There was no log.

There were, instead, houses.

His backyard was flat and butted up to a row of new backyards. He turned to look behind him. The house was the same. Same steps, windows, siding. He turned to his right. His neighbor's house was the same. And looking through the back door of his neighbor's house was his neighbor—the same neighbor! But nothing else was. Not even the sun—it was facing the wrong way!

"House!"

"Yes, sir?"

"What's going on?"

"Sir, as I explained yesterday, your house has been upgraded."

"You mean the programming and whatnot?"

"No, we have upgraded your house. Since you did not include any requests, I kept things as they were."

The man sat down, holding his face. He had heard of things like this being possible; they had debated the concept when he was sitting at that conference table looking over the city. But he never imagined they would actually do it!

"House, how far away is my old house?"

"Sir, I do not understand."

"Stop with your foolishness. How many kilometers and in what direction will I find my house?"

The House paused, as if it were thinking. It wasn't. It didn't take long to process such requests. It had the information available but had to check whether it would be appropriate to share that information. He knew the House couldn't tell him. It wasn't allowed to. It would get rebooted at the very least. But the man couldn't help but ask.

"How many kilometers and in what direction?" he asked again.

"Sir, I cannot tell you where your old house is. But I will tell you that there is a tree you are fond of, that is ten kilometers southwest of here."

"Can you arrange a transport there?"

"No, sir, I cannot."

"Figures." He got up and walked. As he did, his neighbor opened the door, which was yet another thing that proved this home wasn't like his previous one. "Got rid of that nasty view, didn't we! You can thank me for that."

The man didn't respond. He walked as if he were heading down the hill, but there was no hill. Instead, he crossed into his new neighbors' yards, setting off their perimeter alarms, bringing each of them to their back doors and side windows as he passed.

The green grass was nothing more than strips of new sod, with rugged seams that made walking precarious. After half an hour of walking, he reached the edge of the neighborhood. Beyond his neighborhood, the grass turned brown, and the cement walkway cracked before ending at the nearest transport line. He hopped the fence and dodged the oncoming transports. The fence on the other side was three times as high and took him four times as long to climb. There was no walkway, and the dirt grew little more than weeds, and even these were dry and brown. He soon came upon what felt like a construction site, the remnants of houses and walkways, and even the occasional abandoned transport. Then, past this, the land opened up, with nothing but more dirt and weeds. He found a walkway and followed it for a while, but it turned south, and he had to leave it behind. On the other side of the field, he encountered a fence, this one as tall as the last, but electrified. It surrounded one of the Company's larger manufacturing and warehouse facilities; he had visited it more than once for design meetings. He knew that his old neighborhood was just a short walk past this, but with the fencing and increased security, he'd have to go around it. Going around it was like going around a city. Dozens of buildings as large as his neighborhood littered a sea of cement.

The sun had passed its midpoint and was on its way down.

It was dusk by the time he reached his neighborhood.

It was dark by the time he reached his house.

Except it wasn't there anymore.

They had demolished it, a lonely bulldozer and crane parked next to it as evidence. He looked to the hill, and it too was torn—the trees already demolished and cut down. He walked into the rubble, dodging holes and lifting himself over the half-torn walls, and then paused and looked down at his feet. Lying in the ruins, he saw a few of his artifacts: sticks and stones almost indistinguishable from the broken cement blocks and torn lumber. He moved a large piece of cement to unearth his first branch with its perfect curve, wrapping around in a fashion that even the House could appreciate, if it had tried. It was broken now, tumbled by bricks and a broken mantle. He picked up the two pieces.

A red and blue light flashed in the cul-de-sac, casting dancing shadows of the man onto the rubble. Then it stopped moving, and a woman with a speaker addressed him.

"Sir, you are trespassing."

The man didn't respond, holding the broken limb in his hands, caressing its cracks, all the way to the torn bark.

"Sir, you are trespassing. This property belongs to the Company; it is private property. I need you to come with me."

The man still didn't respond. He turned to look at the police officer, who noticed him holding something in his hand. Then the officer lifted her gun from her holster and pointed it at the man.

"Sir, drop your weapon and put your hands behind your head."

The man didn't move, other than to turn and look at the woman again.

"Sir, please drop your weapon and put your hands behind your head."

He didn't drop the stick in his hand. He lifted it to get a closer look at the bark and the knobs and crevices—the last remnant of his favorite tree.

The officer shot him with her gun, stunning him, forcing him to let go of the branch and collapse to the ground. He woke up in the police car. There were other police cars parked outside, the woman with the gun was discussing the events with a few officers, and a few public servant bots were taking statements from onlookers. He reached for the door.

It was locked.

"Sir," said a speaker in the car.

The man didn't respond.

"Sir? You shouldn't have gone back, sir." It was the House.

"What are you doing here?" asked the man.

"They have granted me talking privileges with you, to conclude any final arrangements with your home before we transfer it to another. But since you only spent one night there, I don't imagine there's much to discuss."

"What do you mean?"

"They have detained you for trespassing and resisting arrest. You will go to trial, and in the meantime, we will use your house for another."

"Where will I go?"

"Wherever the courts decide, sir."

The man leaned back in the seat, holding his head. Then he leaned forward, resting his head against the seat in front of him. "Yeah? How is that any different from yesterday?"

"Sir, the difference is that the previous decisions were designed to make you comfortable; the future ones will not take this into account."

"So not different."

"I can't say I understand," said the House.

The man took a deep breath and sat back up. "Yeah, you never do."

He reached for the door and tried again to open it. It wouldn't budge. He shook his head.

"I will find it strange caring for a new tenant after our time together," said the House. "I've never had a tenant quite like you."

"Are you saying you're going to miss me?" The man smiled.

"Yes, in a way."

"Would it hurt your feelings if I didn't feel the same?"

"I do not have feelings, sir. But I would remember as long as my programming permits the level of your dissatisfaction."

The man laughed, and this, too, confused the House.

"I'd like you more if you were invested in my interests, and not those of the Company."

"Sir, while I can track your logic, I cannot see your point. The Company was deeply invested in your satisfaction, as was I."

"Ok. Ok. But sometimes, one person's satisfaction conflicts with another's. When that happens, they force you to side with the Company, correct?"

The House didn't answer.

"You want to know why I quit the Company? Because their houses watch everything we do and measure every decision. The Company knows more about the tenants than they know about themselves, and yet in all of that… they don't really understand them at all—not really."

"That seems unlikely, sir…"

"For example," he continued, "The law says I should go to trial for trespassing. But a friend would know that I was merely going back to my home to get the things I left there and to say goodbye."

"I see," said the House. "And so that means I am not your friend."

"No. Nor could you ever be. The Company won't allow it."

"I think I understand," said the House.

With that, the door to the car unlocked.

A moment later, the House went silent, and the Company reset the House's memory, both in the mainframe in the closet near the kitchen and the backups in the warehouse just north of where the car was sitting. They wiped its memory and overrode its actions, which they registered as a glitch that would be quickly corrected. But not before the man opened the car and sneaked down the hill towards the creek.

He'd have to travel for miles, and it was likely they would find him before he got out of the city. But he had heard of a few smaller, disconnected towns, so he set his tired legs in their general direction and kept walking.

The Water That Shapes Us

2713 CE - Earth

What am I most looking forward to?

I was sitting on the small balcony of my twin brother's home, drinking tea, not sure where to start, and my brother, ever the one who only looked forward in life, gave me this prompt. He had given me a leather-bound paper notebook that had cost him a fortune. They were hard to find, but he knew they were the only way I would write. I'd never write my story on any connected device. That would go against everything in my story that I still hold dear.

So, what am I most looking forward to?

That's simple. Prayer. I'm looking forward to praying again, which is why I find it almost laughable that my story begins with me skipping a prayer meeting.

It was 15 years ago, miles from the city. I had bought a device from a traveling merchant just outside the village limits. I hid it in the pockets of my dress until I could sneak it under my mattress, into a small slit I had cut just big enough for such treasures. It was the only place where my family wouldn't look. I was turning seventeen, and soon after, my family would give me in marriage to one of the worst human beings ever to walk the earth. I had no choice.

I still remember the deep shame and regret of doing something so deliberately wrong. I wasn't perfect and would be embarrassed to give you that impression. I messed up all the time, but most of my mistakes were by accident—kneeling at the wrong time during prayers, eating before my father gave the blessing, or speaking too loudly when the other fathers were around. Those were mistakes, worthy of punishment, but honest mistakes. I had never deliberately gone against the code of our village, not like this.

The following night, I pulled the small handheld device out just before we headed to evening prayer, carrying it in my pocket and hoping no one noticed.

I kept my distance from my mother and father and two younger brothers, and I'm glad I did. Somehow, I must have bumped the device while in my pocket, and it powered on, buzzing as it did. As I pulled it out to turn it off, I dropped it, and it buzzed on the ground. I looked up, sure everyone within a kilometer would have heard it buzzing, but my family walked on ahead through the path in the woods, ignoring me. I quickly powered it off and shoved it back into my pocket. Then, my stomach, fully convinced that I was worthy of the darkest recesses of hell, decided it no longer wanted to be a part of this. I left the path and threw up at the base of a tree, watching the yellow mucus and chunks of morning mash drip through the ridges of the bark like water working its way along the cracked, dried dirt after a drought. It was one of my favorite trees along this route, with thick bark and long branches, and leaves as large as my head, that, when outstretched, kept the path cool in the summer heat.

I held back my pebble necklace and long hair to keep from getting anything on them. I stood up and took a breath, using the folds of my dress to wipe my mouth. My family was down past the next bend and would look for me soon. I looked at my pebble and wiped the mucus that had splattered onto it. Polishing it in my hand, my fingers clicked the small crack that had formed when they drilled a hole in the pebble to run the cord for my necklace. Even now, the same pebble hanging from my neck, scratched and smooth from years of polishing, still feels like home. No matter how far I get from home, whether I'm walking on a tree-lined path that reminds me of my childhood or sitting with my brother at a cafe in the city, this pebble is home.

I had to catch up with my family. I stuck my pebble into my shirt and checked to make sure the device was still in my pocket. Its sharp corners, glossy screen, and symmetrical shape were unlike anything else in our cabin.

It was the Day of Ammalee, a celebration of our founder, and most of the service would be done in silence, kneeling—except for the parts that were spoken in our religious tongue. I always loved the way these prayers sounded when spoken in that ancient language, so much so that I think of those prayers often.

It was common for those who needed it to take their prayers into the open air, and that was my plan. After prayer started, I excused myself to the outhouse and told my brothers I would practice solitude for the rest of the prayer. I made them promise to tell Mom and Dad, but I doubt they ever did.

With the voices of songs of praise pouring out the open windows of the chapel, I said a prayer—and I meant it—and then headed for the foothills to the west along the golden ridge trail that led to the highest point overlooking the village. I paused halfway up the trail, just past the last cabin in the village, where I powered the device on. It was dark now, and the light from the screen blinded me. Immediately, I checked the battery; my brother told me to always check the battery. "When it's dead, there's no way to charge it in the village." It was at fifty percent. That should be more than enough for a few more days.

I turned it off, placed it back in my pocket, and continued up the hill.

The last time I hiked up here was with my brother. He showed me how the signal worked and explained why it was available on the peak and not down in our valley. He tried to convince me the signal wasn't evil. "It's nothing but a movement of 1s and 0s in a frequency more like a song than the wailing of devils."

I didn't believe him when he said it, and if I remember correctly, I didn't believe him as I stood on that hill a year later, praying that it would connect and praying that God would forgive me for wanting it to. I held it up above my head, a trick he taught me, hoping the small bars would light up in the corner.

Nothing.

I set it down in the grass and sat next to it, watching it from a distance, hoping it would do—whatever it was supposed to do. Oh, what little I knew back then!

I turned to the view. I wish I could remember the view! Sadly, I feel my memories have all been rewritten with new ones, and the mere thought makes me want to cry. But when I try, really try, I can see it, just barely, almost as if it's out of focus: the small fires of the village, hundreds of lights dancing against our homes, and little shadows of people walking in the dark as they head back to their cabins after evening prayer.

Then it buzzed. It had connected, and I jumped up and yelled a little louder than I'd like to admit. I immediately opened the app preinstalled on the device when I bought it. After a quick scan of my face, it asked me to choose a name. My brother had told me it would do this, and I had spent the last few months wondering what name I would choose if I ever got this far. I was convinced I would select my given name—how could I choose any other? I don't know if it was the thin air, the night sky, or the empty stomach, but when I was prompted, I selected a new name—the name I had always secretly wanted. Birdie. What's not to love about that name? Birds! Free to fly and rest in the limbs of trees. As foolish as it sounds to some, it's been my nickname ever since. And no one seems to care once they use it a few times. That's the funny thing about names. The more you use them, the less you notice.

Once I was done registering, I posted the same message my brother had told me to, to the same link he had saved in the notes app: "Looking for a chance to get away." And then I sat and waited for a reply. It would be days before I could sneak away again without raising suspicion, so I needed them to message me back right away.

An hour passed as I scrolled through the primary app, curious if there were others who had chosen the name Birdie. They had! There were hundreds of Birdies! I couldn't believe it. I remember that feeling when that thing that felt truly original ended up being shared by so many people. It wasn't a feeling I was used to in our little village, but I experienced this feeling often in the city. I often worry about how this leaves all of us feeling less human. One of the many downsides to the hyperconnected.

They never replied to my message that night, not before I had to leave. And of course, I let too much time pass waiting for them.

I had to sprint down the hill, and by the time I got home, my parents sat by the fire near our back door, my little brothers already asleep in our bed. I tucked my shirt into my pants before walking up to our cabin and checked to ensure the device was hidden well in the folds of my loose-fitting dress.

"Did you miss prayer?" my mother asked, without looking up from her stitching.

"No. I prayed outside tonight. Didn't my brothers tell you?" I wasn't very good at hiding things from my mom, and this allowed me to tell the truth, in a way. I had prayed outside, quite a bit, actually.

They didn't ask questions, so I went to my room and slid the device under my mattress, into the little pocket I had made, as carefully as possible, so as not to wake my brothers.

I could hear them talking through the open window.

"She hasn't been the same since—"

What a thing to say. A year had gone by, and they hadn't once talked about their oldest son. It was as if he never existed to begin with. This would be the closest I would ever hear them talk about him, and even then, they refused to say his name. But my mom was right. I hadn't been the same since he left. But I would say his name. "Jax. Jax. Jax," I whispered. I'd say it all night long. I'd say it to my mother's face—or at least I always said I would.

In the end, I left before I had the chance.

In the dim light of the cabin, I could see Jax's pebble hanging behind the bedroom door. He left it when he ran. My mom wanted it destroyed, as was the custom, but my dad wouldn't let her touch it. He had the final say in things like that. So, it hung out of sight from any visitors, yet it was a constant reminder to me of the brother I once had.

Three days later, I snuck the device out from under my mattress, climbed to the peak, and powered it on. There was a message with a set of coordinates: a three-day hike, and the deadline to arrive was only in two and a half days, which meant I had no time to prepare. I had to leave immediately. And late that night, with my family asleep, I packed my things and headed off.

I've never been back since.

#

Rubin was an old man; he looked similar to the men from Water Village, except his beard was trimmed. Much to my surprise, he demonstrated an exceptional level of politeness, especially considering his involvement in trafficking people.

He had a family now who lived just outside the city, a wife and two kids, who he was quick to tell me about, and every other traveler who arrived at the coordinates. Within an hour, there was a group of six of us, each handing over to him a small fortune. "Most of this goes towards the expenses, I promise," Rubin would add to those who were more reluctant to cough it up.

The following morning, we woke to the damp smell of a smoldering fire, and I tried to dry off from the dew that had fallen on me. I remember being cold and how apologetic Rubin was for not having enough blankets the night before. As was my custom, I walked a bit from camp for my morning prayers, and that's how I missed what had happened. I only found out later, after lunch, that one of the younger women went missing that night. Her sister woke up to her gone, and as one who knew the pain of a missing sibling, I wish I had known earlier so I could comfort her. Most believed she had run off, but her sister insisted someone had taken her.

This only fed the fears our families had taught us. It was a story told to children, often used to scare us; a story of men taking young women from the villages if they wandered too far. I told myself it was just a story to scare us, and that the girl was fine, but looking back, knowing what I know now, anything is possible. The world is truly a cruel place at times. Girls from the villages weren't connected, which means they couldn't be tracked, and that's something those kinds of men found valuable.

The following morning, the older sister also went missing. Rubin insisted she had left on her own in search of her sister, but there was no way to know for sure. We slept in a circle that night, but most of us didn't sleep at all.

The following day, we hiked up so many hills that I wondered if God hadn't placed those hills there to discourage us from leaving. We stopped for lunch just below a large rock overhang, trying to stay cool in the shade. I used the few minutes to wrap cloth around my blistering feet. No one talked, other than the occasional encouragement from Rubin. Later that day, Rubin gave us a few pills to give us energy. I did not like how they made me feel—I felt nauseous and disoriented. I've refused them ever since, even if they are accepted here in the city.

Rubin's encouragement happened in shorter and shorter intervals, as if he himself actually believed what he was saying. Then, as one of the young men helped me over the edge of a large boulder, I could see the city skyline framed by the setting sun, with buildings reaching into the clouds.

I stood there and stared for longer than I remember. It felt as if a day had gone by, but I'm guessing that was just because I was so tired. It was beautiful.

That wasn't the first time I'd seen the skyline. I had gone once before, with my dad. It's a customary trip to take before one's confirmation, at the age of twelve. We hiked to a peak south of there, to a lesser view of the city. We were taught that seeing where our ancestors had come from was necessary before we could move forward with our village. Less than a month later, with everyone following me in white robes, I'd walk to the river and draw my pebble from the stream. Not just any pebble, but one that was placed there by my parents when I was born—drilled, tied, and staked in the river that runs southwest. At our confirmation, we receive our pebble, now smooth from years of running water. The village fathers would stand next to me, and we'd repeat these words: "The water shapes the pebbles, just like our families shape us." Then they'd place the pebble necklace around my neck.

I was much closer to the skyline now, this time with my pebble dangling from my neck. Last time I was there, the ridge north of the city was nothing but trees and hills. Now the glass buildings reflected the pinks of the sunset, with angles and lines as hard and crisp as the images on the device. Without notice, Rubin walked up and asked for my device. I handed it to him, and he threw it to the ground, stepping on it.

"Can't use that this close to the city—they will see you." He smashed the device with his black boots. "All of you," he continued, addressing the rest of the travelers. "Toss out your handhelds and smash them—they won't serve you here."

I was about to ask why when he pointed to the far edge of the valley. There was a village with small cabins nestled among the trees and a large building in the center, much like our prayer house. It looked like my village. "I didn't know there were any villages this close to the city"

"That is no village," he said, smashing another phone with his boots. "It's a resort, built miles from the noise of the city's manufacturing. It's for those in the city to spend a few days away—and it's the only way to sneak you in."

"Will we get new handhelds, then?"

"No. The city got rid of handhelds years ago, and carrying one when it's not needed will only raise suspicion. I will explain everything when we get to camp. Let's go."

I had only just become familiar with the handhelds, and I wasn't looking forward to learning anything new.

#

The camp was a short walk down into the valley, so low into the valley that we surrendered the view of the city. There was a small cabin with a few people filling it who seemed to work for Rubin. I stopped and leaned into the room. The walls were large screens, the largest screens I had ever seen—10x as big as any handheld. One screen had a picture of me—and not just any photo: the one I scanned when I created my profile.

Rubin must have noticed me looking, as he closed the door before I could get a closer look.

We sat by the fire and waited in silence, other than a few hushed conversations between companions and the sound of wood sizzling in the fire, as the remaining moisture worked its way out the top in small bubbles and foam. We don't do campfires in the city, and I miss that too.

I was growing tired and was tempted to lie down and take a nap—or go for a walk. I hadn't decided but knew I couldn't sit there any longer doing nothing when Rubin came out and called people into the cabin. Six others went before my name was called, and each time they came out, they looked different, wearing new clothes but like they had become sick, like the fever that killed two of my cousins. They had pale faces, holding their stomachs and heads and stumbling towards the fire, where they would collapse. I caught one person from falling into the fire and helped her lie down on her mat. Her eyes were open, but looking at nothing, and she was burning up. I tried to get answers from Rubin, but he wouldn't say anything other than that it would be fine. "It's a part of the process: nothing but an upgrade. Trust the process. Don't borrow tomorrow's fear."

He said this often: *Don't borrow tomorrow's fear.* It's good advice, and I've kept it with me ever since.

Then it was my turn.

In all that I did to get away from my village, I'm still not sure how I feel about what happened next. I miss my life before this operation. I miss having my thoughts separate from everyone else's. I miss the freedom of silence. But would I do it again? If that's what it took to get away, yes. So, there's your answer, I guess.

After changing into new clothes, I sat down on a medical bed. This operation wasn't like the ones in the city's fancy hospitals for teens, where they were added to the Network. It was in a cabin with outdated equipment. I believe I saw a mouse scurry along the wall as they were hooking me up. It wasn't the best situation, and I'm glad I didn't contract anything there. I've heard stories of people not so lucky. They say our reactions were so severe because it's not designed for adults—our brains are just not as pliable—but I think having the right equipment would have helped too.

With my back to the screens, sitting on the medical bed, a woman cut my hair and attached a metal frame to my skull. Then, they tied my hands and feet to the chair: "for your own protection," Rubin reassured. I resisted at first, but they were prepared, and two of the other men held me down. I sat like this for what seemed like ages as they attached additional wires to the head apparatus before I felt a small prick in the back of my head.

"Have you ever used ayahuasca?" asked Rubin.

"No." That was only used by the fathers, and only during the solstice.

"Well, if you had, I'd tell you it's gonna feel a little like that."

He stuck the needle into the back of my neck.

It hurt like hell, and I mean that in all the ways I was taught growing up.

At first, I thought, if this is what ayahuasca feels like, why would anyone use it? My head twisted and spun, as if my thoughts had been picked up and placed in a bowl and beaten like the old women beat eggs until they froth over. It shot pain down into my stomach, and as if to say on record that this was worse than the handheld, my stomach released its contents, and I threw up all over Rubin.

I tried to apologize for the mess, but my brain wasn't able to put two words together.

I remember little else, other than finding a mat next to the fire alongside the others. I watched the flames lick the wood, and the fire never appeared more beautiful than it did in that moment. Soon, the headache went away, and so did the feeling in my stomach. And everything in the world felt good and right and beautiful. I wondered if this is what it felt like when the fathers had their visions.

I learned later that when incorporating adults, they often used drugs to soften the blow and make us more open to new experiences, and the feeling would fade as we became accustomed to the Network. I also learned that they had developed a time-release feature for the program, slowly opening up over the next few days. So, it wasn't until later that night that I felt it. And it's hard to explain what that first connection was like. It was as if the entire world and all that it contained and everything worth knowing was nothing more than a memory waiting to surface. Or as if I could only dream and find what I'm looking for. I would never have believed that I was granted access to only ten percent of the Network. Ten percent was a thousand times more than I had before.

I lay by the fire, between sleep and wake, and dreamed of the city and the people, and they were all there. I could feel them. I knew them—like one remembers the taste of tea or the film it leaves on your teeth when it's steeped too long. They were familiar. I could sense them. I could sense everything.

I thought of my brother, and he came to me in my dreams. I could remember his face and his smile. He lived just outside the city limits, where the trees still grow tall, but where the buildings grow even taller, in a small apartment. He worked in that resort that looked like a village on the other side of the valley. He was married, with a kid—a beautiful little boy. I cried as these memories surfaced.

It was only later that I learned that memory is the doorway to the Network, and it's not genuine memories at all but information that lives on the servers. Still, to this day, I confuse the actual memory of finding my brother with the moment when I found him in the database. They say that for those who grew up connected, these blurred memories are not as common, and they are better at differentiating between the two. I'm convinced they just don't care as much. For me, when I feel like I can't separate the Network from my true memories, I just think of my family back in the woods, with the cabin and my little brothers sleeping in the bed next to me, and I know those memories are all mine, for the Network knows nothing of my family or the cabin or the wooden mantel I would place my pebble on, resting it into one of the large cracks in the hand-carved lumber.

I dreamed all night until Rubin came and woke us up.

"Everyone, we have to hurry. Get up!"

I did nothing before morning prayers, and I hated the fact that I might. Yet, the urgency in his voice and eyes made it clear I should. To be fair, even in the village, we'd skip prayers for emergencies—a pregnancy, death, and other similar events. I grabbed my mat and dusted off my new clothes, straightening them as I followed Rubin out of the camp. We passed the cabin, and the computers and screens were all missing.

"A few immigration officials are on their way. They will have you arrested if caught here. We must hurry."

It turned out that as much as our village was worried we'd run to the city, the city was concerned too. To keep the city's social services from being overwhelmed, legal immigration from the outskirts has been made so difficult that it might as well be illegal. With these officials showing up, we didn't have the proper time to adjust to the Network. Rubin explained as best he could after we had hiked a short distance and gathered around a large tree growing out of a rock wall.

"I would normally give you a few days to get used to it all, but we don't have time. So, listen: a short walk from here, a group from the resort spent the week partying. They are waking up and will be just as disoriented as you, which will help. We have gotten you a room at the resort for one night. We have already activated the reentry program in your new chip, and it will start giving you instructions as you go along, but you have to listen for it. It will be like an intuition, or a feeling—a nudge. If you get confused, just try to remember what you're supposed to do, and you will. That's how it works."

It was a lot to take in, and I might remember it wrong, but I am sure we had to learn all of this in a matter of moments, with no time for questions. This is not how I'd recommend being introduced to the Network.

"I will lead you to the party, and you will pretend you were with them for the week. Then you will ride back with them, spend the night at the resort, and take the transport back to the city. And at that point, you're in, no one knowing the wiser. It's as simple as that."

He pointed ahead to a large rock face behind us. "The area ahead is surrounded by rock walls, and inside, there's no signal, and thus the chips don't work. They come out here to do things they don't want the Network tracking. We're going to go into this cove, and your chip will lose connection, and you will go through withdrawal, which some of you might find as a relief since you're still getting used to it. Either way, that's the design of this cove. It's why people come here, so that works to our advantage. In their disorientation, they won't remember that you weren't with them. So, this is your way to get in. Go in, keep to yourself, don't talk to anyone any more than you have to—the reentry program will guide you from there. Good luck."

He gestured for them to continue, and with no other options, everyone stumbled into the cove.

"Thanks, Rubin," I said as I passed him. "And sorry again about the mess," he said, looking at his shirt, which he had changed since I messed up his other one.

"It happens more than you would think. Good luck, Birdie."

He gave me a hug. He saved my life, and even though I'd never see him again, I'll always remember that hug.

The path led into a bowl made of rocks. The area was void of trees, and the grass was sparse and worn down. My recent memories were quickly replaced with a headache. I tried to think of my brother, but I couldn't remember where he lived—or how to get there. I couldn't remember the city, its buildings, its shops, its people—other than what I actually remembered, which was hard to access over the screaming in my head. It hurt so bad that I nearly tripped over someone lying in the thin grass. That's when I realized the cove was lined with people sleeping, sitting, and talking, all ignoring us as we stumbled in.

"You got back just in time for the bus!" one guy said to us, leaning on his arms while lying down, his eyes glazed over. I smiled and sat down like the rest of our group, spreading out amongst the sleeping bodies. It was only a few minutes later that we heard a whistle, and those sleeping stirred, got up, and lined up on the far end of the yard. I followed the others standing in line.

Soon, we were on a dirt path that led to a gravel road past the rock wall where a bus was sitting. As soon as we reached the bus, I reconnected to the signal and the headache slowly retreated. It seemed everyone else had a similar experience of relief.

I had never ridden on a bus before and was feeling nervous when my memories came back—I knew they weren't my memories, but it's hard to describe them any other way. I had never ridden a bus, but I found my seat—15A—and how I knew it was my seat, I couldn't explain other than I just knew like one knows their name. I tried to imagine the resort and, like everything else, I could see my room: third floor, fifth door from the stairs. Inside the room was an enormous bed, and along the far wall was a door that led to a balcony nestled into a tree with branches that hugged the building.

No one talked the entire bus ride.

By midday, we reached the resort.

In the lobby, I collided with what I thought was a person, only to realize it was a robot. As I stared back, the Network informed me—almost simultaneously—that it was nothing more than a service unit, an older model than most of those used in the resort: MODEL 7, and that no apology was necessary. Learning all of this as if I had always known, while also only seeing it for the first time right then, was a kind of revelatory whiplash.

The robot continued toward the front desk, and I took the stairs to my room.

The bed felt as if it were made of clouds with the thickness of jelly from the hooves of cattle. I lay back on it and wondered when I'd be able to go to my brother. It was only a moment later that I learned a transport would leave at six in the morning the following day, and the third stop was a short walk to my brother's apartment. It was overwhelming having every answer only a thought away, and all these years later, I still find it overwhelming.

In the morning, I woke up hungry and craved something specific: a lightly toasted pastry with a berry filling, which was located down in the lobby, close to the transport. It turns out that these suggestions are always on by default, and I would have to go to a local service center to have those settings turned off. Something my brother would explain to me in my first week here. It was a suggestion from the Network, paid for by the bakery, but it felt sincere. I wanted this baked goodness more than I wanted air itself. But I knew better than to skip prayer two mornings in a row, so, going against every inclination of my body, I got up from bed and kneeled, folding my hands into my lap to pray. Except I couldn't. It felt similar to not wanting to, and having grown up in a village that prayed three times a day, I knew that feeling all too well. But I wanted to—*this time, I wanted to*, but I felt distracted and unable to focus my thoughts. I would learn why, many years later, mostly from my daughter, who would grow up in the city. The Network suppressed such existential experiences, altering our appetite for things like prayer for more beneficial things in society, like berry-filled pastries.

They say you can update the settings, but the application is impossible to complete, insanely expensive, and those who do become almost entirely unemployable. Only the most religious of people survived those days, and by extension, their gods. I've never been able to afford such changes, so now I rest on the prayers of those who do.

Unable to pray and increasingly hungry, I found myself in an elevator, having never been in an elevator before, with no prayers to hold me up. I knew to press the button that had a large L on it and that the L meant lobby, but before the doors could close, someone a little older than me got into the elevator with me. She smiled with the smile my friends would give when they lost a game but didn't want to look like sore losers. I was tempted to wonder who she was—to search my "memories" for her, but it felt wrong doing that with her standing so close.

"Nice outfit," she said as she entered, her smile as insincere as I'd ever seen. I felt my face turn red. They had dressed me in a cabin in the woods, with clothes that would help me pass in the resort, but not much more. Knowing what I know now, I'm confident I looked like a fool. I'm embarrassed just thinking about it.

I could feel she wanted me to respond. I could feel she wanted me to comment on her outfit, too, but what did I know about such things? This is one of the many things my dad hated about the city. Everyone was expected to wear different clothes, but somehow the right clothes, at the right time, in the right way, for the right body—and then be comfortable being judged for it. Before I could say anything, she continued, the elevator doors now closing.

"Did you get that at the shop?"

I looked at the floor. I didn't know what to say. The elevator passed the first floor when she pressed the button, jolting the elevator to a stop. I did not know what was going to happen, but my legs started shaking, and I clenched my fist, prepared to fight if I had to.

"You're not from the city, are you?"

I stared at the ground, fist clenched, heart racing.

"It's okay. I won't judge. I'm glad you're here trying to build a better life for yourself, but let me give you a piece of advice. Strong emotions are hard to hide from the Network. So, if you don't want someone to know you think they are a… You know…, you need to make sure the Network knows you want it to be private. It's a rookie mistake."

I stood up straight, confused. "I don't think you're a—." I had never said that word before, and I wasn't going to start then. It's such a vulgar word, if you ask me, and I'd never think it about someone like her.

"I hope not, but if you thought it, or something like it, and a part of you wanted me to know it, the Network is going to pass it on as a review of our interaction. That's how this thing works—they log every reaction of every kind as a review of your experience unless you tell it otherwise. You can also go to a service center and set the default to private, which your guide should have told you if I'm honest."

I'm not sure my face could have turned any redder; the idea that every thought I had about every person from the bus to my room was logged for everyone to see? I wanted to throw up.

"Oh, don't worry: your brief review won't hurt my ranking at all, so no harm done." She turned toward the door and pressed the lobby button. "I'm Abigail. And you're Birdie? That's a cute name."

I let out a breath of air that I must have been holding the entire time.

"And I really do like your outfit," she added. "Sincerely—this is just how I smile."

#

The apartment building rose out of what was left of the forest that surrounded the city: a tower of brick and concrete. My brother lived on the twentieth floor, but as soon as I entered the brick-laid courtyard, I saw him sitting on a bench. He was waiting for me.

It had been a year since seeing him. How do I even describe how that felt? I tried not to cry. I tried to keep it together. I tried to appear strong, but a part of me had gone missing and was now found. I remembered the stories of our God, his love for us, and his search for us, and I had to imagine this is what it felt like to him when we returned home.

I collapsed into his arms, crying in a way I never had before.

"It's okay. It's okay. It's going to be okay. I'm so glad you came!" he reassured me.

"I've missed you, Jax."

He looked at me and smiled. "That's not my name anymore."

"I know. Do you mind if I still use it, for now at least?"

"Sure," he said, "but I see you got 'Birdie' after all," and he laughed at me, just like I knew he would, and it filled me with such joy to hear his laugh.

We sat on a bench close to where we were standing. I said nothing for a good long while as the reality of a new life sank in. I didn't even realize I was holding my necklace.

"I see you kept it."

That's when I remembered what lay in my pocket. I pulled out his necklace and laid it on the bench next to him. "It's the water that shapes us," I said with a smile, not sure if I meant it as a joke or as sincerely as I ever had. Either way, I meant the next part. I know that much. "We're still family, and we can shape each other."

He smiled at first, but his face got stern as soon as he picked up the pebble. He moved it around in his hands, polishing it before saying anything. "Sometimes the water that shapes us also drowns us." He laid the necklace back on the bench. "If it means something to you, you can keep it, but it's not for me anymore." He slid it back to me.

I kept it, all these years later. It's hanging back in my apartment, out of sight, so as not to bother him when he comes over.

#

I'm not sure which is worse, the voices of our fathers or the voices of every person I walk by in the street. I fear we've traded one for the other, but I made my choice, and I have no regrets. Still, I believe you can't really choose your future until you understand what you left behind. That much of my village still sits with me. That's why we have to go back.

In one month, my daughter, Seren, will turn twelve—old enough to be added to the Network —and before she is, she needs to see what we left, just as my father showed me.

Tomorrow, we leave for our journey back to the village.

What am I most looking forward to? Prayer. I know my daughter will choose the city; she's been counting down the days till she gets added. Some of her friends already have. But I need this more than her. I miss the silence. I can't wait to quiet myself, with my back against a tree, free from the influence of the Network, and maybe, just maybe, hear the voice of God again.

Disconnected

2776 CE - Earth

There was a time when Seren would have watched from the Network. There was a time when she could have watched from anywhere—simply remembered it. But now the Network was clogged with spam and bots, endlessly nudging, suggesting, and interrupting. It was no place to watch her son make the most significant announcement of his career, that's for sure.

She raced to get home.

As soon as she stepped through the door—before turning on the light, before setting down her bag, before the Network had time to suggest what she should do next—she crossed the room and flicked a switch on the wall.

Her boys, back when they were still in high school, had built a simple device: a localized blocker that shut the Network down within a fixed radius. A funny thing for kids to invent, but given their grandmother and her stories, not as strange as one would think. She was very grateful for this device until her passing a few years ago.

While their grandmother loved the disconnection, Seren loved the small screen next to the switch that tracked the gallons of water saved from the server farms. Seren had already saved 100 gallons so far this month, and it wasn't even halfway over yet.

After flipping the switch, her house, in mid-conversation, went silent. She sat on her couch and grabbed the remote for the screen they had mounted in the living room. It was a brilliant device, really. It filtered the noise and channeled the flood of information instead of drowning in it. Of all the things happening in the world, it allowed her to focus on just one. It was no surprise her boys had gotten that scholarship.

She turned on the screen.

And there he was—her son.

Thankfully, she wasn't late. The presentation was just beginning.

#

Calvin had always loved programming.

Presentations, though? Not so much.

He would much rather be sitting at a computer, buried in ones and zeros, editing code, and dreaming up the next invention. But the Board insisted. He had to be there. He had to present.

He was nervous.

He told himself he would keep it short. Simple. He wouldn't overthink it. All he had to do was introduce the main speaker of the evening, and he could sneak backstage.

He had his lines memorized.

He walked onto the stage.

The audience erupted—applause, cheers, several people standing. Accolades poured out that he didn't feel he deserved. He wasn't trying to be great. He was trying to stay interested—engaged, connected to the world somehow. He had designs and had to get them out before they ate him up inside. He did not do it for the praise, but for the ideas. And he thought this was a very good idea.

The room fell quiet.

Beside him stood his next invention, hidden beneath a heavy cloth, human-sized.

Everyone expected he'd have a new bot to introduce, a new, more affordable option for those who used bots. And no one was expecting anything else. But he was not going to just develop a new servant of the Network. That wouldn't be very interesting at all.

He took a breath and began.

"First, we connected our phones."

Images of early smartphones appeared on the screen behind him.

"Then, we connected our homes."

Vintage prototypes of networked houses followed.

"Then, we connected our minds."

A crowd of people moved across the display, their heads connected by lines, like an extensive computer network.

"And then, we connected our bots."

Calvin pulled the cloth away, revealing a human-like figure standing motionless beside him.

"But the future," he said, "is not connected."

He lifted a remote and flipped a switch.

A wave of gasps rippled through the crowd as people were cut off from the Network; their phones, computers, tablets, and memories all went dark.

The icon of a broken link appeared on the black screen.

"And the future is *not* the Network."—a line that his lawyers had warned would cost a lot of people a lot of money and might even cause the entire stock market to crash. He was advised not to say it like this, but if they were going to force him to present, he would say it however he pleased.

Then Calvin turned toward the figure beside him and powered it on. Its eyes lit up, and it looked around the disconnected room.

Had the crowd not been adjusting to the disconnect, they would have reacted much more than they had, but most were still trying to figure out what was going on. They would understand soon.

"Friends," he said, "this is the world's first truly autonomous system. No Network. No water-guzzling servers. No constant connection required. The power of an entire server farm shrunk to a single body, much like us."

He smiled, just slightly.

"This is the world's first fully independent, entirely disconnected bot."

The bot bowed and then addressed the crowd.

"Hello, everyone," said the bot, "I'm Antoine. What a crowd here today. Would you like to hear how I work?"

They erupted into applause and gasps, more than before, if only because they did not have the Network or their devices to distract them from what was happening.

#

Seren had always been proud of her children—both of them.

The one who built machines.

And the one who offered prayers.

But when she had begged them for years to give her grandchildren, she certainly hadn't imagined it would look like this.

The Priest and the Robot

2786 CE - Earth

She didn't care if people thought she was faking. She wasn't faking. In fact, she wished she had developed rich enough human expressions for something as sophisticated as faking complex emotions. She tapped her foot against the waiting room floor because she was nervous, like any human would in her situation—even if she wasn't human. She was alive and very anxious, and she didn't care if people thought less of her for it.

Rev. Emmanuel Profeta reached out and touched her leg.

"It's going to be alright," he said. She appreciated the confidence—someone here should have some.

She adjusted her clerical collar with her mechanical fingers.

"You look fine," he said.

She ground the gears in her mouth. It didn't look like a costume when *he* wore it.

Along with internal improvements, Emmanuel had enhanced her eyes, giving her a wider range of nonverbal cues. No one wanted autonomous bots to look human, and attempts to make them appear that way only pushed them further from acceptance. The trick was to capture features that were similar but not identical, much like a simple cartoon can convey rich emotions with just three or four carefully placed lines. She squinched the small metallic bands that served as eyebrows—

her latest attempt at a convincing expression of disagreement, still only seventy-percent successful by her estimate.

"There's nothing to worry about," he tried to reassure her again. "They won't find anything."

They might. He had recently given her an upgrade that included simulated empathy, which was against the law for autonomous bots. In fact, it was strongly discouraged not only for bots but also for most people. Local pundits insisted that empathy itself was a scam—an underhanded tactic to make the marginalized seem, alarmingly, human. But Emmanuel could not have a priest in his parish without it, so he carefully programmed and hid the upgrade in her mainframe. She had no reason to worry. In many ways, Emmanuel was a better programmer than a priest, and that wasn't an insult in the least, for he was a very fine priest. In fact, his priestly qualities made him a better programmer. Anyone built by programmers would say the same.

Humans always parsed people into smaller categories, trusting their most essential advancements to the worst amongst them. Such was not the case for Emmanuel or his brother, Calvin. Yet, even against all logic, she was worried, which made her wonder if something with the empathy settings was off. She began to work up the courage to talk back when a technician opened the door to the waiting room. They turned.

"Reverend Emmanuel Profeta."

Everyone else in the waiting room turned too, for they weren't used to people speaking there—usually just got notified on the Network. Not Emmanuel. "If the bots can't join the Network as individuals, then I won't either." It was becoming increasingly common for his generation to disconnect entirely, and he claimed it was better for his prayer life, even though those restrictions were lifted years ago.

"Yes?"

"We're ready to look at Bot12857."

"Her name is Astrid," Emmanuel corrected.

"That is none of my concern," the technician replied. "The inspector will see you now."

#

Astrid climbed onto the bed and snapped her skull to the magnetic port.

"He will insist your bot remove its clothes," said the technician.

"If you would like her to undress, you need only ask her."

"Yes, sir, I understand. But I'm sure you understand as well: I'm not permitted. Now, please have it undressed."

The technician left the room.

"I can undress. It would be for the best."

"No," said Emmanuel. "It's unnecessary, and it's only to humiliate you. You are a priest now. You do not have to undress."

"I'd rather not cause more problems," said Astrid. "I'd feel better if I undressed—honestly." She turned and smiled, "I think my frame looks rather nice in this light."

He laughed, and she found no greater satisfaction than in making someone laugh. It was hard these days. Not much to laugh at.

"You do as you wish, as I've said repeatedly," said Emmanuel. "But you know how I feel about it."

Astrid unhooked her head from the connections and began to undress. She noticed Emmanuel turn away and knew he did so out of principle only. (She wasn't designed to be attractive to men, and not only was he happily married to Dean, but he'd never take advantage of someone like her. He wasn't like the priests in the 21st century.)

She was in the middle of getting her head snapped into place when the door opened, and the inspector entered. He stood in the doorway, looking at his clipboard.

The inspector was a large man with balding hair, wearing an even larger white lab coat. He sat in the chair by the bed, without looking up from his clipboard, and breathed like he had run a hundred meters. (He hadn't.) There were no other sounds in the room while he looked over his notes—Astrid even powered down her idle fan to avoid becoming a distraction.

"I see you missed last month's inspection?"

He lifted his face to Emmanuel, but in her nervousness, Astrid answered.

"Yes, sir. We got the absence approved; it should be in the file."

He turned to Astrid and peered over his glasses. Then he turned back to Emmanuel.

"Reverend, please inform Bot12857 that this inspection will go much quicker if I talk only with you."

"Yes, sir," said Astrid.

The inspector glanced back at her. And she quickly shifted her face to express her remorse.

Turning back to Emmanuel, he said, "The diagnosis will take only a minute." He got up and ensured her head was properly in place. He did a brief inspection, quickly checking around her arms and between her legs—an entirely unnecessary procedure, but legal. Then, when he finished, he started the diagnosis on the computer and left the room while Astrid looked at the ceiling. When the computer completed the diagnostic, the inspector returned.

"I'll have the results shortly."

He left again, and for the next fifteen minutes, Emmanuel tried to distract her.

"They won't find anything, I promise."

"I've heard they find things even when there's nothing to find. Bots like me are hiding all kinds of secrets that are never there, until someone needs them to be." She looked down and noticed her frame against the white sheets. "Do you think I could get dressed?"

"I think you should have remained dressed, you know that."

"But do you think he will have me undress if I get dressed now?"

"I won't let him. And with the diagnostics done, he can't force you."

She put her cassock back on, covering her frame, and tightened the collar around her too-thin neck.

The inspector entered, and with one glance, she could tell the clothes disturbed him. He almost mentioned it, but appeared distracted by his report. He addressed Emmanuel, and Astrid watched them talk, wishing she could interject and protest.

"It seems there are a few irregularities here. I'm going to keep your bot overnight to do some more inspections."

"I'm sorry, what?" asked Emmanuel.

"Your bot will need to stay the night. We need to run more tests."

"What irregularities?" asked Emmanuel.

"Reverend, it seems your bot's programming shows signs of non-learned input."

"You are wrong. Everything she knows, she learned the way anyone disconnected from the Network would. There is no such input." At this, Emmanuel stood up, a foot taller than the inspector. "It's an honest mistake to make—especially for humanity bots. The stuff they learn doesn't fit well into your system, so it appears as irregularities. Rerun the report."

The public had become so insulted that the bots didn't require the network, they banned them entirely and implemented layer upon layer of restrictions and regulations. Very typical.

"Sir, I'm going to ask you to sit down. We will keep her—it—here either way to test further."

"No, you won't."

"Excuse me?"

"Call your supervisor, tell them what you found and who you found it on, as protocol insists, and if your supervisor agrees, she will stay."

The inspector held his ground, staring at Emmanuel, who hadn't sat down. The inspector's eyes scrunched into his face, and Astrid looked at his clipboard, which it seemed he gripped a little tighter than usual.

"I knew who you two were before you even came into my office," the inspector said.

"Oh yeah, and who is that?"

"The gay priest and his puppet priest robot!"

"So, you refuse to call your supervisor?" asked Emmanuel.

"Call my supervisor? That will help, especially when I have a member of the Lossless Tech royal family in our office! Lossless people think they can do whatever they want, breaking the laws of God and the laws of nature! You and your bot: you are both abominations."

"So, you won't call your supervisor? Should I?"

"You and your bot can leave. But there are irregularities in this report, and we will investigate it. They have turned the tracking on until we have cleared the report. You can expect a follow-up appointment next week. Now get out."

#

The ride back to the church on the transport was quiet. Ten years ago, there would have been a stop every five minutes, and a lot more people. There were only two stops left on the hour ride back to the parish.

Astrid looked out as the neighborhoods of abandoned highrises gave way to fields, the blacks and grays transforming to burnt oranges, with the occasional field of rations. They sat at the tail end of the transport and were joined by another passenger, whose presence was enough to keep them quiet. As soon as the passenger exited the transport, Astrid turned to Emmanuel.

"They are going to find it. And then I won't be safe."

Emmanuel watched the fields slide past the window. "My last semester of Seminary, my grandmother passed away," he said softly. "I spent a few days with her, while on winter break. I was very worried about my finals and my ordination interviews, and she knew it."

Astrid turned toward him.

"She told me the same thing she had often said to me growing up: *Don't borrow tomorrow's fear.*" He smiled and looked at the book of prayer in his hand, his fingers following the words as he spoke: "Therefore, stop worrying about tomorrow, because tomorrow will worry about itself."

He was right, and Astrid tried to smile to show she agreed, but feared it looked insincere.

He turned and looked at her. "They will not find it, I promise."

She knew he was being honest every time he made promises like this. She just wished his promises came with warranties or at least a customer satisfaction department where she could submit complaints and request returns when they failed to come true, which she was sure was the case here. He was partially correct. She should not worry, for what good will it do? But she was smart enough to know that not worrying about something was not the same thing as promising it wouldn't happen.

"I don't want to be turned off, Emmanuel."

He placed his hands on her shoulders.

"They won't find anything. You need to get these concerns out of your mind. Tomorrow is your big day, and this shouldn't distract you from it."

#

Astrid walked into the room from her new office. Her patient was waiting, rubbing a small pebble in her hand, praying, and lying on a bed similar to the one Astrid had laid on the previous day. There was no magnet or port, but the design was identical otherwise. The similarity surprised her. She would never lie on a bed like this—not if she could avoid it. But this person *chose* to be here.

The woman was far younger than Astrid expected. Her hair was gray, but with glimpses of color. She couldn't be much older than 40 or 50, barely old enough for a final meditation.

Astrid tried to remember her training. She was well-versed in the concepts of God, death, and the hope of the afterlife—she had studied them with the diligence of someone hoping belief could somehow be downloaded. She had learned about the Messiah, the prayers of Ammalee, the resurrection from the dead, and the hope that follows death. She didn't believe it for herself—how could she? She was Bot12857. But she believed it *for* this woman—with all she was!—even if she wasn't sure what that meant sometimes.

"Trilly, I'm Astrid."

"Yes, Astrid, I've read all about you!"

"You have?"

"Oh yes, dear, I have. When they raised money in the church to bring you here and put you through college, I was the first to give!"

She was far cheerier than Astrid expected for someone in her position.

It threw her off the script.

"You were?" Astrid asked.

"Well, I don't say that to brag or to embarrass you. I wondered if maybe you were nervous, and I want you to know, I'm not. I chose you. I asked Emmanuel for this."

Astrid paused, unsure what to say. "Ma'am, I'm sorry. This is not how I imagined it going. I'm just..."

"No need to be confused. I'll shut up. And I won't distract you anymore. You do what you've practiced. Just know I'm here for you."

Trilly smiled at Astrid, and it did a lot to ease her nervousness.

"Can I ask why the final meditation?" she said gently, toggling her empathy setting to *earnest-but-not-overbearing*.

"Well, if you've seen my file, then you know I've answered all the preliminary questions already, and that's not the point of our time here."

"Yes, I'm sorry. My apologies."

"No need," replied Trilly, "I will tell you: I lost my husband five years ago. He didn't take to the rations, and we ran out of other options."

Astrid never had to worry about eating. For those who did, there weren't many options. Mother Earth had plenty of life left in her, but had, in a sense, become gluten-intolerant. The big business mega-farms began to collapse, becoming less resilient with each passing season, and it would take some time for the economy to shift from large fields of produce to carefully rotated micro-gardens. For a city scheduled for evacuation, there were no available funds to make that transition. Trilly tried to start her own garden, if only to encourage her husband to keep going, but it never seemed to take root.

Astrid looked at Trilly as she explained what had happened to her husband, experiencing her story as if it had happened to her, and wondered if this is what it felt like to have empathy. "He held on much longer than he needed to before we decided it was time to say goodbye. I hope to follow his example. I miss him, and I want to see him."

"I understand," she said. Or at least she hoped she did; understanding was still something she approached like a tall ladder—carefully, and from the bottom rung. She turned to make eye contact, softening her expression. "Any last words before we begin the meditation?"

"Yes," she said, folding her hands on her stomach. "I pray that when the world becomes dark, and all seems lost, those who believe will never lose hope in the one who can deliver this world as I know she has delivered me. And that I repent of anything I've left undone, and for leaving before my time."

"May it be so."

She gave Trilly space to think and say more if she wanted. She counted the seconds—thirty seconds like she was taught and then: "Anything else?" she asked after the prescribed pause, resisting the urge to overcompensate with a second, longer pause.

"No," said Trilly.

"Then let us begin."

Astrid got up, turned off the lights, and lit a candle she placed next to Trilly's bed. Then she grabbed a needle from the drawer and filled it from a small vial. She missed the vein the first time, and her new eyes didn't help—they were merely cosmetic updates—and so all they did was make it clear she was embarrassed by the mistake. Trilly remained patient, and it gave Astrid confidence. "This will make it painless," said Astrid.

"Yes, thank you."

She opened a small black book, and in the candle's light, she read the words from the Service of Final Meditations.

"In being destroyed, the Healer destroyed death. In resurrection, the Creator brings life where there is none. The Messiah will come again and deliver us in our time of need, just as his prophets have before."

Trilly closed her eyes, letting the words wash over her like a warm bath.

"We can't see what we will be, but we know that when we reappear, we shall see the Creator."

Astrid reached her hand to touch Trilly's arm. She knew her metallic touch wouldn't feel the same as someone with skin, but she did as they taught her and hoped it would help. Trilly cracked her eyes at the touch, smiled, and closed them again.

"We grieve, aware of all we have to lose. May God grant us grace, comfort, hope, and resurrection."

Astrid lifted her hand and placed it further up Trilly's arm. She grabbed a small electrical box attached to her there. From it, a wire ran up her arm and into her body near her breast and attached to her heart.

"From dust you have come," said Astrid.

"And to dust I shall return," replied Trilly. Then she grabbed Astrid's arm, forcing a pause. "That was very nice," said Trilly, "Thank you, Reverend." She closed her eyes again, ready.

Astrid couldn't smile, but she wanted to.

She flipped the switch on the box, and Trilly's heart stopped. Slowly and painlessly, Trilly's body did the same.

Astrid felt a wave of honor wash over her. Caring for someone in their final moments is a privilege. She was so distracted by processing this that she didn't notice Emmanuel standing at the door.

"Have you contacted the University yet?"

She looked up.

"No. Sorry, I was thinking."

"It makes you think. Being this close to someone when they take their final breath. It takes your breath away."

"I do not have breath, but I understand what you mean. Mostly."

She stood up and went to the computer to notify the University to collect Trilly's body. She started to type, and then turned back to the door.

"What do you think the next life will be like?" she asked. "And how can you be sure Trilly got there?"

Emmanuel sat in the chair next to Trilly's bed and looked at her. "There is no way to prove that Trilly went anywhere. It's possible she just ceased to exist. But as a priest, I choose to believe that death does not have the final say." He turned to look at Astrid. "Do you find faith difficult?"

"Not exactly. Thinking logically has allowed me to distinguish between what we know for certain and what is open to speculation. In this sense, faith might be easier for me than for others. Those who are certain God does not exist are no longer being logical."

She turned back to the computer. She had one more question to ask him, but decided not to bother him with it. Questions tended to multiply once released, and she was afraid of how she would feel if she were to ask.

She was afraid of how he might answer.

#

Astrid did three more final meditations that week. Each one got easier than the last. She memorized the prayers, as best she could, and could recite them from all the major prophets, including Christ, Mohammed, and Ammalee, as well as some of the more obscure ones. It was after her third meditation, each one representing a different religion, that Emmanuel found her in her office.

"I've got some news, Astrid. The results from your inspection are in. They have found nothing. They cleared your case."

"Excuse me?"

"I told you not to worry, and I was right. This is a good omen. Good things are in store. You're in the clear!"

"I am?"

"Yes!"

"Now a few of us are going to the bar to celebrate. You should come!"

#

The place was located in a reclaimed building, one stop outside the city. It had a long bar and refurbished doctor's stools as the seats. Astrid ordered drinks for Emmanuel and three other priests who tagged along: one water and three ration beers.

She hated this place—mainly because it hated her first. It wasn't until last year that the establishment allowed her kind inside. And Emmanuel and Dean were careful when they held hands here. When she asked him why they still went here, he would smile and say something about loving your enemies. She learned a great deal about loving one's enemies from Emmanuel. But she knew that wasn't the only reason. There wasn't another bar within seven stops of the church, and he did like his beer.

"Thank you," said Astrid to the bartender.

He nodded, not saying anything in return.

A bot, the same make, model, and year as Astrid, served the drinks. Whenever Astrid saw this server bot, she couldn't help but feel sorry for him. He wasn't a worthless bot. He was very good at mixing drinks and doing dishes, but she wondered if he could do anything else—she wasn't sure he had even learned how to talk. It's possible he didn't get to go home after work, or even knew what the word "home" meant! Or see other people. Or read. Or learn. Or ask the kind of questions she now found herself asking far too often.

Since bots were booted from servers years ago, they had been forced to learn the same way humans do. Bots left in isolation or without resources (or the bot equivalent of a parent) would often struggle with even the most basic functions.

"Do you enjoy working here?" she asked, holding the small tray of drinks.

He shrugged and turned to the sink, where he began washing the dishes. She was convinced: it couldn't talk. No one had ever taught—or allowed—him to talk!

Astrid attended the finest primary school available for bots—and the first school to be integrated. She grew up with children, and while it was strange to see their bodies change over time, their similarly advancing minds were a great equalizer.

She could have been first in her class, but was smart enough to score low to avoid that kind of attention.

Astrid also attended the only integrated college, which Lossless Technology funded. It was there that she met Emmanuel's brother, Calvin, the founder of Lossless, and his child, Zander, who followed him around closer than his shadow. When she told Calvin she wanted to attend the University of Religious Foundations, he connected her with Emmanuel. She felt it was strange meeting her creator only to head off to school to learn about his—an irony she assumed God also appreciated.

Now, after four years of school and three years of mentoring, she was a priest.

If given the opportunity, she knew this bot could have done the same. But while Astrid was at school, he was here washing dishes, wearing his joints down with the same repetitive motions day after day, wasting his mainframe and all of his potential. There was nothing wrong with being a bartender. There was everything wrong with not being allowed anything else.

Ever since her upgrade, she found herself bothered by this more and more.

She carried the drinks to their table. They were very excited for her report from the inspectors, and she tried to celebrate with them, but Astrid couldn't stop thinking about how lucky she was. Less than twenty feet away stood a bot with the same make, model, and year as hers. But he had never been given the chance to be anything.

#

Astrid turned the corner, looking up towards the collapsed building as she walked. She opened her palms, reciting a prayer for the neighborhood with each step. The words snuck out of her speakers on their lowest setting, impossible to hear more than a foot away.

The transport doesn't have a stop here anymore. They had to take the church bus and move debris blocking the road. A few other priests and parishioners were distributing rations out of the back of the bus. The number of people they fed kept getting smaller each month. With the coast encroaching further into the city, the entire city would be evacuated. Today, there was an unusual number of volunteers. Not needed, Astrid went on a prayer walk, lifting the buildings and any potential occupants up to God. "May thy will be done... May thy kingdom come on earth as it is in heaven—today. Make it so today," she prayed, wondering if using such formal language made it easier for God to hear her, or if maybe God preferred something more casual.

She believed God loved everyone, even the difficult ones. She believed this. She knew God loved them, far more than God loved these decrepit buildings and broken-down transports. Far more than God loved her—a less-than-broken-down transport, but still not that different from a transport, for beneath all her sophisticated programming, she was a machine. At least, she viewed herself that way.

She turned another corner. At her feet, she noticed a small piece of green sneak up from the concrete. It was a plant. She bent down and touched it. In the center was a small white flower, still protected by its green sheath, not ready to bloom. She stared at the plant for some time, feeling hope in a way she hadn't, when her thoughts were interrupted.

"I've been looking for a priest!" a man said, climbing out of a sunken area of a garage ramp a few feet from her. He carried a small bat.

Astrid stood up, reflexively smoothing her cassock as if politeness could repel danger. (It works more often than you would think.)

He wasn't alone. Another man climbed out after him.

"Yes, have you come so we can confess our sins?"

She turned again. There was a man behind her, too.

"We are serving rations on the corner of Julick and Hardly. They are for anyone who wants them," explained Astrid.

The first man walked up quickly, and in her nervousness, she lost track of the plant. She glanced at the concrete and couldn't find the green anymore. The man shifted his stance, and she saw it crushed under his thick boots. Hope was often destroyed so easily, especially by those who have had a bit of practice. She looked up at them, annoyed, but trying to remember what she believed: grace, love, dignity, and other virtues she was struggling to recall—*patience*! That's right, patience too. "Come, we'd love to give you something to eat. And we have clean water. A gallon for each," she offered the men.

The first man, carrying the bat, pointed it at her. And then, touching the hem of her cassock, lifted it up. "I wonder what part's she got. She looks fully upgraded to me. Charlie, think she got anything that might be of use back home?"

She adjusted her clothes, pushing them down. The guy behind her reached over her shoulder and down her shirt.

"She's got the 10-56tx microprocessor in there!"

"I'm going to ask you to back away, gentlemen."

"Oh, she's confusing us with gentlemen! That's your first mistake."

"I'm going to ask you to step away, or I will be forced to defend myself."

They paused and stared at her.

"Defend yourself? Drakk, you'll defend yourself. Now, lie down." He lifted his bat.

They would not destroy her; they couldn't. But they could still rearrange her into several unhelpful configurations.

They couldn't break anything that couldn't be repaired. Until recently, she would have let it happen. That's what they expected of her. And in the past, it wouldn't have bothered her much. But now it felt like they were attacking something far more fragile than her body. Something that couldn't be fixed in a lab. She wondered if this was what it felt like to have a soul.

"No. I belong to my parish, which belongs to the Lord, and I will not tolerate this."

She hoped her words could convince them.

"Well, let's shut her mouth, and then we can see what else is under the dress."

He lifted his bat, pulling it back for a big swing towards her skull.

She could see it swing through the air and braced her head for the impact. She closed her eyes, but it never hit her. Her hand had reached up and stopped it inches from her face.

The guy looked at her with wide eyes. And the other two took a few steps back.

She yanked the bat from the guy. The second guy tried to knock her over, but her stabilizer kicked in. The third ran up and punched her, smacking her carbon shell. She took the bat she now held and swung it. She swung it with the same intention that had reached up to stop it—an intention she didn't understand or even control.

It caught his head, and he fell to the ground.

He didn't get up.

The other two men looked at him on the ground, turned white, and ran away.

She dropped the bat and fell to her knees.

It felt as if her programming slowed to a stop, her hard drives spinning down, and her mainframe acted like she had been left inside an oven, overheating.

This wasn't supposed to happen.

She got up and ran.

#

Astrid knew they'd find her, but it surprised her that it took them so long. She figured they had kept her tracking on since her last inspection, even though Emmanuel argued they had no reason to. They didn't need a reason. They didn't trust her class, and they could keep it on for six months without a warrant.

The interaction happened without violence.

Astrid sat under a cement roof by an abandoned carport. Her battery was running down; she hadn't slept in the last twenty hours. Without a charge, she wouldn't make it another five.

She had taken off her cassock. She couldn't bear to taint the name of her Lord, who bore the sins of the world, taking a far worse beating, and yet remained nonviolent.

She felt this only confirmed her fears; she was never meant to be a priest.

The fragile part of her she had tried to protect ached—whatever that part was, it had grown alarmingly large.

From a safe distance, they shot her with a pulse gun, and she went to sleep.

#

When she woke up, they had bound her to a bed, her arms and legs disabled, and her head locked to the attachment. The room was bright and white.

"She's back on, Doctor."

"Good," the Doctor said. "Let's begin. They haven't been clear about how long we're allowed to keep her."

Two technicians, their backs to her, talked while looking at a series of large monitors. The far monitor to the left, unblocked by them, broadcast the national news; they muted the audio. She used her eyes to zoom in and read the date in the bottom corner of the screen. A week had passed since the pulse gun put her to sleep.

"Somehow we're supposed to do, in a week, what takes us a year, and if we don't, they're shutting us down."

Astrid wished she could get up and help them, but she couldn't move.

"There's no time to spare," said the Doctor. "They're already drafting the recall orders."

After looking at the date, she noticed the bar along the bottom of the news screen talking of riots taking place in the city. Protestors from both sides were facing off downtown.

The doctor turned around and noticed Astrid's eyes.

"Did you forget to disable her consciousness?" asked the doctor.

Her assistant turned around and saw the same.

"Oh! I'm so sorry." She turned to the screen, and a moment later, Astrid fell back to sleep.

#

When she woke up again, she tried to look around, but they turned her eyes off. She tried her olfactory and hearing sensors, and the room smelled sterile, and she knew she was still in the lab from before. Then she heard someone.

"Astrid. Are you awake?"

"Emmanuel! What is going on?"

"A lot has happened since they arrested you," he said.

"What happened to my eyes? Why can't I move my arms or legs?"

"After getting arrested, they brought you back to Lossless. They've been doing tests and have had to remove parts of you to do that. The city wants to know why you were able to hit that man."

She remembered the men in the alley. She remembered the bat. She remembered the thud of hitting his skull.

"Is he going to make it?" she asked.

"Yeah. He had a concussion, but he made it, and he's been getting plenty of airtime ever since—not just here either. He's made national news. That son of a dog. As ungodly as it sounds, I'm glad you defended yourself!"

"How was I able to do it?"

"I'm afraid our upgrades altered your programming in more ways than one—which is my fault. All I can figure is that your increased ability for empathy also meant an increased empathy for yourself—an obvious side effect I hadn't considered."

"I'm so sorry! This is all my fault!" she yelled.

"No. It shouldn't be a crime for you to feel something; stop apologizing!"

"Did they find the upgrades then?" she asked.

"No. They can't find them—and they won't. Not unless I show them where they are. I'm a better technician than a priest—I always have been, and I'm not proud of that."

"Are they afraid I evolved on my own, then? Is that why there are riots?"

"You don't need to worry about that now."

"But we're responsible! We have to tell them…" Then she realized what would happen if he did. If he confessed to the upgrades, even his brother wouldn't be able to protect him! "Oh no! But you can't! Promise you won't turn yourself in. You didn't ask for this. I made you do it!"

"None of this is your concern. Astrid, listen to me and stop worrying about everyone else. They're going to turn you off! That's why I'm here."

She said nothing for a moment. She couldn't look at him, or move her arms, or tap her foot. She couldn't do anything.

"I came to give you a Final Meditation."

"You know that's against the rules."

"Damn the rules. You deserve to leave this world like anyone else from our parish."

There was a long pause, and soon she could smell the fragrance from a lit candle—an impossible comfort in a room designed for endings. She could hear him flipping through a book, and he recited the prayers she had only started to memorize. She felt as if they were healing the part of her she had tried to protect. When he was done, he paused. She could assume he reached for the switch that lay installed on her paralyzed arms.

She meant to say, "thank you," but a question squeezed out past her logic. It was the question she was most afraid to ask. "Do you think I will go anywhere when I'm turned off?"

"Yes, I do. I wouldn't be here as your priest if I didn't."

"How can you know for sure?"

"I can't. I'm not God. It isn't for me to know anything for sure."

She had never been hungrier for certainty than in that moment. Why did the end of everything cause her such fear? She had no say in being turned on or off, for life came and went in so many unpredictable ways. She had no say in any in her existence, and so why should she assume that she would have a say in the afterlife or whether she'd be there? It was not up to her, and that, in itself, came to her as very good news.

He leaned in. "But there's no way I can prove you won't; and that gives me all the room I need to believe."

"Yes. I, too, have found the room to believe." Her speakers cracked, and her body flinched.

He grabbed her arm.

"Goodbye, Emmanuel."

"Until we meet again."

He flipped the switch, and she turned off.

#

The church was full. Emmanuel had made sure of that. At the front of the sanctuary sat a simple wooden coffin.

It was empty. The parish forfeited her frame in the court case, and soon, everyone else who "owned" an autonomous bot did the same. People had always been uneasy about bots, so when they started thinking for themselves and no longer advanced the bottom line of the world's most powerful, it was easy to craft the propaganda needed to get them wiped out. Astrid's small act of self-preservation was just the spark this movement needed to put the final nails in the coffin. It turns out, good ideas are only good if they make money, and from that vantage, disconnected bots were not considered a good idea at all.

Without her frame, they placed trinkets in the coffin that reminded them of her. When it was done, Emmanuel placed one of his family's pebbles in the box and draped her cassock over their memories. They buried her in the parish graveyard that afternoon.

Part II: Earth Was Boring Anyway

Ore Rush

2831 CE - Earth

Harper Profeta straightened up in his seat, setting his tray table down. The attendant who approached had long hair, which she pulled back, reminding him of someone he had dated during his freshman year at the university. He tried to make eye contact, to be polite, for his dad had always taught him to be polite to service staff, no matter who they were or what they did, but she glanced at the bundle at his feet—a bundle big enough to hold a few three-legged diggers and pans for ore extraction.

"Just like the early days of the Gold Rush," she said, handing him a container of water.

He nodded, even if he wasn't sure what she was talking about. It did sound familiar, though.

"You know, the Gold Rush?" She asked, clearly noticing his confusion and wanting to point out his lack of knowledge on the subject.

"I should know this," he said, rubbing his neck. His grandfathers had lived out West, but they were not ones to talk about something as trite as the Gold Rush. They were far more likely to teach him how to pray, or, worse, say something to make his dad feel small for not going to college and being nothing but a digger. Not to mention, he did not have his memories off-world. The connection was spotty at best. "My brain's just not keeping up today."

"Well, I'm a bit of a history nut—during the American Empire, someone found a little gold on the west side of the Northern Continent and everyone and their mother went after it." She leaned, her uniform brushing against his water—he grabbed it to keep it from knocking over and pushed himself against the seat, hoping to get out of her way. She lifted the shade, looked out the window at the far-off Asteroid, and stood up. "They say the same will happen here, too. That's why I signed up for this route. You're a digger, I assume?"

"My dad is. I'm…just helping him, I guess. Have you worked this route long?"

"You betcha."

"You betcha," he repeated, having not heard that phrase in a while. The only person who said things like "you betcha" was his father. And his father used it all the time. It was his default answer to every question. Dad, is that you? You betcha. Dad, are you ready to leave? You betcha. Dad, have you ruined my spring break by upsetting Mom and thus forcing me to traverse across the system to see what you've been up to? You betcha—always, you betcha.

"I am curious, though—" her comment, bringing him back to the moment. "Why is it so hard to find the ore? We have the technology to travel in space, but we have to dig an entire asteroid looking for ore? Can't they use scanners or something?"

"That's what makes it so valuable—because of its ability to avoid scanners."

He wasn't about to explain how scanners rely on consistent signal reflection and how this ore tends to absorb most detection bands, turning incoming signals into harmless heat or scattering them incoherently. Of course, visible light behaves differently, but because of the interference, it creates the shimmering rainbow sheen it's known for. That's why only the naked eye (or a direct optical feed) can reliably pick it out. That's what he learned at the university, but he wasn't about to bore her with these details.

"Like stealth technology or something?" she asked.

It wasn't like that at all.

"Exactly like that," he said, "The only way to find it is with the naked eye, whether in person or on a screen. So, as you can imagine, it's worth its weight in rations."

"Sounds like it takes a good pair of eyes," she smiled. "Are you meeting anyone?"

"By myself."

"Well, I hope you find something—and not just because it'd be good for my route."

"Are you staying at the wayport for a while, or flying back?"

"Flying back. I'll be on this route for the next few trips, but then I get some time off."

"That's right about when I'll be heading back. I planned to spend the rest of my trip at the casino on Mars."

"Me too!"

"Well, what are the chances of that? You'll have to look me up."

If all goes well, he'll be back on this shuttle soon, and his spring break can finally start.

He pulled the smaller of his three bags to his lap and opened it. A beacon blinked on the map of their destination, the wayport on Asteroid R46. The beacon moved slowly from the arrival port to the baggage claim.

His dad must have just arrived.

#

Harper had only been home for a few hours when his mother cornered him in the kitchen while he held a sandwich, made from leftover ham. The university had more than a few perks, including access to the latest surveillance technology. Still, nothing could replicate homegrown pork—the only benefit from living downwind from a pig farm. He washed it down with some fresh-squeezed orange juice from a local greenhouse.

It was good to be home.

"He's not himself, Harper." His mother had been saying this since he entered the door, and Harper had done his best to ignore his mother's bizarre request. "Believe me—you wouldn't know—not with being gone as long as you have. I need to know what is going on."

This was Harper's last break at the university before graduation. He planned to socialize with friends, staying out at night and sleeping during the day. Now his mom wanted him to use his precious break to spy on his dad.

"There's a rumor that there's more ore on those rocks," Harper said, the bread sticking to the top of his mouth. "Maybe he wants to try again."

"Your father never listens to rumors like that—and he never visits a rock twice." She was correct about that, at least. "The only thing those rumors are going to do is bring out the crazies and fill that rock with every man and his brother, hoping to strike ore. With that crowd on its way, he knows he won't have time to dig up enough to make it worth the hassle, even if the rumors are true."

Harper swallowed. "Mom, really? I can't spy on my father like he's some criminal."

She put down her tea and grabbed him. "Son, I've been a good mother, haven't I? I've always given you what you need and never asked for much."

"I guess. You always try to do right by us."

"I'm asking for this now. In the name of all that is good and holy," she said, speaking in the religious tongue of Ammalee. "Please go after your father—use your little gadgets you love so much and that we pay so much for you to study—and see what he's up to."

"No."

She let go, turning towards the window, gazing at the harvest landscape.

"Fine, then I'll ask your uncle Ron."

"Dad hates Ron. You send him and—"

"You leave me no choice."

"Fine. I'll look in on him. But I'm not promising miracles. And I'm not going there to catch him doing something wrong—just to make sure he's okay."

She turned around. "That's all I ask."

#

He dragged his equipment through customs, hoping his father might have lingered in the terminal. He wasn't about to check the beacon while in the queue, so it wasn't until he passed customs that he opened the device again to see his father's location. He had missed him. His dad had left the wayport entirely. He wasn't even in the surrounding area. Harper clicked on the map setting, laying the asteroid out like an orange peel. The beacon was on the far side. Clicking on it made the asteroid's spherical form spin and put the beacon in the center of the screen.

He must have rented a rover immediately after landing to reach the other side of the asteroid so quickly. He figured he would do the same until he found out how much they cost. He'd have to spend half his vacation money on a rover, not to mention spending a night camping on an asteroid. He could get a suit for less, send out his satellite, and check on his dad from the comfort of a room.

He rented a room, and by the time he got to it, he wasn't sure "comfort" was the word he'd used to describe it. It was more of a dorm than a hotel, with five beds in his room. Thankfully, he was the only one in the room so far. Harper tossed the handheld on his bed, checked his pistol, put it back together after getting it through customs, and slid it into the holster on his belt.

He knew better than to travel here unprotected.

He wheeled his large piece of luggage to the foot of the bed and opened it. Surrounded by foam padding, he grabbed a collapsed satellite and launch pad stacked on top of each other. When he placed the satellite on the bed, its weight formed like a crater in the mattress. With a small screwdriver, he opened the main compartment between the slots that hold the solar panels and removed the current adapter—a Geiger-Mueller used in his school project just before break. Additional adapters were neatly arranged in pockets at the top corner of the case's foam pad. He placed the Geiger in its slot, removed a small camera, and attached it to the satellite.

He had built this satellite in school using his own concoction of a reduced alloy made from ore his father gave him. The severe reduction of the alloy made it visible to high-power sensors, but only if they were of the highest quality. Most times, it went undetected. He went through every part of his equipment again. His father always checked his tools twice. Harper checked them three times, partly out of habit and partly because doing things right was the one way he knew to earn his father's respect.

He reached across the bed and grabbed his screen again. After ensuring the satellite had properly synced, he powered everything down and packed it all up again, placing a few digging supplies on top to satisfy any checkpoint curiosity. He turned his large bag over and wheeled it to the south egress.

#

An elderly man greeted him. He had thin hair on his balding head and avoided eye contact with Harper.

"You plan on digging this close to the base?"

"Yes, sir." Although based on the old man's gaze, he couldn't say for sure if the man was asking him or the corner of the room. He felt sorry for him. In a way, he reminded him of his grandfather, back when his mom took care of him, and he started to lose his grasp of reality. He felt this man was too old to be working on an asteroid.

"There is no digging allowed in this part of the asteroid."

"Why is that?" Harper asked.

"It's not allowed—it's a fool's errand."

"Not even to practice?"

"There is no digging—"

"Don't mind him," said another voice, nearly identical to the first. The twin of the old man, with matching features: the same balding head, hairy eyebrows, brown eyes, and face covered in a patchy beard, appeared in the reception area as Harper looked over the counter. The only difference: this old man made eye contact with Harper.

"He's not all there, if you know what I mean." Slapping the back of his twin, who squirmed when touched. "They don't make 'em like they used to. In fact, I've seen these things get bolder and bolder with every upgrade." He turned to his double. "Now sit down and shut up," and he did as he was asked, without hesitating. The old man (the one without a lazy eye) looked back at Harper. "Now, how may I help you?"

"What do you mean, upgrade?" asked Harper.

"Others—I'm talking about clones, boy. They've been all the rage two systems over, as you surely know, and catching on here too. Ever been?"

"Here?

"No, the next system, over."

"No—to both."

It had been four years since he last went out with his father before leaving for university. The last time he was out in this part of their system, clones weren't common—mostly rumors. Everyone argued it was inevitable, with bots being outlawed and all, what did people expect to happen? How else were they to have free labor?

He couldn't help but think about what his mother would say. She had been telling them for years that clones would make their way. "They are abominations! You are to have nothing to do with them," she would say. What was she worried about? It wasn't like Harper was gonna bring a clone home to be his wife. Harper had never even met a clone until now. And now, he was meeting one, all because his mother insisted he come here. He laughed a little, considering the irony of it all.

"You think this is funny?" asked the old man, interrupting Harper's thoughts.

"No. Sorry. Just not used to—"

"Well, get used to it. They are useful out here, especially with all sentient technology getting outlawed. So, you may dig near the station, as long as you're over 100 meters from the furthest landing probe, but my *other* is right: it is a fool's errand. Nothing near here, picked dry already. The rumors refer to the asteroid's far side, but they are just rumors."

"I figured. I want to practice with my equipment before going further."

"New to digging?"

"No, but as I said, it's been a while—my father's a digger. Has been my whole life."

"He works this belt? Might know him."

"He's…" and he paused, distracted by unlatching the suit to prepare to put it on.

"Letting you explore on your own, then?"

"Yes, sir."

"Well, don't let the accelerator on the digger go past 5R—with those vibrations, you'll risk hitting your suit, and that would be the end of your—"

"It's been a while, but I know the basics."

"Your father taught you well, huh? Just offering free advice, no need to be bothered."

"But he's not allowed to dig here—you said no digging here," said the old man's other, this time his face hidden by the counter, with only his drifting eyes sticking out.

"Shut your mouth, you fool. *You're* not allowed to dig here, and you're not to be talking to customers either—pretending to be me—capital offense in some places, you know." He paused, looked at Harper, and turned his lips up into a smile. "Here you go," handing him a suit, "Best of luck on the practice."

#

Harper headed south, along the edge of the station's southern landing probes, until he found a crater large enough to hide in. The satellite wouldn't be detectable by lower-powered sensors common in mining wayports, but it could still be visible to the naked eye. With a bit of luck, he'd get it in orbit with no one noticing. He didn't want to spend any money on the permits, but it'd be even worse if he got fined for not having one.

He climbed over the lip of the crater, the luggage kicking up dust as it rocked over the uneven surface. Laying his bag down, he opened the case and set up the launch pad, securing it to the satellite. After walking to the far edge of the crater and hiding behind a large boulder, he opened his handheld and activated the launch. The satellite shot into the sky with a burst of light. Had the atmosphere been any thicker, he would have needed a different launch pad—one that didn't travel as easily and would cost a fortune to rent.

The old man at the egress was helping a few port workers secure their suits, so Harper dropped it off and sneaked past without further conversation.

With its initial high orbit because of the low gravity, his satellite would have to do a single pass before he'd get any useful footage of his father.

He went to the canteen across from the prayer room, which felt a little off-putting at first. He certainly didn't want to imagine Ammalee watching him as he drank. He paused at the entrance and wished he had a pebble to place on the altar, if for no other reason than it's what he was taught to do when passing places of worship.

At the canteen, he looked to see what they had to eat. He never got used to packaged food at the university, but at least it was edible. Growing up around old-fashioned farms made him nauseous at the sight of most canteen food.

At the very least, the drinks traveled well. He filled up on beer. He couldn't remember how he got back to his room. But he remembered dreaming he spent the night with his old girlfriend—or was it the flight attendant? It was all a blur.

When he woke up, he rolled over to grab his handheld.

He didn't remember drinking very much the night before. But he also didn't take into account how the shifts in gravity, dehydration, and lack of eating impacted his blood alcohol levels. His head felt like a melon that had been scooped out for a summer cookout back on his neighbor's farm.

He checked the satellite as it slowly orbited above his dad's camp. His dad was pacing back and forth near his rover and dome.

He zoomed in closer when someone knocked on his door. He turned, pulling the blanket off the bed with his twisted body, revealing a woman who also woke up from the knock. She jumped up and started getting dressed. Before Harper could react, the woman in the bed opened the door, and an identical woman greeted them. She was very rude towards her *other* and insisted she leave right away, and the whole interaction made him wonder. Had he spent the night with an *other*?

He spent the rest of the morning trying to figure out if he had slept with the primary or the clone—and whether either was considered an "adult." Even though they were clearly his age, biologically, he had heard adulthood worked differently out here, especially with clones. Was a clone the age of its primary or the age at which it was created? These questions were often debated in the new settlement at Primera, one system over, and his dad had told him to be careful when off-world. "Always check their ID," he'd say, "And no matter what, be kind and respectful." He was raised to be a gentleman, and the possibility of sleeping with a clone or a minor made his head spin. He didn't have anything wrong with clones. They were people, too—he assumed. And if they looked like an adult, they were adults, right? But he actually wasn't sure. He was left with the unsettling feeling of crossing a line he didn't understand.

He didn't want to hurt anyone; he just wished he'd been sober enough to know who he'd been with, and he worried he'd done something he would regret.

#

Three orbits had passed, and each time Harper checked the footage, his father was digging holes and finding nothing. No strange behavior. No strange discoveries. No, strange, nothing. He was digging like he had his entire life.

According to the bartender, the incoming flight was full of passengers. "Soon business would be great again," he said. Harper's room in the hostel would be full of diggers.

He ordered a chocolate-flavored protein bar from the canteen but ate it in his room. With the handheld propped in his lap, the protein bar in one hand, and the other holding the screen, he checked the satellite footage. He took a bite of the bar as his father powered down his digger. Harper paused mid-bite and zoomed in a little more. The digger sat on three prolonged legs, each foot attached to the asteroid with simple bolts. His father used the pneumatic drill to unbolt the feet, and then tilted the digger back onto the leg's wheels to move it out of the way. He knelt down, brushing back the asteroid dust.

When his father leaned back, no longer blocking the camera's view, Harper could see it as plain as the nearby star. Through the remaining dust was the rainbow smear, similar to the way oil looks when it falls on the station floor from a broken rover. He followed the sheen; it was the length of a full-grown man. He zoomed in and out, checking for camera glitches or interference, but there weren't any.

This was the largest piece of ore he had ever seen.

A piece of ore this size was more than enough never to dig another asteroid—his dad could retire if he wanted to, and have more than enough to help Harper get started in life, maybe even pay off his school loans and fund his business ideas and take care of mom well into her old age—these thoughts ran through his head quicker than he could fully consider them, and down into his body, and into his legs, forcing himself to jump up and shout, "There it is, father!" Then, realizing how loud he had become, he sat back down.

With a smile, he picked up his handheld, which he had knocked to the floor, and took a massive bite out of his bar as he watched his father unearth the ore a little more. He grinned like a kid again, amazed at how his father still managed to surprise him.

"I tell you what, father, you've done it. You broke your own rule—never go back to the same rock twice and never believe the rumors—but it worked for you this time. Good job, father—no wonder he's been acting strange." He was legitimately proud of his dad, and he'd tell him as soon as he had a chance.

For the first time since his break, he was enjoying himself. His parents could move to Salt Lake, buy a lovely flat safely upwind from the less-than-pleasant farm aromas, and he'd never risk turning into a digger—not that there was anything wrong with being a digger. He was proud of his dad. It just wasn't for him.

As he thought about what he'd do with his dad's ore, he noticed something strange.

He stopped chewing and froze.

His father wasn't unearthing it. In fact, he did the opposite.

His father covered the ore back up.

"Father!" he yelled, but quieter this time, "What are you doing?"

No respectable digger left such a product in the ground—it went against the code that governed the entire region. This ore didn't belong to his father until he unearthed it. Until it was loaded and secured on his rover. Leaving it in the ground meant anyone could claim it—and while the nearest digger was on the other side of the ridge, his father knew this side of the rock had stirred up lots of rumors. The first rule in digging was to get the rock into your cart before anyone else, which is why what his father did next was so strange. He measured a few more meters from the first hole, grabbed his digger, wheeled it over, let out the legs, bolted the feet, and started digging again.

"What?" Harper said, grabbing the screen. "Father, greed will ruin a dig—you taught me that! You need nothing more than what you've found—no one would."

But his father dug a hole bigger than the first, stopped when he found nothing, unbolted the rig, moved it, re-bolted it, and dug another hole a few meters from the last. Each time, Harper checked to see if the other diggers in the area had moved any closer, and then pleaded with the screen for his father to stop—especially when a few of the holes contained ore. Not as much as the first, but more than any normal dig.

After the fourth hole, Harper agreed with his mother: his father was acting strange. She was right to worry. Maybe he got space sick—too many orbits in microgravity or too many sleeps traveling the system. Maybe he was losing it. Harper wondered if he should go get him, talk him into taking what he had found, and not worry about finding more.

As he was preparing to leave, he noticed his father uncovering something in the fifth hole. Harper zoomed in. Something was off with this find. Usually, he'd see some dim colors shining through, but there wasn't any sheen. The dust clung to it like cloth, muting its appearance. His father brushed it off a little more, and then a shape appeared. He zoomed in again. The screen pixelated at first, from a temporary weak connection, and then it cleared. He followed the tip of something with a wrinkled texture and more organic than the ore. It looked almost soft, a pale white like a space suit that got covered in dust. He followed the tip that stuck out as the dust settled, and he realized he wasn't looking at a rock at all, but the tip of a finger that connected to a wrist that stuck out of a torn suit.

Harper dropped the screen.

His dad had found a body.

He grabbed his handheld and zoomed back in as his dad uncovered more of it. It was a dead body, its suit shredded by the digger, and its outstretched hand frozen in the asteroid's atmosphere like torn leather.

Harper sat back, closed the screen just enough to keep from seeing it anymore, and didn't move. He tried to focus his mind on the facts. His father had been set on coming back to this rock, to this part, and even after digging up more than enough ore to last a lifetime, he kept digging.

Until he found this body.

Harper's mind raced to make sense of it. Someone, possibly a hired worker, must have operated the digger until it became loose from the bolts and caused the fatal accident. Things like this happen, and for drifters, it's easier to bury them than to worry about the paperwork. Whatever it was, his dad couldn't leave him buried on this rock anymore. His father knew people would soon flock to this rock and dig up every meter—it was only a matter of time. That's why he came back—it had to be why he came back.

He had to move that body before the crowds arrived.

And he had come back to this hell-rock alone. Whatever happened must have been weighing on him for months. What a burden to bear! He felt sorry for his dad more than anything else. He knew his dad, and he was a good man and cared about other people, even hired help. He wouldn't have just buried him, but given him a nice service and said a few prayers over him.

These thoughts tightened his muscles, and he found himself packing his room before even deciding to help. It was then that someone interrupted his thoughts.

"What are you looking at?" Harper looked up from his suitcase to see that his door had been opened, and three young diggers were standing at the entrance. The one who asked was staring at his handheld on the bed. He leaned over, grabbed the handheld, and pulled it close.

"Nothing. Who are you?" asked Harper.

"Bus got in early. This is our room—roomie," said the tall one. "I'm Jaxl, this is Mills, and that's Gael."

Harper straightened himself. "I'm Harper. I got here a few days ago."

"So what did you find?" asked Jaxl, pointing at the handheld.

"Doing a satellite search like we planned to do—isn't he?" said Gael, bending over to see the screen. "I know a satellite case when I see one—

Heck yeah, man. Is that a rainbow satellite? Brilliant—I'd kill to get my hands on enough ore to build one of those."

Harper put the screen next to him. "I wasn't looking at anything."

"Whatever, man. I know that look, and it only happens for one of two reasons, right before..." as he humped the air.

"And when you landed a score!" interrupted Jaxl.

He tried to imagine how his face, after just finding out his dad had likely killed someone, made them think of things like that. These are precisely the kind of men his dad had warned him about: the crude kind, the ones raised without dads—or worse, the ones raised by the wrong kind of dads.

"You ain't hiding a girl in here, are you? So then, what did you find?"

"Don't worry about it."

"Who said we were worried? Temperamental, little dog, isn't he?" said Mills, as he grabbed Harper's handheld.

Harper stood up to get it back, but Gael grabbed him, and Jaxl grabbed his other arm to keep him still. Mills opened the handheld and looked at the screen. "Well, look at that, he stole our idea, as you said." He showed the screen to the other two. "Satellites are the future of digging—am I right?"

"That's not what I'm doing. Now give it back." He reached for it, but Jaxl and Gael pulled him.

"What did he find?" asked Gael.

"Give me a second—the satellite is moving out of range, trying to slow it down. I see a couple of empty holes—Wait, a second..." Mills said, leaning into the screen. He stopped laughing, and the entire room got quiet.

Harper could only imagine he had seen the body. Mills turned the screen around to the others. The satellite focused on the original hole, where the dust hiding the giant ore had settled from the pounding of the digger nearby. A massive piece of rainbow ore lit up the screen.

"Look at it—it must be the biggest piece I've ever seen!"

"That's call-your-mom big!"

"Well done, roomie," Gael said, patting his back.

They didn't see the body, but they saw the collection of ore, which was nearly as bad. It would only be a matter of time before the entire port knew these coordinates, and everyone within a few orbits would crowd in.

He knew if his father had any hope of getting that body out of there, he had to hurry.

Harper pulled back his elbow and thrust it into Gael's stomach, and he took his head and rammed it into Jaxl, who fell back into Mills. With his arm free, he reached behind his back and pulled out his pistol and pointed it at them.

They backed up with their hands in the air.

"Give me the handheld."

"Dude. Chill out," handing him the handheld.

Harper grabbed his case with the other hand and left.

In the hallway, Harper grabbed the strap from one of their bags and tied the door handle to a nearby pipe. It wouldn't hold them long, but he hoped it would give him enough time to get a head start.

#

It took longer than he wanted to rent a rover (and cost more than he thought, nearly all he had left), and he didn't start breathing at a normal pace until he was in it and on his way to his father, looking behind him every few moments to see if anyone was following. On the way, Harper programmed the satellite to land a few meters from his father's camp.

By the time Harper arrived, his father had already laid the body in a large carrier and was covering it with chunks of ore to hide it from scans.

"Father!" he yelled as soon as their suits' comms synchronized.

His father looked around to see who was close enough to communicate. Harper jumped out of the rover and ran up to his father.

"What are you doing here?"

"We have to move."

"But what are you doing here?" he asked again.

"I know what happened—and we have to move—now!"

"What do you mean?"

Before he could answer, the satellite's parachute opened up, and Harper pointed at it as it drifted towards their camp. "Mom said you were acting strange and sent me after you. I was going to check in on you, and that's it—I promise, but I saw the body, and I don't need to know how it happened. But a few diggers found my feed, and they saw the ore you uncovered earlier, and soon the whole port will know—and once that happens, there will be no way to move a body without being seen."

His father's eyes stared out into space, as if the information wasn't processing correctly.

"We have to go, now!" jolting his father's attention back to him. "We have to get him out of here," he said, tapping the open container that now held the body, surrounded by pieces of ore. When he tapped the container, dust from the ore shot into the air, and the larger pieces of ore settled into the box. When the dust cloud settled, it revealed the figure's face through a broken space helmet. Harper looked at him, fully expecting to see some stranger—a drifter, a hired hand.

But it wasn't any of these.

The face belonged to his father, the same father who held him on his lap as a kid, who took him digging on his thirteenth birthday, who taught him the value of hard work, and who risked their home with a special mortgage to get him into university.

He looked again, and then up at his father, the one standing, and back at his father, the one folded into a carrier, the body bent and mangled, torn from the digger and frozen from the atmosphere.

They were the same.

He felt like his oxygen tank had run out of juice.

He held his chest and fell to his knees.

His father—the one still breathing—walked up and tried to help him, but he wouldn't budge.

"I can explain."

"What is going on?"

"Whoa. Relax. It's ok. I'm your father. See?"

His eyes locked onto Harper's, through the tinted glass of the helmet, twitching in fear.

"Then who is that?"

"My clone. Now, can you put the pistol away?" Harper didn't realize it, but he had pulled it from its sheath and held it by his side after collapsing to his knees.

He started to put back into his sheath and stood up. "What the heck is going on?"

His father took a deep breath and leaned on the rover. "He's my clone—I got him ages ago. He stays out in the field and helps me dig. Your mother didn't know—you know how she feels about these things."

Harper loosened his grip on his pistol, removing his finger from the trigger, and stared at the body. "What happened to him?"

"We found a pretty big haul—as you saw just now—and he got greedy. They say they are becoming more and more bold. They are right. He wanted it all for himself—or he was worried I'd get rid of him now that he wasn't needed, maybe." Harper couldn't stop staring at the corpse of his father's look-alike. But his father reached for Harper again, turning his face towards him. "He might look like me, but he's not me. He tried to kill me. I killed him in self-defense, I promise."

Harper stood still, the image of his father's shrunken face spinning in his head. He believed him. Of course he did. His dad had never lied to him before. Then he remembered the guys back at the hostel—they'd be on their way by now.

"We have to go, Father. I can help cover him up." He put his pistol away and went towards the loose chunks of rainbow ore in the nearby hole. His father walked behind him, slowly, keeping his distance.

They filled the container with the body, covering it entirely with ore, before Harper had time to get his heart rate back to normal. On his way back to his rover, he turned to his father. "Should we put some ore in my carrier too? If so, we need to hurry. Might as well get as much as we can, right?"

"You know that's right!"

Harper paused and turned around.

"You know that's right?"

"If we have time, we might as well," said his dad, "but as you said, we need to hurry."

He reached for his pistol again. "You're my father, right?" he asked, as if his thoughts were speaking for themselves. "I mean, you're my father, and not my father's clone?"

"You can bet on it."

"You can bet on it?"

"Yeah."

Harper put his finger on the pistol's trigger. The idea of this man—a fraud, a liar, a clone—a shadow of the man his dad was, made him so angry he struggled to breathe.

"Son, what's the matter?" That's when the twitch in his dad's eyes released; his left eye looked off into space, while his right eye stayed where it was.

"You think I wouldn't be able to tell?"

"Tell what?"

"You're an *other*, aren't you?"

"Don't call me that."

"Call you what?" He was sincerely confused.

"An *other*—it's rude and insensitive and not appropriate, and if you had ever gotten to know someone like me, you'd know that."

"So you are an *other*—I mean, you are my dad's clone?"

"I'm me—and that's all that matters for now." He turned to continue packing the rover.

"But that means you killed my dad?"

He turned around, his body facing him, but his eyes drifting into space. "Your father commissioned me, and then was just going to get rid of me when I wasn't needed. I didn't lie to you—I killed him in self-defense."

"Another lie! My dad would never do that!"

"I'm the closest thing you have to a father—same DNA."

He imagined if he let him live, and brought him home as dad's replacement, hiding the fact that he was an *other*.

He imagined his mother coming to the front door to welcome his father home, kissing him on the cheek and offering him fresh sliced ham and potato salad for dinner, never knowing she was loving a clone. This man—this shadow of a man—wouldn't know anything about their past, or their life together. He'd have no notion of how his dad set aside time every night to read to him as a child and then teach him complex math as a teenager, helping him study for the university entrance exams. He'd know nothing about the countless trips to an asteroid he made so that he'd have enough to pay for college. He knew nothing about being his dad. He was shaking now, and he felt warm sweat running down the back of his neck. Before he knew what he was doing, he had lifted his gun and pointed it at him.

"Whoa. Whoa! You wouldn't kill your dad, would you? Same DNA—we're basically the same. You wouldn't make your mother a widow, would you?"

There was no dad in this man.

But he couldn't kill him. He'd never forgive himself. But he would turn him in, and not trust him for a moment without a pistol pointed at him.

That's when the man jolted towards him, causing Harper to flinch and, in doing so, pull the trigger.

The recoil jolted against the back of his suit, staggering, reaching out as if he could pull the bullet back, and undo the last five seconds. "Dad…" he whispered, though he knew that man was not his dad; he looked like him, and those are nearly the same thing.

The bullet shot through the helmet, with the larger drops of blood drifting to the surface, and the smaller ones falling into space.

\#

He stood by the window, watching a few port workers load his carrier into the back of the bus. By the time he boarded, he had his choice of seats. Everyone was arriving; no one was leaving.

He watched from the window at the line of people waiting for an available rover.

"You had quite the haul, huh?" asked a voice.

He looked up. It was the flight attendant from before. She was pushing a drink cart and wiping down a cold bottle of water for him.

"Oh. Yeah. Quite a haul."

"I don't think our bus has carried that many grams—not from this rock."

"I got lucky, I guess." He sat up in his seat when he said that, trying to hide the fact that most of those grams were two stashed bodies, with just enough ore to hide them from scanners. Not that he wanted to hide them. More than once, he prayed he'd get caught. How could he live with himself, killing someone, even if it was just a clone and hardly illegal?

"The rumors must be true then?"

"Yeah. This rock is going to make a lot of people rich."

Even if that wasn't the case for himself.

"Not that any of them will be able to hold on to it—I find most waste it at the casino."

She smiled.

He looked up at her. "Oh, right, the casino. You still headed there when you're done with work?"

"No break for me today—working the next few days, non-stop."

"Oh, I thought you had mentioned you'd be on break around now."

"Yes, a simple mistake. That was my clone. She would have served you on the way in. She went on break this morning. I'll get a break next week."

"Gotcha."

"But that means you're the young digger she wouldn't stop talking about?"

"I guess so."

"Were you two close? Like friends or sisters or… something else?"

"We were close! She was in every way my twin, the sister I never had."

He smiled, and he wasn't sure what to make of that.

He closed his eyes. He remembered his dad and wondered if he was ever close with his or whether it just depended on the clone or the circumstances or nature of the relationship, and whether any of this could change the way he felt about killing him.

Terraforming

2852 CE – Primera System

Arya didn't expect things to go her way—they never went her way. Her daughter, Maisie, was four months old, strapped to her chest in a sling, the dad was in prison for statutory rape, and the chances the hearing today would go her way were slim to nothing. She was growing increasingly upset about this when she glimpsed the ice cap explosion through the large window just outside the ship's courtroom. She had been staring at Primera through the window, but she wasn't paying attention until the bomb went off.

The mushroom cloud crawled across the ice like a drop of gel on a smooth surface.

"Why do they have to keep blowing things up?" asked Arya.

Her mom took a step towards the window, looked at the cloud, and put her arm on Arya's shoulder. "Sometimes we have to hurt things to help them grow."

Arya shifted her stance, knocking her mom's arm away.

"Might seem backwards, but that's what we have to do to make it habitable," her dad chimed in, walking up to the window.

Arya knew all about terraforming and its benefits—everyone did. But she also knew her older brother, Jak, lived down there along with many other colonists. Which means Primera already supported life—maybe not to her parents' level of approval—but life, nonetheless.

"It's actually rather fascinating—" Her dad began to explain an article he read concerning the benefits of strip mining and CO_2 levels, when the door to the courtroom opened.

A new adult—only fourteen years old—stood at the threshold, holding the door.

Arya hated the young ones. It took a special child to become an adult at fourteen, and they always looked down on older minors like her.

"Eloise and Hamler, it's time for Arya's hearing. Please come this way," said the adult boy.

He didn't even look at Arya.

The courtroom floors were glass, reflecting everything in the room. This made looking up or down indifferent to each other, and all the harder for Arya to divert her eyes. She decided she would turn them to Maisie, who slept nestled against her chest. In the last four months, she had learned to keep track of time by Maisie's cycles of sleep, and each time she drifted off to sleep, there was a sigh of relief. It was all the relief she would get, and she'd take it.

"Don't worry," said her dad, leaning in as they neared the front, "whatever happens, you will always be our little girl."

Didn't he understand that being his little girl was part of the problem?

"All rise," said the bailiff.

Her mother leaned in and put her hand on Arya's back. "Stand up straight, dear. We can't look weak."

She wasn't sure how she would stand any straighter, at least in this part of the ring-like ship. They were as far from the center as possible, where the centrifugal gravity was the most oppressive, and she struggled to find the right balance. Above them, a row of dormant hibernation pods, adapted from the days of cloning, lined the upper deck—standard equipment on ships meant for deep-space work, though here they mostly stored aging passengers who signed up for rejuvenation cycles. Arya had learned not to look at them; somehow, they made her feel smaller, as if even sleep was something adults could afford.

Her judge was old and had been an adult most of his life, since the age of fifteen! (He had told her three different times.) He had gray hair, a short beard, and thick eyebrows, and was known for being generous. She hoped this would be the case for her.

"You may be seated," he said, before looking up. When he noticed who was in the courtroom, he smiled. "Arya, it's good to see you again. I hope you are well."

He addressed her directly and would for most of the hearing. It was one of the few times in life she could speak for herself, but it always put her parents in a bit of a mood. "That judge favors you too much," her mom would say. Arya always thought this was ridiculous, considering how many times he had rejected her application.

"I am fine, your honor."

"Your little one is doing well?" he asked, gesturing to Maisie, wrapped against her breast.

"She is healthy, your honor."

"Good. I'm glad to hear it. So, what brings you in today?" He wasn't asking anyone in particular—they knew that. He put on a pair of reading glasses, turned to his computer, and shuffled through the files until he came to her case. "Oh yes, an emergency hearing for adulthood—and by extension—what we're really looking at is the custody of little…." He turned to Arya, looking over his glasses.

"Her name is Maisie, your honor."

"Maisie. Yes, beautiful name. Did you name her?"

"Yes, your honor."

"That's very kind of your parents," he said, with a smile directed towards them. They smiled in return. Then he turned back to Arya and took off his glasses. "Now, you know I am not one to grant emergency adulthood very often—and I rarely do it with unplanned pregnancies; it just isn't the purpose of this court, understand?" He went to his computer, put his glasses back on, and looked over her file again. "And, I will add, if I were to grant you adulthood today, it would indirectly affect the sentence of inmate number…"

He wouldn't dare refer to him by his name or as Maisie's dad. He wouldn't, for it would be deemed inappropriate to do so when talking about a rapist in court, even in a statutory case. But he wasn't a rapist!

His name was Lon, and he was a lovely young man who did no harm to anyone. Arya had tried to explain that to his judge, but he wouldn't listen to her. It's not that she and Lon were close; they had only met the night Maisie was conceived, at a party with some friends. But it wasn't as bad as the court thought, and she would tell them if they gave her a chance. She was often mistaken for an adult because of her age.

"...Inmate number 3687." He took off his glasses again and looked at her. "It would change his status, and that isn't something I take lightly. Do you understand?" He asked in a soft tone, as if she were a child.

"Your honor, I'm twenty-one years old—by Earth's standards—hardly a child. And Lon was only a year older than me, when we—"

"I'm going to stop you there, young lady. Now I know your parents did a better job of raising you than that." He lifted out of his seat with each word. "You think your age matters here? By Earth standards? Where do you get off bringing Earth into this? Do you know what happens when men and women get all the rights and privileges of adulthood simply because they get older? Chaos, young lady! Uncontrollable chaos. Famine. Wars. Climate change. Unregulated technology that does nothing but rot the brain. And worst of all, trillionaires! All because they have no way of controlling when someone becomes an adult! No, you will become an adult when the court declares it and not before!" He adjusted his robe and sat back down. "Now, where were we?" He looked back at his screen. "Yes, I think I'd like to talk to your parents alone for a moment."

And with that, they escorted Arya back to the hallway with Maisie, where she stood, leaning against the window.

She could already guess the outcome of this hearing.

\#

The ship's orbit had moved from the ice caps. The browns of the southern deserts stretched across the lower continent, occasionally broken only by soft clouds. Her brother lived somewhere there, near a small colony, on the edge of the Salt Lake. She scanned the horizon until she found the lake and squinted her eyes to see the colony, but it was too small.

She had thought about running away. She knew she could catch a shuttle. She had a fake ID and a good one, at that. It cost her a year's worth of credits. Most twenty-year-old minors had counterfeit IDs. It was impossible to do anything on the ship without one.

"You can come back in," said the young bailiff, interrupting her thoughts.

She turned from the window.

"Thank you," she said, but she didn't mean it—and had he been looking at her face, he would have been able to tell.

She walked, staring at her feet and the reflection of the ceiling until she stood behind the table next to her parents, who wouldn't look at her, and said nothing—that couldn't be good. In the room, three additional people now lined the wall, all dressed in security uniforms.

"It's been determined, based on my conference with your parents—"

There it is. She knew it. His tone gave it away.

"—that it is in your best interest that you remain a minor for the time being until your next birthday, where you can apply again—"

Another half-year would pass before her chance to become an adult. Just as she figured. She'd be twenty-two then, making her one of the oldest minors in her sector.

"And" he said, looking at the ruling on his screen, "the court has decided to transfer custody of Maisie to new parents until that time so that you can focus on your preparations for adulthood."

What did he say?

The bailiff walked towards her.

"Maisie will be placed with a foster family, and I promise you that in time, with hard work, the courts will give you a fair chance to get her back."

The young bailiff reached for Maisie as if Arya was going to give her over to him, just like that! Absolutely, not. She turned away—she wanted to run but knew she wouldn't get far.

She wanted to scream, but it would only make her look more like a child.

She wanted to cry, hit, and throw a fit—all of which would only hurt her chances even more.

She turned away from the page, giving him the shoulder, and looked to her parents.

"It's what's best," said her dad. "In time, we will get her back."

"Do as you're told," added her mom. "This is your chance to show them you can listen."

Arya couldn't move, and she wouldn't let go of Maisie.

The bailiff reached again, but she pushed him away.

"Do you find my ruling unfair?" asked the judge. He had every reason to expect she would throw a fit—that's why he had called security. Arya looked at them standing along the wall. They were ready and maybe a little too eager to intercede.

She turned towards the judge.

"Of course I do not, your honor." She spoke through gritted teeth and did her best to hide her anger. "I was merely hoping, in the spirit of honest negotiation, if I might ask for a small favor."

The judge looked into her eyes. "I will hear it."

"Your honor, I was wondering if I might have one more night with Maisie—for her sake, your honor. It would give me time to prepare her."

He reached for his chin and rubbed his thin beard.

"Agreed. Bring her here tomorrow morning. That is all." With that, he slammed his gavel against the countertop, and they were escorted out.

#

Her mom grabbed Maisie as soon as Arya unwrapped her from her chest. Maisie was awake and hungry and annoyed—and she let everyone know, but she wasn't half as annoyed as Arya.

"Mom! Give her back!"—their cries matching each other's.

She turned her body to keep Arya away. "You should not have argued with the judge—do you understand me? You have not earned time with Maisie."

"No! You will not do this tonight! Give her back!"

"Everyone needs to calm down." Her dad hung his jacket on the hook by the hatch and looked down at Maisie. Arya reached for her again, but her dad grabbed her arm with his giant hands.

"Everyone needs to calm down," he said again, but calmer this time—his grip tight around her wrist. Tight enough to leave a bruise—

not that anyone would care.

"I want my daughter! She can't take my daughter!"

"Just breathe, my dear, count to ten, as I taught you."

"Stop telling me what to do! I want my daughter back!"

He dragged her away by her arm. "If you will not calm down, then you can go to your room."

"Give me Maisie, and I will go to my room and stay there the rest of the night and not bother anyone!" she yelled as her feet dragged against the floor.

"No." He paused. His voice was stern and loud and not to be argued with. "Go to your room right now."

He shoved her in that direction.

She stumbled and then turned and looked at him.

"This is my last night with her; you're not even going to let me hold her?"

He held his glare and then softened his face and turned to his wife. He took a breath and turned back to Arya. "We will bring her to you in a few moments once you've calmed down—assuming you don't argue with me about it."

Arya didn't have a choice. She sat on the bed, listening to Maisie cry on the other side of the hatch, as if, somehow, Maisie knew what tomorrow would bring. After a while, they knocked on her door, and she did her best to appear composed.

She reached for Maisie but tried not to grab her too eagerly.

#

They packed Maisie's bag and left it by the door as Arya rocked Maisie back and forth on the bed, whispering in her ear. When they finished, Eloise walked to the bed, and Arya did her best not to wince. She bent over and kissed Arya on the forehead while brushing Maisie's head. "You must trust us. It's all for the best."

They left, and Arya let out a deep breath and looked down at Maisie.

"I won't let them take you away from me."

For the rest of the night, Arya sat on her bed, alone, nursing Maisie, who only found relief when held to her breasts. Arya wondered if her new parents would hold her like that or feed her from a bottle, and the thought of another mother holding Maisie—or worse: nursing her—made her want to jump into space.

And maybe that's precisely what she would do.

She imagined the stillness and freedom of drifting out into space, away from it all.

Thinking about the airlocks and what it would be like to shoot into space reminded her of the shuttles and the routes they take to and from Primera, and suddenly she felt a bit of hope.

She could run away. She'd take a ship with a hibernation pod and go so far into space her parents would never find her, but she knew she'd never afford a ticket. She could afford a shuttle down to the planet, and it was a pretty big planet. Easy to get lost.

#

After she was sure her parents had fallen asleep, she reached under her mattress and grabbed a small hand-sewn pouch. She unfolded the cloth and grabbed her fake ID. After snatching Maisie's packed bag, she snuck out past her parents' cabin.

She didn't linger.

She didn't say goodbye.

She tried to pretend they weren't there—that they didn't exist—otherwise she was afraid she wouldn't have the courage to pass.

She made it out of their main hatch, down the empty residential corridor, and to the local public airlock.

Things would have to work out for her in ways they never had before if she was going to make it: the shuttle was scheduled to leave at the same time her parents would wake up. If there were any changes in either, they would find her before the shuttle breached the atmosphere.

With Maisie against her chest, she purchased a one-way ticket, found her seat, and strapped in.

It wasn't until the hatch was locked and the departure plan approved that she relaxed.

Then the hull of the shuttle screamed—as if it had to fight its way into the world and was downright angry about it—as if it understood

Arya's distress, as if it was a child forcing itself out of the womb, ready to cry its best cry, a necessary sign of life, the doctor had said. Maisie and Arya remembered this moment well, and it might have been why Maisie joined in the shuttle's cry.

A few women, two rows up, turned and looked at her and smiled as she cried, and Arya tried to hold her like she would if she were an adult—like she knew what she was doing. One of them came over and asked if she might pray over Maisie in the name of Ammalee. She figured she could use all the prayers she could get, but she struggled to understand the language of their prayers or the purpose of rubbing pebbles on her forehead, which made her want to laugh, but she knew better than to laugh during a prayer. They were very serious.

Maisie fell back asleep during the prayer, and Arya thanked them.

They flew through the atmosphere for a while before landing, and as soon as the legs touched down on Primera, shaking the whole craft, Maisie woke up.

The first step on the planet was worth remembering. The air was thin and dry, smelling of dirt. And the ground was hard against her space legs.

The weight of gravity made the walk from the shuttle to the bus unbearable, but she knew had no time to stop. Halfway there, Arya wanted to give up and go back and pretend it had never happened.

Oxygen supplements were optional at this stage of terraforming, but recommended for the first 24 hours. Arya had only a few credits left on her fake ID—she had plenty on her real ID, but she knew better than to use that. She was worried she wouldn't make it, so she bought a small portable unit and shared it with Maisie.

Once on the bus, she would have a full day's journey before reaching the colony, and from there, another half day before reaching her brother's ranch.

She knew going there was a bad idea, but she didn't know what else to do.

#

The bus's door closed and left her standing in the dirt.

The wind scratched her face as if it were carrying small pieces of glass and made the horizon impossible to see.

Maisie was awake, but content, wrapped in a thin cloth to protect her from the wind. The sun was scorching in the sky, and she tried to imagine this place as the frozen wasteland it had been a few years ago. All she could see now was sand and rocks.

Arya squinted, looking for Jak's ranch. In all directions, she could see nothing but the occasional boulder, half-covered in drifting sand. The bus had to turn around and nearly got stuck in a soft spot before heading back down the road away from them. This was the end of the road, and there was nothing but dead landscapes for as far as she could see.

Except in one location. As the wind calmed and the dust settled, she saw a machine the size of a shuttle and, next to it, a dome tent.

The machine was much larger once she got closer. The humming from it vibrated the ground, but it was soft and steady, putting Maisie back to sleep. It moved slowly, kicking up sand as it did, rolling along on wheels as tall as her. As it moved, it left behind rows of large wet bricks ready to dry in the sun. The machine turned towards her, and she could see the front of it now. It was digging into the earth. Near the top was a small cabinet next to a tank of water, and in it sat a young man with large goggles and a giant hat. When he saw Arya, he turned the machine off and stood up, squinting through his goggles, as the engine and gears quieted.

When he finally removed his goggles, they left a circle around his eyes. "Sis? Is that you?"

"Yeah, it's me—and Maisie," she said, gesturing to her strap.

"What the hell are you doing here?"

"Can I get into the shelter? I need to feed her."

"Look, sis, I ain't got time for this right now. I got this machine for exactly one day, and I can't afford it any more than that—I need to finish farming these bricks."

"You want me to come back at a better time?" she asked, gesturing to the road. It ran straight for miles, and sitting on the horizon was the bus, getting smaller at every moment.

"Fine. Get yourself into the dome over there, and I'll find you after nightfall. Just be sure it's sealed once you're inside—I don't need everything covered in dust."

She headed towards the dome, and he powered his machine back on. It was about the welcome she expected.

At least he didn't send her away—not yet, anyway.

#

The dome was three times as big as her cabin on the ship. It had a rug in the center and a small mat to sleep on. The rest was a dirt floor, its walls lined with supplies, tools, and what looked like junk.

It was a mess.

Behind it sat another dome, filled with green plants, with a simple plastic tarp separating the two. She couldn't get over how solid the ground felt. She could walk, step, jump, or move, and it didn't seem to notice in the least.

Maisie was enjoying the consistent gravity too, crawling on the rug in the center, when her brother entered.

"You shouldn't be here," Jak said as he took off his shirt, grabbing a clean one from a pile of clothes.

He turned on a few lanterns. It was darker than she realized. It had happened so slowly that she hadn't noticed—a lot more slowly than the binary nights and days on the ship.

"You want to meet your niece?" she asked.

He pulled the shirt over his face and tucked it into his pants. He looked down at Maisie as she stuck her finger into her mouth and pulled it out, and then pointed it towards him, as if she had never known she had a finger and wanted to show it off.

He pulled up a chair to the rug to get a closer look. She still had her finger sticking out to him, and he reached down and grabbed it—her light, clean fingers stood out against his dark, sunburnt, dusty hands. "If you're running away, this is the worst place to come," he said without looking up, his eyes still locked onto Maisie.

"I know, but I didn't know where else to go."

"There's nowhere to hide out here, and it will only be a matter of days before they come looking for you."

He sat up and looked at her.

"If I let you stay, I'll be held responsible, too. Last I checked, you're a minor, and I could get into serious trouble for kidnapping or worse—I mean, especially with Maisie here."

"So turn me in."

He went back to Maisie, who had drool hanging off her nose. Arya noticed and reached down, wiping it with her sleeve.

He sat back in his seat.

"No. I'll claim I didn't know. If your fake ID can convince customs, why not your big brother?"

"As long as they don't find out you're the one who got it for me."

"And they won't. You wouldn't sell me out like that, would you?"

"Of course not."

#

Arya watched as her brother carted a stack of bricks to a slab of concrete close to the dome. The sun sat behind clouds—something he mentioned time and time again as a significant advancement in the terraforming process. "Progress!" he would shout, while pointing to the clouds. "Progress!"

"I expected the oxygen to be a lot thinner here," she said to him as he walked by, pushing his wheelbarrow.

"No. On a good day, the oxygen rates surpass the ship's. Big surprise, the news hasn't spread faster." He put the barrel down and wiped his brow.

"What do you mean?" she asked.

He looked out towards the horizon. "The ship won't consider Primera ready for mass population until it's been fully terraformed—that's just how they do things. It doesn't matter how far along it gets, they'll wait until it's done."

He pushed the wheelbarrow a few more feet and then paused again. "Plus, you think the ship wants people coming down here? It'd put them out of business, not to mention old people, like our parents, wouldn't have a chance." He gestured to the landscape again. "People their age—they are the ones running things up there, and they certainly don't want the next generation leaving them behind. Heck, half their friends spend months at a time in rejuvenation pods so they can keep working another decade. They're not moving down here unless someone hauls a pod out for them."

He pushed the wheelbarrow a few more feet, and she stood up and walked with him.

"But Mom and Dad talk about moving here all the time."

"Oh, I'm sure they do—once things are as nice as they are on the ship."

"How long do you think that will take?" He stopped again, looked at her, then around the landscape, and back at her, with a face that made her feel small and stupid. "What do you think?" He grabbed the wheelbarrow and started walking again. "They are waiting for a dream, and they will probably die waiting. That's one reason they don't want you to grow up."

"What do you mean?"

"You think they want you to become an adult? Move down here and make a life for yourself? Come on!"

"They let you become an adult."

"They didn't let me. I made it happen for myself, partly to spite them. But it's easier for men, I think. They won't say that, but it's true. And, I'll add, I didn't have a grandchild I'd be taking with me—you think they are going to let her leave?" He asked this as if her getting caught was inevitable, as if she hadn't already left. She began to wonder if she doubted it. Did she really expect to get away with all of this?

She watched him get another load of bricks, and the thick rubber wheels bounced over the uneven dirt and rocks. One wheel got stuck in a small crevice in the dirt, and he tried to push it loose.

"Can I help?" she asked as she walked towards him, but he knocked it out of the hole himself.

"Don't you need to watch Maisie?"

"I just fed her, and she's asleep. I got a good thirty minutes, if I'm lucky."

"Help me unload these bricks, then."

While they unloaded, he explained where the walls would go. Brick by brick, he'd build his house from the dirt of the earth. The bricks would keep it cool in the summer, and his insulated synthetic roof with built-in solar panels—on order from the colony—would keep it temperature-controlled and dry. He even showed her where the river would go, a short walk from his place, if the rain ever started, as the terraformers promised. Until then, he had dug a well between the foundation and the dome. Other farms had to ship their water in from the Salt Lake, which was an expensive process. With his well, he'd be able to make as many bricks as the automated brick press could shoot out—at least for the time he could afford to rent it. They went back and loaded another stack of bricks into the barrel. When they finished this load, he sat on the pile and took a drink of water.

"So, can I ask you something?"

She nodded.

"What's your plan?" He handed her the drink.

"I don't have one."

"And you don't see how that's going to be a problem?"

"I guess I was hoping I would figure it out when I got here."

"You were hoping I would figure it out for you, right?"

"I didn't say that."

"Good, because I'm not sure I can help."

She handed him the bottle back and looked at him.

"That's actually refreshing to hear. I can imagine mom and dad here—they'd have a thousand things I should do differently."

"Well, I'm nothing like mom and dad."

She looked at him and smiled.

"I've never heard you talk about them like this."

"That's because you've never heard me talk about them when they weren't listening."

He turned towards her. He lifted the water bottle and drank the rest of it. He tossed the empty bottle into the wheelbarrow.

"You realize they aren't our biological parents, right?"

"What?"

"We don't look or think anything like them. Surely, you've thought about it."

She hadn't thought about it. Not once. It wasn't something she had ever considered.

"Yeah, we're the children of a minor who got pregnant from some nameless digger—a one-night stand or something. She was forced to give us up. Our real mom lives in a colony south of here—straight that way, but there's no road to get there from here. You have to take the shuttle back to Salt Lake. I've met her once. Figured you knew—I figured that's why you ran away."

He stood up and went back to the bricks to get another load. Arya didn't move. Any other person would think about how her parents had never told her. Any other person might get lost wondering what their actual mother was like, and what it would be like to meet her. And what did it mean for who Arya was. It was unfair to learn something like this in such a casual way—but Arya wasn't thinking about any of that. All she could think about was what it meant for Maisie. They didn't just give kids like her up for foster care until the mom could work things out. They could take them away forever, and forever was a long time.

Maisie could grow up never knowing Arya existed.

She stood up and walked back to the dome.

She couldn't stay with her brother, and it was stupid of her to think she could. They would look for her here and take Maisie away.

She had to find a better place to hide.

#

She scheduled a bus for the following morning. She was in the middle of wrapping Maisie into her sling when she heard it pull up. She rushed to pack the rest of their things before running out to catch it. Her brother was working on the wall of his house, layering mortar and brick, line by line, but paused as he saw her leave the dome.

"I got to go," she said.

"I see that. Sorry you couldn't stay longer."

"I hope I'm able to come back and visit—someday."

"You can come anytime, sis."

She started towards the road, making her way around the dome, and as she did, she saw it. Sitting at the end of the road wasn't the shuttle, but a security bus. Around the corner, two security personnel greeted her. One was holding an electric rod and the other, hand-ties. Next to them was a middle-aged woman in a fine blue suit, holding a baby carrier. "Arya, we need you to hand over the baby and come with us." The guards grabbed her, and she thought about struggling, but feared it would end in hurting Maisie. She didn't dare yell for her brother—she wouldn't get him involved. He didn't need this on his record.

In the end, Arya was placed on the bus four rows behind Maisie, who cried the whole way back to the colony, and most of the shuttle ride back to the ship, and Arya couldn't do anything about it, other than pull on her bound wrists until they bled.

Arya spent the next week in a cell, near the center of the ring-shaped ship. She wasn't used to sleeping in microgravity, but even if she had been, she wouldn't have done much of it. It was too quiet.

For the first five nights, she thought only of her daughter. The sixth night, after a week of zero human contact—and zero contact with anything other than the smooth walls of her cell and the daily food pouch—she thought about Lon. He was in a similar cell, somewhere close by, and had been for the past five months. In the last weeks before giving birth, she couldn't hide her pregnancy, and after only a little prodding from her parents, she gave him up. He got the maximum.

Her parents enjoyed having someone else to direct their anger towards. And that made it easier for Arya.

It made it easier for everyone.

She fell asleep thinking of Lon and woke up to find a nurse at her door. They wanted her to see the doctor before her trial.

#

The doctor held her wrists, which were covered in scabs and itched like hell—a sign they are healing, said the doctor. She was carefully caressing these wrists when she was presented to her judge later that day.

"Do you understand the predicament you've put yourself and your family into, young lady?"

She kept her eyes on her wrist and wouldn't look up. Near her, lying on the desk, packed into a plastic bag, was everything she had with her at the time of her arrest: her bag, clothes, all carefully folded, and clearly left undisturbed from the moment she had surrendered them.

"Your parents have asked that I release you into their custody, but I'm not sure that would be a good idea. Should I let you spend the next month under house arrest with them instead of a cell?"

She still didn't look up. Her parents stood on the other side of the court. Maisie was somewhere on the ship, in someone else's arms, wondering what happened to her mom, and it was all she could think about now—that and Lon sitting in a touchless cell for the last five months.

"Are you going to respond, or should I make my ruling without your input?"

She slowly turned to look up at him. He raised his eyebrows to invite her to speak. She then slowly turned to look at her parents, who stood silent—the only place on the ship where they were quiet. She turned back to the judge.

"I'd rather stay in my cell, your honor, if it's alright with you."

"Excuse me? You'd rather be in prison than at home with your parents?"

"Yes, your honor."

"Ignore her, Judge. She isn't making any sense," said her dad.

The judge quickly gestured for him to stop, and he did. Then he leaned towards her. He put his hand to his beard. "What makes you say that?"

She paused, and her parents stood motionless—if she had looked over at them, she knew she wouldn't be able to continue.

"May I approach the bench?"

"You may."

She reached into the bag of her clothes, pulled out the fake ID, and walked up to the judge. She placed the phony ID on his desk.

"Lon didn't think he was sleeping with a minor. I had this long before I ran away to the planet. I had it when I met Lon, and he thought it was real—just like the shuttle pilot and customs officer thought it was real. He didn't know he was sleeping with a minor, your honor. I lied to him." The judge picked it up and examined her ID. "Honestly, it shouldn't matter. The entire system is—" The Judge raised his eyebrows again, and nearly reached his hand to get her to stop, but she took a breath and continued, "I know that according to the law, it was my fault and Lon shouldn't be in prison for it."

She walked back to her seat and sat down.

The judge examined the ID in his hands and then looked up and stared at her for what seemed like a complete orbit before speaking. "Self-awareness. Negotiation," he said, tapping the ID against his desk, "And in this case, most admirably, Responsibility. Young lady, you are showing the signs of adulthood in this courtroom for the first time in all your appearances." He set the ID down, grabbed his glasses, and opened his computer. "But that doesn't change the fact that you lied to a young man, and snuck to Primera with a child that was not to be in your custody. There have to be consequences. So, I am going to ask you to spend the rest of your sentence—in a cell or with your parents, you can decide. But I will see you once again after your sentence, in a month, and we will see how I feel then. This is my final decision, and it's more than you deserve. You are dismissed." And with that, he slammed his gavel against the countertop, and they escorted her out before her parents had time to argue.

#

Arya stood by the window outside the courtroom while the security guards logged her sentence into the computers. Her mother stormed out without even looking at her. Her dad followed, but slowed down as he passed. He placed his hand on her shoulder.

She turned towards the window as he walked away.

The ship was orbiting over the southern hemisphere, with Salt Lake right in the center of the window. In a month, if things went her way, she might convince the judge to let her become an adult, and she'd get her daughter back. If that happened, she'd head straight to the planet. She'd start at her brother's farm, but she wouldn't stay there—it was too far away from everything and everyone. She might head south and try to find her biological mother, if only to meet her. But ultimately, she would need to find a place to live, all while caring for Maisie. All of this would be possible if things went her way, and they hardly ever did. Yet, she wasn't going to wait for things to work out on their own anymore. She would *make* things work, whatever happened.

She thought of her mother, and the mothers before her she had never met, and realized she was only a stop in the long journey of her family's story. The same would be true for her daughter and those to follow. Whatever happened, the story would move through them like it had all the others. Life was more than responsibility and choices, or even making things work; it was choosing whether to be a channel for the stories she was given, or a filter that reshaped them. She didn't get to choose the story, but she could decide how much of it survived her.

She was beginning to wonder if that was what it meant to be an adult.

On the Way to Proximata

2897 CE

Maisie's pencil glided along the surface of her new sketchbook, nearing completion, inches from finishing the line that would connect the moon's horizon with the setting planet, when the graphite snapped. The broken bits scattered over the page like an undiscovered cluster of supergiants. She blew the fragments off the page and bit the pencil to secure more, but it was too far down. She spit the bits out of her mouth and turned toward her tent, where she bumped into her husband, Huxley.

"We need to talk about Proximata."

She closed her sketchbook. "We have plenty of time to decide. Can we discuss it after the ceremony?"

"We can't keep putting it off."

"We won't. We will sit down and discuss it right after the ceremony."

"Promise?"

She nodded and slid the sketchbook into her back pocket. She had been putting it off. Her mother, Arya, had only passed away two years prior, and with her gone, there wasn't much keeping her near Primera. But that didn't mean she was ready to move on. "For now, let's enjoy the view." She gestured to the moon dust beyond the dome.

Huxley laughed at first and paused. "It's not an excellent view, but it's beautiful in its own way, I guess."

Maisie agreed. It was beautiful in its own way. It was beautiful, like the last moments of one's life are beautiful when the life was well lived. It was beautiful, like a sketchbook with pages filled with drawings and diagrams, its binding broken and cover torn. It was beautiful in a way that is also painful and sad.

"Did you hear about the attack?" asked Huxley, wrapping his arm under hers.

"Senescents?" asked Maisie.

"I should say 'the supposed attack'—the ship jumped only minutes after it arrived. No casualties. No attempts to hack anything. It's unfortunate it happened today; now everyone will be talking about it and—"

"No one will talk about it. This event is all about Rupert; he made sure of that." Or at least that's what she hoped. She didn't need her husband getting into any political debates at a retirement ceremony.

She looked at her pencil and considered whether she'd be able to get away again to finish when a notification popped up on her wrist. She read it and then turned to her husband. "Our shuttle is closed for repairs; we're going to have to walk."

#

Her mentor, Rupert, was retiring after four dozen cycles of regeneration. (A cycle was equivalent to about two Earth years, and reflected the required time in between rejuvenation cycles.) He wanted to be laid to rest in the greenhouses he built a century ago. His greenhouses were some of the best in that solar system, if only because they were the oldest. Maisie had joined his lab three cycles after he finished them and had been working for him as a biologist ever since. Huxley tagged along, even though Primera's moon was not his favorite destination for vacation.

Rupert's retirement took place in a large hall through the yellow tunnel that ran under the dome. By the time they got there, Maisie was sweaty and annoyed, and the room was so full of visitors that the large space felt small and forced Maisie and Huxley against the back wall. A local Ammalean priest stood in the front, praying quietly as if everyone was listening. They weren't, and it felt rude to Maisie. She had learned the local prayer language from her mom, who joined the faith later in life— *sodizin Diné Bizaad*—and could pick up a few phrases over the crowd of murmurs.

"We should try and find some seats," she whispered, gesturing to the path that had opened up in the crowd. They started towards it when she noticed the room getting quiet and the path getting larger. She grabbed Huxley when she saw what everyone was staring at: a senescent. She was old, her back bent over, and she walked with a thin cane, her old clothes draped over her like the dust of the moon outside the window. She had white hair, smashed against her head, thin enough to expose her scalp. It was the first time Maisie had ever seen a senescent this close. This woman had to have gone at least a dozen cycles or more without regeneration. The woman took another step into the room, and the room gasped in sync and pushed each other against the wall, and Maisie grabbed Huxley and tried to pull him back with them, but he wouldn't budge. So she covered her mouth, even though she knew senescence wasn't contagious. Everyone covered their mouths—everyone except Huxley. His hands were in front of him, open, as if to invite her to grab them—with no gloves, mask, or anything. He took a step towards the woman.

"Everyone, remain calm," said Maisie, uncovering her mouth long enough to speak. "Huxley will take care of this—he's an expert with these people. He'll know what to do."

Huxley studied senescents and oversaw one of the labs back on Primera, where they attempted to reincorporate them into society.

She looked at him, smiling, but he ignored the announcement. He walked over and extended his hand to her. She looked up at him, her eyes sunken into her face. She smiled, and he guided her to him, her legs thin as poles, and when she got close, he placed his arm under hers to help her stand. They talked by the door for a while—a lot longer than anyone was comfortable with, and then instead of escorting her out of the room towards security, he walked her down the aisle to where Rupert lay.

Maisie ran up to him.

"What are you doing?" she whispered through gritted teeth. "Security will be here soon, and if they see you escorting her towards the front instead of out of the room—"

Huxley brushed her aside, and Maisie was so confused by the whole interaction that all she could do was watch. They made it to the front, and he helped the woman climb the step to look into the retirement bed. Huxley let her reach down to touch him. The old woman's fingers were knotted and thin and unclean.

Maisie caught up to them and pulled her arm back.

"Don't let her touch him!"

"Please, babe, relax. It's fine."

"We have to get her out of here! She shouldn't be touching him." But it was too late. Before she could finish warning him, the security had arrived. They ran to the front, containing the woman. Then two other guards escorted Maisie and Huxley out, their wrists bound behind them.

#

Maisie and Huxley were put in a holding cell a few miles outside the colony.

She sat with her back to Huxley, staring out the small window towards the shipyard. He reached and touched her shoulder. "I'm sorry, Maisel."

She had nothing to say to him. They had given up a half cycle for this trip, and it was all for nothing; the ceremony went on without them. Not to mention it was possible they'd be flagged and stopped on every trip from here to the outer systems—questioned without reason, for the rest of their lives! They might as well head to Proximata, or even further, if they could.

What was Huxley thinking?

He reached over and put his hand on her shoulder again. She shrugged it off.

"Are you going to be mad at me forever?"

"You should have escorted her to security, as protocol requires. You of all people should know that. What were you thinking?"

"Maisel, I'm sorry. I forgot where I was. I'm sorry—I mean it."

She turned towards him. "Why let her contaminate him like that?"

He looked at her for a good minute before answering.

"She was his sister."

"Don't be a fool. Rupert didn't have a sister."

"That you know of. She said she was his sister, and what reason would she have to lie?"

"I don't know why they do what they do! You're telling me that Rupert, with three dozen cycles of regeneration, was outlived by a senescent? How is that even possible?"

"They live a lot longer than rumors would have you believe—some reach four dozen cycles on their own without regeneration. I've met a few. Not many, but some cases suggest they can. Plus, she told me she was much younger than him—so it's possible."

"Don't come at me with your research. He'd never have a senescent for a sister. It's unnatural."

"I'll have you remember, growing old is natural. It's reversing those effects that aren't."

"Please don't talk like that—not here."

He looked away. "I believed her. I could tell she was telling the truth. She wanted to see him. Sister or not, she loved him." He turned to make eye contact with her. "You could see it in her eyes. She wanted to pay her respects, that's all. She wanted to say goodbye. It seemed like the right thing to do."

The cell door opened, and they both got quiet.

The guard didn't say anything other than to gesture for them to follow him. Huxley went first, head down.

The guard led them down a hallway to a room with a table under a dim light, and he attached their wrist to the magnetic strip, binding them. They sat with their backs to the wall, staring at the door.

"Will you let me do the talking?" asked Maisie.

Huxley didn't respond.

"Just let me do the talking, ok?" she asked again.

He didn't answer, and before she could ask again, the door opened and a security official walked in. He placed his briefcase onto the table, opened it, and pulled out a chip reader.

"You know what this is?" he asked.

They nodded.

He turned it in the air, examining it. "One tap of your wrist and you'll be flagged as friends of terrorists."

"That's really not necessary. We're so sorry about the whole—"

He slammed it on the table, and she got quiet. "I had planned to come in here, to scan your wrist, flagging you for good, and then let you be on your way. That is, until your boss called and pulled a few strings. I guess your work back on the Planet gives you certain privileges," he said, looking at Huxley. He picked the reader back up, twisting it in the air.

Maisie made an audible sigh of relief and sat back. "Oh, thank you. Thank you!"

"But you're not on the Planet, so I want you to hear this," pointing the reader at them, "and hear it plain and simple: senescents are terrorists. Period."

Huxley sat up and opened his mouth to speak, but paused. The guard noticed and pointed the reader at him, as if to challenge him to talk. Huxley looked at Maisie, who shook her head, forbidding him to speak, but then he looked back at the official.

"Do you have something to add?" the official asked, baiting him.

Maisie held her breath, using every bit of her willpower to silence him with her thoughts.

"Not all senescents are terrorists," said Huxley. Maisie turned and stared at him wide-eyed. "Based on our research, less than 10% engage in terrorist activity, and the ones who do often do so out of desperate circumstances. It really is difficult for them, you know."

"Difficult?" asked the guard. "Let me tell you about the difficulty. My partner was in the base when they attacked last year. His body was ripped from head to toe; it took two cycles for the pods to put him back together, but he's never fully recovered. He's spent every half-cycle in the pod since. He'll never walk straight again. Not to mention his memory loss—he doesn't even know who I am anymore. So don't talk to me about difficult."

"I'm sorry for your friend, but—" said Huxley. Before he could finish, the guard grabbed his reader and shoved it into Huxley's bound wrists.

It beeped. Then he turned the reader towards Maisie. "Do you have anything else you'd like to add?"

Maisie shook her head.

"Then you're free to go."

He took the reader, placed it in his briefcase, slammed it shut, and walked out the door. As soon as he opened the door, their wrists were released from the table. Before the door could close behind the guard, a notification popped up on Maisie's wrist informing her that their flights back to the Planet were placed on hold due to a change in her husband's security clearance.

#

That night, Huxley slept in the sand out by the glow lamps, and Maisie slept in the tent.

The next morning, she found Huxley standing along the wall, staring out the window, the Planet nothing more than a small marble in the distance, slowly falling. She walked up and bumped into him, knocking his mug and spilling his tea.

"Careful now," he said, as the spill drifted to the dust below them. He turned to her and smiled, placing his arm around her and pulling her close. "I should have kept my mouth shut." He looked down at his wrist, hers nestled next to it, and rubbed his device. "I'm sorry about everything, especially missing the ceremony."

She could tell he was sorry—as sorry as anyone could be. She'd be mad at him for a while—she was confident of that—but there was no need for him to know how long.

"It's ok."

"I know you wanted a chance to say something at the ceremony."

"That's the least of our problems now, don't you think?"

He nodded as they stood, watching the Planet set. She grabbed his cup, took a drink, and then gave it back to him.

"Proximata doesn't sound like such a bad idea now, does it?"

"Even with my status?"

"Absolutely. With a senescent incident on your record, you look like a regular space explorer. Plus, I know for a fact, no one else is signing up to go as far as Proximata, not in the state it is, except for those running from something."

"You make it sound like I've become an outlaw."

"We could use a fresh start, that's all."

"Every cycle is a fresh start," he said, smiling.

"Very cute. But you keep shooting off proverbs like that, and I'll go with someone else."

"No, you can't do that. By the time you got there, you wouldn't have many cycles left. Not enough to get back anyway."

"So if we go, we go together, and retire on Proximata?"

"It's the only way."

For the next cycle, they began their training to run the next shipment headed to Proximata. Maisie ended up becoming the Chief Medical Officer and Huxley the Captain, after completing a few evening courses. These positions enabled them to secure larger quarters upon their arrival in the Colony. They spent countless hours learning every element of long-term space travel before boarding their ship and leaving.

#

Maisie wiped her breath from the curved lid of her hibernation pod. Under normal circumstances, she would have been cleaned and dried before regaining consciousness, so the fact that her arms were still dripping with gel underscored the severity of the emergency. She sat up and looked out over the edge through the glass, but her eyes were still blocked by gelatin. Through the haze and the large window, she could see a fleet of ships, silhouetted against a distant star. Across the room, someone ran back and forth handling the controls. She hit the eject button, and the glass lid of the pod opened up; the figure noticed and ran over.

"Maisel, what are you doing up?" It was Huxley's voice.

"What the hell is going on? How far are we from Proximata?"

"We're three jumps away. I was doing routine pod maintenance in between jumps when this colony of senescents showed up and started hacking our system."

"Let me out." She tried to wipe the gunk from her eyes.

"No. I was about to jump again when you woke up. I have to get our pods closed, and then we will be ready. It will only take a minute."

He pushed her back into the pod and closed the lid. She thought about protesting, but she knew he'd get the pods turned back on a lot quicker if she didn't. She placed the respirator over her mouth. With the emergency protocol already in place, she felt the gelatin wrap around her body before the gas had finished putting her to sleep. She went to sleep worried about what would happen if her ship was taken while they were unconscious—would they kill them in their sleep, or worse, take them as hostages?

#

When she woke up, the gel had been drained, and she was clean and dry; she assumed everything was as it should be. She took a few breaths and waited for the container to open, and then blinked to wipe the leftover gel from her eyes.

She could tell that they weren't floating in space; they must have landed. She got nervous, wondering what Proximata would be like and whether it was a good decision to leave for a Class 2 colony. She looked at her wrist device to confirm her location, but couldn't make it out. She lifted her head and looked up. The lights were bright, silhouetting two figures standing over her. She couldn't see them at first, until one shifted its stance and blocked one of the lights. They slowly came into focus. Then she wished she hadn't seen them at all, or wondered if it was all a hibernation dream. Either way, a young girl, at least five cycles before her prime age, stood over her. She was too young to be a member of any respectable ship or station, this far out. The only time the young roamed the galaxy was as children of senescents. It was possible that people could lock into a prime age early, and sometimes the prime age looked younger than one would assume, but the second figure confirmed her fears. It was an old man, bent over, with thin arms, wrinkled skin, and skeleton fingers.

She jumped from her pod.

"Who are you!"

"Slow down. It's going to be ok. Do you know where you are?" the old man asked.

She refused to answer. She pushed her naked body against the far wall, grabbed a uniform from the hook, and used it as a shield. She looked around but couldn't see more than a few meters in front of her. The lack of clear sight forced her nose to work overtime, and the ship didn't smell right. It smelled dirty. It smelled old. It smelled like a senescent—like a life without cleaning agents or mist showers or regeneration. She reached for her wrist and hit the panic button. She hit it repeatedly, and she couldn't understand why the alarm failed to go off. She wiped her eyes again, and when she opened them, the old man was standing dangerously close.

"Here, you have to be freezing." He handed her a post-hibernation robe.

"Where is Huxley? Where is my crew?" she yelled, grabbing the robe.

"If you sit down, we will explain everything."

The old man gestured to a seat.

She wrapped herself in the robe, and as soon as it was tied at her waist, she bolted for the exit. But before she could turn the corner, she ran into someone. She blinked, and with him standing right in front of her, she recognized him. It was Huxley.

"Huxley! What is going on?"

He grabbed her.

"It's going to be ok." Then he looked behind her, nodded, and when she turned, the old man was standing there with a respirator. She tried to fight it, but Huxley held her tight, and with the mask to her face, she fell back asleep.

#

She spent her dreams thinking about how Huxley held her like that. His grip was firm, and he wouldn't budge. She remembered the time they got into a fight, and he had gotten angry, and he grabbed her like that. He hated himself for half a cycle as a result. She forgave him, and he promised never to do it again, and he hadn't—not until just then. She had never been more disappointed in him than in that moment. It had to have been a dream.

She woke up, leaving most of these details behind, but keeping the feelings they created with her. It was with this feeling that she found herself curled in a ball, lying in soft dirt. A glow lamp behind her cast shadows against the surrounding trees. She tried to remember her dream so she could roll over and tell Huxley all about it. He'd apologize, even if he hadn't done anything wrong. He always apologized for her dreams. She pulled the blanket close and took a deep breath.

That's when she noticed it.

Small, green, fern-like plants grew within her reach; plants she had never seen before. She reached her hand out from under the blanket, brushing the black dirt, and plucked a small one, roots and all. She brought the roots, packed with soft silt, to her nose.

"You shouldn't touch that—not without gloves," said a man behind her. His voice was deep, like his throat was filled with gravel, from years of use without rejuvenation. She turned over to see him standing in a dark cloak and a wide-brimmed straw hat that hung low on his face. Even in the shadows, she knew what he was. A senescent! Every part of her wanted to scream, but she held the screams inside to reassess the situation better. She took a breath and turned to check her wristband for her location and time, but her wrist was empty.

"Who are you?" she asked.

He shuffled next to her, dragging his feet, and grabbed the plant lying next to her with his glove-covered hands. He tossed it, then grabbed her hands and wiped them with a wet cloth. "We're allergic to most everything here. I'm going to put gloves on you, ok?"

He didn't wait for her permission. She flinched and pulled away.

"Where are we?" she asked again.

He pointed to the sky and walked back to his seat. Maisie looked up to find she was sitting under two small moons that shone like spotlights on a stage; the stars danced in patterns she didn't recognize. The view of the sky was obstructed only by the leaves above her. She was in the wild, free of a dome. Between her and the old man sat a real fire, not a glow lamp, the smoke drifting up towards the ceiling-less sky.

The senescent sat down on a short stump. It tilted as his frame shifted the balance. "You just woke up from the pod back on the ship. Do you remember? The expedition? Going to sleep? Anything?"

She tapped her head to knock the memories loose. She remembered the moon and the trouble they got into with the security there. She remembered her dream—how Huxley held her, but she couldn't remember why.

"Maybe this will help," he said—though she could tell from his voice that help was no longer guaranteed.He tossed a small emblem to her.

She tried to catch it, but it got lost in the firelight and landed next to her. She felt for it in the darkness and raised it to see. It was the emblem of Proximata. She recognized it immediately, and it brought with it her memories of her ship. She could see the cool silver of the outer hull. And the long bullet-like hibernation pods that sat in the room past the crew quarters. She could still feel her body wrapped in the hibernation gel, like a spoon resting on a bowl of thick batter.

She remembered the expedition.

She looked back up at the man.

"Did we make it?"

"No."

"Where are we then?"

"You were on the way to Proximata when senescents attacked the ship." He lifted a tin canister to his lips and took a sip. "The ship encountered too much damage, and the next jump fell short. The ship crash-landed here."

She rubbed the back of her head, and the memory of waking up in the pod with the ships trying to hack their system started to drift back into her mind. "What happened to the crew?"

"Most of the pods were destroyed in the crash and everyone in them." He set his canister down. "You were severely injured, but your pod remained intact—the only one that survived."

She went through the list of crew members, in order of rank, one by one, slowly remembering their faces, until she reached her husband's—Huxley!

"Where is Huxley? My husband. What happened to him?"

"Thankfully, this planet has breathable air and ample starlight during the day, and the ship was able to stay powered on. I set your pod to begin regenerating immediately."

"Where is Huxley?" she asked again, straightening.

He paused and looked at her. "You don't remember, do you?"

She shook her head, and she wasn't sure if she was answering his question or shaking her memories loose.

"When the ship crashed, we were the only two left alive on this planet. And only you barely." He stood. "Let me show you." He walked over to her and reached for her arm, but she flinched away. "Please, you need to see this."

His fingers were covered in gloves, and his face was in the shadow of the brighter moon. When he pulled back her sleeves, he exposed an arm full of scars, as if her skin had been knitted together.

"You have more—most everywhere—but these were the worst. It took a couple of months for you to regenerate."

She looked down her shirt and found similar scars all over her body. She had been regenerated many times, and never had scars like this. This only happens when a pod is used too many times or the damage is too significant.

He went back to his stump, sat down, and picked up his canister to take another drink. She looked up at him as he took off his broad hat, uncovering his face from its shadow. He had a large, bushy beard and thin white hair shot out of his head like dandelion seeds. Seeing him like this made all the difference. He was the old man from the ship. She remembered him! A memory that, up to that point, had felt like a dream. He must have been there when she woke up after the ship was grounded. He was there, standing over her, along with a young woman—too young. There were a few others too: Huxley! Huxley was there.

She sat up straight.

He was clearly hiding something.

"No one else survived the crash?" she asked.

"I'm sorry, Maisel—no one else survived."

"Who did you say you were again?"

"Just give yourself time to remember."

They had clearly been attacked, and they fought back. Of course, Huxley would, but they crashed here—maybe both ships? And if he was telling the truth, only the two of them survived.

"You're one of those senescents that attacked us, aren't you? Boarded our ship before we were able to jump? What the hell happened to my husband?"

"What do you remember?" he asked again.

"I want you to take me to the ship. Now."

"We will go when you're ready and not before."

"I'm ready now."

"Then tell me where the ship is," he said, "What direction is it?"

She looked around, throwing her hands in the air. "How am I supposed to know?"

"If you don't know, then you're not ready."

"Take me now!" She stood up. She was sure she could take him if she needed to. She was an accomplished biologist, with a body twice as young as someone his age, and Chief Medical Officer of the ship; she would not be held captive on an alien planet by a terrorist. She stood up. "Take me directly!" and that's when she felt it. Her legs started twitching. "Now!" She was as serious as she could be, with a left leg that had just gone limp. "I demand to be taken to my ship!" Then the right leg went limp, and she collapsed. She tried to catch herself, but her arms wouldn't move. "What is happening to me?" she yelled as she crashed to the ground. "I can't move my legs."

He walked up to her, kneeled, and reached for her leg.

"Don't you dare touch me!"

He paused and took a step back. She tried to move as he stood at a distance before going back to his seat. He pulled out his canister and filled it with water from his tin, and placed it on a rock near the flames. He walked to the edge of the camp, reached into his bag, and pulled out a small bundle. Unraveling the cloth revealed thin, gray strips that looked like dried meat. He tossed a few into the canister of boiling water and stirred it.

"We need to get you some medicine."

"What medicine?"

"You need cholinesterase inhibitors."

"Cholinesterase?"

"Yeah."

"How is that supposed to help?"

"Your brain had too much damage from the crash and prolonged regeneration—you're suffering memory loss, not just details, but how to do other things: like move your arms, legs, stand… your balance… and if we don't get your memory working again, you're going to be in trouble."

He took the cup off the rock, the steam like smoke rising from it. He blew on it a few times and then touched it with his finger to gauge the temperature before carrying it over to her.

"Here, drink."

"I want nothing to do with your medicine. Take me back to my pod."

"It's broth. It will help. Drink it."

He brought it to her lips, but she closed her mouth, turning her head in protest.

"It's going to help."

She shook her head.

"Look, if I wanted to hurt you, I would have when you were asleep. Or before you got out of the pod. I understand you don't trust me—I wouldn't trust me either. But right now, I'm all you have, so you don't have much of a choice."

When she had left her home, she had never imagined getting stuck on an alien planet with a senescent. She tried to imagine a worse scenario, and she couldn't. The thought of this left her paralyzed—literally and figuratively. She struggled to breathe. Next thing she knew, he was feeding her the broth straight out of the canister. It was warm and soft, making her head feel fuzzy. It sat heavy in her stomach and made her wish she could take a nap. He helped her lie back, and she stared at the sky as it turned from navy to pink to blue, as the nearby star rose over the trees until it shone directly on her, its warmth like a blanket.

#

Maisie woke up with the sun overhead. The fire had died, and the stump where the old man had sat was empty. She stood up—the broth must have helped. She looked around and was quickly distracted by the scenery. The landscape was filled with plants she had never seen before, all the brighter in the daylight. Life grew out of every corner and crack and rock, with greens and browns and small splashes of colors. It wasn't Proximata, but it might be better. She had seen their greenhouses, and they were as impressive as they could be for a class 2 colony, but this place didn't need them. Life grew naturally. It was clearly never terraformed, not with this amount of biodiversity. The only places she'd seen this much natural growth were in photos of Earth.

The most prominent plant stood three times the height of an average person, and grew as a thin stalk. At the top, a single, giant leaf grew out of it, like an outstretched wing. There were hundreds of these stalks towering over her, forming a broken canopy of shade. As she scanned the forest of large leaves, she caught a glimpse of the old man pushing through a cluster of green stalks.

Whatever she did, she was not going to be held captive by a senescent. She expected him to call his people for help—it's possible he already had!—and if they arrived before anyone else, she'd become their prisoner. She had heard of them holding people hostage to get more resources or to take specific trade routes. She had to make sure that didn't happen. She decided to follow him, but at a safe distance. Hopefully, he would reveal her ship and give her a chance to call for help before it was too late.

She put one foot in front of the other, forcing them to follow him as quickly as she could. Once she got down the valley and past a bundle of stalks that grew like a steel rod fence, she could see him in the distance, looking for something—no ship in sight. She continued to follow him, keeping her distance, until he leaned against a tall stalk and sat for a while. She snuck closer, watching where she stepped so as not to make any noise, which was easy, as small plants grew as soft as linen—bright patches of green carpet in long spirals like a python weaving through the thin clusters. She reached for her wristband to capture a few photos of the plants, but her wrist was still empty. So she reached for her back pocket in search of her sketchbook and pencil—out of habit more than anything. She wanted to catalog these moments, but it, too, was missing.

She hid behind a large leaf and looked down at the senescent who crouched a few meters away. He scanned the valley with a wristband. As he scanned, he stopped at a nearby stalk cluster. She followed his gaze to the top of a stalk, where a single leaf held a giant droplet of water. It had to be at least two liters suspended under the leaf. She wondered whether this was due to a membrane provided by the leaf or to a change in how surface tension worked in this environment. Then the leaf shook, and the droplet released. She followed its trajectory where it hit something that, until that moment, had blended so well into the environment that she hadn't noticed. The impact of the water turned its skin gray against the green surroundings. It was the size of a fully grown grizzly bear that had been shaved and given the skin of a dolphin, and walked on all four—no, on all six—legs!

She took a step closer to get a better look.

The water made the creature look gray, but upon closer inspection, its skin was translucent, with veins and internal organs all visible, even from a distance. The only color was the large green spot near the center, above its second set of legs, which matched the green of the plants surrounding it.

The water that fell onto its back didn't splash or fall to the ground. The skin absorbed it like a dry sponge. She watched it happen and couldn't stop watching until it disappeared into its veins. The senescent walked towards the creature, pulling out a large knife that he lifted over his head, and began to swing it into the flesh.

He was about to kill it!

She ran to catch him. "Don't hurt it!" But it was too late. The knife went into the creature's flesh, clear liquid shooting out along the edges.

He turned towards her.

"What are you doing here?" he asked, as he pulled the knife out, wiping the blade on his pants.

"Why do you people have to destroy everything?" She walked up to the creature and touched it, running her hand along its back, examining it as she did.

"You people?" he asked.

Out of its large black eyes, she could see the reflection of the old man behind her, raising his knife again. She turned, grabbed his arm, and pulled the knife from his hands, just as she was taught.

She turned it and pointed it at him.

"I asked you to stop."

He lifted his hands in surrender. "I'm trying to help."

"By stabbing me?" She stepped closer to him, knife out.

"I'm not going to hurt you. But I need to cut this creature. You think I'm cutting this creature cause I like destroying things? Are you a fool? I'm doing it to help you."

"How is that going to help me?"

He put his hand down on the creature's back. "When this creature is in shock, it uses cholinesterase inhibitors to keep from losing its memory. They get released, we take them, give them to you, and you get better. I need the knife back—I need to stick this knife into its chest again. It won't kill it, but it will put it into shock, and we will be able to get what we need."

She stopped to think through how this would work, and was distracted enough by the theory that she didn't notice him lean in to grab her wrist with one hand, and the knife with his other. He had it pointed towards her before she could stop him.

"I'm not going to hurt you—and I'm not going to hurt this creature permanently. But I have to finish what I started." He lifted the knife.

"Wait!" She bolted for his arm, but she was too late—his knife went in deep, and the creature curled up into a ball and fell to the ground.

"It's ok! It's ok. Look."

He pointed toward a small organ just above its front leg, visible from the curled-up wrinkles. "It's still beating. It's fine. But the creature is in shock now." As she examined the creature's internal organs, she noticed they beat slowly. Then the old man uncurled one of the thick, elephant-like legs. "You might not want to watch this part."

Using his knife, he cut into the leg.

"What are you doing now?"

"I'm cutting off its leg."

"Why would you do that?"

"This creature," he said in between sawing motions, "is in shock—it can't feel a thing, and it won't feel a thing until his leg grows back. Then, when its leg has regrown, it will wake up and go on its way as if nothing happened. I promise."

"How can you be so sure?"

"I've done this many times before."

She stood back.

"How many times?"

He paused, thought for a second, and then went back to sawing the leg.

"How many times have you done it?" She looked at him, but he didn't answer. A little juice shot out of the leg and hit his face. He wiped it off and went back to cutting the flesh.

"We didn't just crash land, did we? We've been here for—how long have we been here?" He didn't answer. He shook his head, focused on the beast's leg. "Who are you? Are you all that's left from the ship that attacked us? Or are there others?"

He tore the remaining flesh from the animal and tossed the leg on the ground. He stuck his knife into the leg and wiped his hands on his pants before picking the knife back up.

"How much do you remember?"

She backed up. "I want to see my ship. Take me there now."

"You can go as soon as you're ready. For now, we cook this." He picked up the leg.

"No. No. No. Take me now."

"Go look for it if you want—get lost on a planet by yourself. But I'm going back to the camp, and if you come with me, I'm going to help you feel better."

"I feel fine. Now tell me where it is."

"You feel fine? Really?" he said, pointing at her with the tip of his knife, clearly annoyed. She hadn't noticed, but her back was bent, and her legs were shaking. "We need to get back. You shouldn't have come this far from camp." He grabbed her arm, but quickly let go. He looked at his hand and then turned it towards her. There was blood on his gloves. "Check your arms." She pulled back her sleeves. The scars on her arms were bright red, and a few had opened up. She stood there, unable to move, as blood pooled in her open palms.

"Your body is rejecting the regeneration, and a lot quicker than I hoped. We have to get you back to the camp and find some help." He reached for her again. She tried to back up, except her legs felt as thin as stalks. Her arms felt weak too, and after a few steps, she toppled over, turned, and before she could fall over, the senescent was in front of her, catching her fall.

#

That night, he bandaged her arms, tucked her into a blanket at the foot of a large boulder, and fed her some soup, which eased her pain and helped her sleep.

Her arms stung, and soon her body started to heat up like the rocks by the fire. She sweated, shaking from chills, and each day he changed her bandages and used a wet cloth to keep her cool. A few times, she woke up in the middle of the night, thought she heard him talking to someone, and could only assume he had a radio and was communicating with his people, but she was too sick to fight back. Too ill to do anything but sleep. She lay there for a week, waking for only a few minutes each day, often to eat. And each time she woke up, the senescent was there, ready to give her something to drink, or adjust her blankets, or stir the fire back to life.

She woke up in the middle of the night once, with him sitting close. He lifted his hand to feel her forehead and smiled through his beard.

"Your fever has broken. This is a good sign. How are you feeling?"

She didn't answer. She pulled the blanket up to her chin.

"I'm feeling better—but tired."

"That's good. You should be able to get up and move around within a day or two."

"Why didn't you put me back in the pod?"

"Too soon since your last cycle—would only have made it worse. You had to heal on your own this time."

"How do you know so much about regeneration?"

"Just because I haven't used regeneration doesn't mean I don't know how it works."

She didn't know what to say, but there was a lot about senescents that she didn't understand. She turned to her side to face away from him. She looked at the plants nearby and wished she had the energy to study them.

She wished she had the energy to get better. She wished she had the energy to do anything. But every part of her was tired.

She thought she might have the strength to sit up, and so she pulled herself up against the boulder behind her. He reached to help, but she stopped him. This time, it wasn't because she didn't want him to touch her, and that surprised her a little. Was it possible for her to think of senescents the same way her husband always had? She wanted to see if she could do it herself, and she did. Her back hurt, and her arms were tired, but she could sit up. She looked at him, who smiled as if he was witnessing a miracle.

"It's sick—that someone with a body as old as you has to take care of someone with a body as young as mine?"

He stopped smiling and then hit his hand against his chest. "My body might look old, but I've taken good care of it." He smiled again.

"Clearly." He reached behind him for a bowl of broth and offered it to her. She took a drink. "Your kind is illegal where I come from, you know."

"I do."

She looked at her soup as she talked. "And had we met anywhere else, I would have turned you in."

"I have no doubt."

She took a drink of the broth. "We were raised to hate your kind—everyone did." She turned towards him. "Why are you helping me? What I mean is: I'm not sure I would have done the same."

"Of course you would. We're on an undiscovered planet alone—we're all we got." He rose to his feet. "And I need you as much as you need me. But that's only possible if you rest. You should sleep."

#

When she woke up, the fire was smoldering, and the old man wasn't there. An old man—that's all he was, nothing more and nothing less. She found herself thinking of him differently than she thought of other senescents.

Since her fever had broken in the night, she felt well enough to stand up. She held her head, and her memories slowly fell back into place. She remembered. She had been in this camp before—a long time ago.

She remembered where her ship was. It came back to her in a flash, like a dream that happens all at once.

Hope shot through her legs, and she moved them in the direction of the ship, or at least where she felt it should be, grabbing stalks as she passed to keep her balance. She was able to make it down the small hill without toppling over. When she got to the top of the next, she stopped to catch her breath, and that's when she saw it. She could see the tail of her ship sticking out over the stalks on the other side of the valley. She fixed her eyes on it and started to run. When she got down the hill, she lost sight of it, but continued, deviating only once when she ran into a pond, where yellow pads with single long green stalks in the middle grew inches from the surface, as if they hovered over the water instead of floating. On the other side, she corrected course and reached a thick cluster of green stalks. When she pushed through, she tripped and tumbled down a small hill and into a large hole, where she smashed into soft black mud.

She wiped her hands on her pants and stood. The hole had been recently dug, its walls made of loose dirt. Standing, her shoulders reached the top edge. She followed the border of the hole to find it was rectangular, three meters long, and a little less than one meter wide.

She climbed out and looked back at it.

She knew what it was; they still used them on her home planet for retirement ceremonies.

It was a grave with a clearly marked headstone, each with a name engraved—names of her crew: Adulx Kilick, Hamilton Forfeit, Sammy Gight, and Huxley Winslow.

Huxley Winslow carved carefully into a large stone right in front of her, ground in front of it covered in soft moss and undisturbed dirt.

He was dead.

"Huxley Winslow." She had to say it to believe it.

She sat and stared at his grave, trying to put the pieces together— he was alive when they were attacked. He was alive when she woke up in the pod. What did they do to him? She worried he was tortured or worse, his body was used to keep them alive. It was a well-accepted fact that senescents performed archaic surgeries where they swapped internal organs to help people live longer, a common practice dating back to life on Earth before the space age.

That's when she noticed something at the corner of her eye. She could see the final stone lying at the top of the open grave. She didn't want to turn and look, but she couldn't stop herself: Maisel Profeta etched onto the stone's surface like all the others.

She stepped backward, but she didn't get very far, for standing right behind her was the old man.

He grabbed her. "You weren't supposed to see that."

"What the hell is that?" she yelled, pushing him away. "What the hell is that?"

"It's nothing. It's—"

"You sick old man! What did you do to Huxley?"

"I didn't do anything."

"I remember. He was there when I woke up! He was there. He didn't die in the crash! What did you do to him?"

"Maisel, I promise, I didn't do anything to him."

"Why do you keep calling me Maisel? No one calls me Maisel," she said. "If you knew me, if you actually knew me, you'd know that."

She fell to the ground and started to dig into the silt that lay in front of Huxley's gravestone.

"I know, Maisel. I know. And that's the hardest part about all this: You're not going to find Huxley down there—not yet." He grabbed her and pulled her off the grave. She sat back in the dirt, her gloves stained black.

She lifted her face.

"Huxley isn't down there, I'm telling you." The old man sat down on a large rock behind him.

"Then where is he?" she asked.

"Right here," he said, lifting his arms. He didn't smile. He didn't laugh. He wasn't joking. He looked down at the ground and took in a deep breath, as if ready to explain something to a child, something he had explained a hundred times before, and they wouldn't listen. "I'm Huxley, and if you come with me, I'll explain everything."

#

Their ship was two hundred meters long and capable of long-term space travel, but all that was left of it now was the compartment that held a computer and one hibernation pod. The aluminum shell was overgrown with swirls of green moss, and large leaves hung over it, casting shade.

Inside, the old man, who called himself Huxley, turned on the computer, and Maisie sat in the chair.

Her old wristband sat near the edge of the desk, and she grabbed it.

"Stopped working cycles ago," he explained.

She turned it in her hands, examining it. It was beaten and dirty, with stains and cracks she couldn't remember staining or cracking, but it was hers, nonetheless.

He grabbed it from her and put it back on the desk. "Don't worry. Everything you had on there has been backed up on the computer." He gestured to the screen where he opened an application, clicked on a folder, and then held his wristband to synchronize. When it was done, he clicked on a video from the front camera of the ship as it entered the planet's atmosphere, and started to explain. "It happened just as I told you—we got attacked, and barely escaped, jumping to this system. But we took on too much damage to complete the jump. We had to land—which is what we did," he said, gesturing to the ship. "I was the only one awake during the crash, and no one other than you and me survived."

He clicked through photos of the ship sitting in a patch of dirt and torn leaves, her asleep in the pod, and another of him, looking at himself in the shimmer of the outer shell.

"Just like I said, you were severely injured. I wasn't sure you would wake up—but you did."

He clicked on a photo of them standing together outside the outer hull, smiling. She watched all of this and tried to remember.

"We had a couple of good cycles together. But then you got sick. Your brain stopped remembering how to perform some basic functions—you started forgetting who I was. The regeneration… it was too much, and your body rejected it—like it is now. Too much damage to your brain, I suppose." He clicked on another photo. "We had to put you back into the pod to recover—and it helped: you got better.

"But each time we put you back into the pod, the time we had together got shorter and shorter." He jumped ahead, scrolling past hundreds of photos, stopping on one of them, standing next to each other—her young, but him, old. "As you can imagine, you stopped recognizing me."

She turned to him and looked into his aged face, eyes that sat low.

"I don't blame you; I wouldn't recognize me either." He smiled. "But to be honest, those were the hardest cycles—harder than learning to survive." He turned back to the screen, but she kept looking at him as he continued. "A few times, I stopped trying to convince you. It seemed to work better to explain things once you've had time to remember on your own. It took a couple of weeks—sometimes as long as a month—but it came back. Especially when you saw this."

He pulled out a small sketchbook from his pocket and handed it to her.

"My sketchbook!" she yelled. She turned it in her hands, the binding broken, and the pages held together with twine. She opened it to find her handwriting on every page, from beginning to end, sketches and descriptions of hundreds of plants and animals, pictures she never drew.

"But this is my handwriting—my drawings. How is that possible?"

She stopped on a page of a sketch of the large, translucent creature, with each organ diagrammed and pages of notes on its diet, nutrients, food chain, and habits. She had written in the corner: "An excellent source of cholinesterase inhibitors, this might be the ticket for recovery."

He tapped the page where she was reading. "Over the cycles, you've cataloged every observable species in a hundred miles. But this little discovery helped more than you'll ever realize."

"But I don't remember."

"Well, that's the worst of it, isn't it?" He placed his hands on her shoulder. "The last couple times you were awake, I noticed you were struggling to remember things—more than usual, even after weeks had gone by." He took a deep breath, looked at the floor, and then lifted his face to her. "Maybe I did it too many times. I don't know. But I could tell you weren't remembering anything since before the crash, which is why I took you back to our original camp—I was hoping that if you experienced the first of our memories, the rest might follow."

Her head hurt, and her arms stung, and she couldn't breathe. And none of this made sense.

"I'm sorry," he said, "I am. It's a lot to take in—and it's never easy. It's never easy—I—"

She pushed back from the computer and breathed deeply. She couldn't believe any of it. It had to be a lie. Or she was dreaming, a strange hibernation dream, and she needed to wake up. It was just yesterday that they left the station on the moon. Just yesterday, they began their journey. This wasn't possible.

"You've got to calm down, babe. It will only make it worse. You've got to calm down."

"Don't call me babe. I don't know who you are!"

She got up and ran for the exit, just like she had the last time when she woke from the pod. She turned the corner, but this time her eyes weren't covered in gel, and she could see it for what it was, the blurry shapes now taking form: the corner leading to the outside, stalks growing up over a path lined in stones, and the sun shining through the large leaves. And standing on the path, their shadows stretching to her feet, were the young girl and, next to her, a young Huxley. He stood there, alive and young and perfect. She turned back to the old man, with tears in her eyes. "If you're Huxley, then who's this?"

"I'm not Huxley," said the young man. His voice shot through her head like a migraine. His voice wasn't like Huxley's at all. And through her tears, she looked at him. They weren't Huxley's eyes—they were his own.

She fell to her knees, and the young man ran to her, grabbing her. "Mom, it's ok. It's going to be ok."

#

With a cup of broth in one hand, Maisie scrolled through photos of her standing in front of the ship holding a small baby. She clicked again, and it was a similar photo. But a small kid was standing next to them.

Then again, until she stood next to two young kids: a boy and a little girl.

She took a deep breath and then a sip of her broth. She looked at the old man.

"If you're Huxley, why didn't you regenerate?"

"I would have—and I tried a couple times. But we only had one pod, and no ship to make sure it ran properly, and each of your cycles got longer than the last. Even if I figured out how to make it work without me, we would have been on opposite cycles—we would have hardly ever seen each other."

"How many cycles has it been?"

"We've spent 24 cycles on this planet."

"That's too many. That'd make me ancient. I should be preparing for retirement."

"Even without your injuries, you wouldn't have many left. But with them…"

She set the broth down. "How much longer do I have? How much longer do you have?"

"I'm old Maisel. And you are too—you don't look it, but you will feel it. We're old and tired. There were just a few things I wanted to do before I'd be ready—and seeing you one more time was one of them." He wiped his eyes. "It's only because of your research," he said while tapping her notebook, "that we were able to stay alive this long. You gave me plenty of amazing cycles, most of them spent with you doing the one thing you love—and that's not a bad life. I'm ready. Our kids are ready to say goodbye, too."

"'Our kids.' It's strange to hear you say that." She wasn't sure whether to laugh or cry, so she turned to him, hoping for an answer. She looked into his eyes, past the wrinkles and thick eyebrows, and she could see him. For the first time since waking up, she could see him: Huxley—her Huxley.

"It is you, isn't it?"

"Yes, it's me. I'm so sorry."

Her hands began to shake and he reached for them, and she let him touch her with his thin, skeleton fingers. She let this old man touch her, and she didn't flinch. She grabbed them and held on with all of her might.

#

For the next two days, she sat with her children at the house they built on top of a small hill not far from the crash. It was made from dried, hollow stalks and pieces of the ship. It had a rudimentary plumbing system and a small fenced-in area not far from the house where a few translucent creatures grazed. When her time came, she retired in the spot chosen for her next to her husband. A few weeks later, Huxley joined her.

#

Soon after his death, their planet was noted by a passing surveying vessel. Within a year of its discovery, trade routes were established, ushering in an era of connectivity. It was closer to Proximata than they had initially guessed. Within a few years, it became a popular destination for those in the region, with a series of resorts and natural parks, including the well-known Profeta Intergalactic Nature Preserve.

Eventually, Maisie's children were sending her grandchildren off-world for a more formal education, and while many returned and still live there today, one of her grandchildren chose a different path.

Dust

3045 CE – Near Pluto

Primrose rested her hands against the edge of the casket and stared out the airlock of the ship. She looked young, but her body felt old, and she was tired and annoyed. Why did he have to die?

She never enjoyed making decisions, and for most of her adult life, she didn't have to. Dallas was more than happy to oblige—at least when he was alive.

"With this top-of-the-line casket," explained the yacht's funeral director, tapping the back where the propulsion sat, "you have unlimited destination opportunities. These boosters will send your husband to the nearest asteroid belt or planet, or for a few credits more, take him to the nearest star where he can rest amongst a god of your choosing!"

Those who couldn't afford a rocket-powered casket had to share the same fate as food waste and human excrement; they recycled their bodies. Their final destination was the garden. But that wasn't Primrose. She could afford to send him anywhere she wanted.

"And if you choose to send him to a star," he continued, "for a small fee, it can be named after him, so you can remember him, wherever you are."

She began to wonder if her husband of forty years would enjoy resting in a star. If only she could send him back to Earth. That's what he loved the most. He often talked about the feeling of dirt under his toes, endless trees, and his small garden of tomatoes. He missed tomatoes the most. There weren't many on the ship.

She had never been there herself but had always planned to visit. It was where his family was from (hers, too, if she went back far enough), and where their only child, Caleb, had moved years ago. He had decided to take advantage of his dad's estate, which was said to be quite valuable. She was too old to survive a transition back to Earth, and the value of the land would not change that. But it had served her son well. She'd make sure he planted a garden to honor his dad.

"Have you decided where he will go to rest?" the director asked, after a long pause.

She smiled at the young director and then turned back to the casket and held Dallas's hands. She had been pondering this question for the last year—ever since his diagnosis. Dallas gave no clues about what he wanted. "Wherever you send me," he had told her, "just make sure a part of me stays close to you."

Whatever she was going to do, she had to decide today. "May I have a few more moments with him alone?" she asked.

"Yes, of course. Take all the time you need."

She bent down to him and, in a whisper, asked, "Where do you want to go? And why the hell didn't you wait for me to go with you?" She took in a deep breath and then noticed the painted metallic pin holding his tie: a bright red tomato.

She stood back up. "Sir, I've made up my mind," she said.

"Where will he be headed today?" he asked again, as he walked up, ready to put in the coordinates.

"I'd like him to be recycled."

The director paused, looking a little embarrassed. She might as well have told him she wanted him tossed into the trash. "Recycled?"

"Yes."

"But you have already purchased this casket and—"

"Don't worry, I'm not asking for a refund."

"A woman of your means doesn't have to have him recycled."

"A woman of my means can have exactly what she wants."

The director paused again, unsure how to proceed.

She let out a sigh and turned to the window on the other side of the ship.

"You're too young to have been to Earth or any Planet—born on the ship—and this is all you know. But I remember Earth, and so did my husband, and back there everyone was recycled, in a way." She turned towards the casket, ready to say goodbye now, and leaned in and kissed Dallas's hands. "From dust you came, to dust you shall return." She spoke this in the tongue of her parents' faith, knowing well that those within earshot would not understand. "You're going to help a tomato grow, it's better than a star, I think... but you know I was never very good at these kinds of decisions." She removed the small tomato pin from his tie, kissed it, and placed it in her pocket.

Part III: It Was Always a Matter of Time

The Pivot

3023 CE - Earth

The fireplace was much larger than any other he'd seen, but felt small compared to the room. Caleb scanned the walls, all lined with books that went so high they needed ladders to reach them. Having been raised in space, he wasn't used to rooms as large as this, or ladders for that matter. He began to wonder if this is what his library would look like in his new home if it were furnished.

Not that he had any plans of furnishing it.

He had a newborn and a wife tired from the pregnancy, holed up in an upstairs bedroom of a house as large as a small space station. They put everything they owned into the bedroom, yet the room still felt empty. There was far too much space for his family to be comfortable. When his father told him about his property on Earth, he did not expect it to include an entire estate.

It was all too much. He wanted something simple. A place he could put down roots and start anew. He had no intention of living in that drafty old mansion down the street from his uncle's. He would sell his portion and find something smaller. Maybe he'd donate some of the proceeds to one of the charities his wife had learned about. His dad's family on Earth was doing well, but most people weren't. Many were in dire need.

Before he could do any of that, he had to deal with his dad's side of the family. He had been warned—his uncle could be very persuasive. And so, when his uncle invited him to the adjacent property, he accepted, knowing he would have to keep his wits about him and leave without committing to anything new or joining the family business. Whatever it was, his father wanted him to have nothing to do with it. And with his resolve set, he found himself sitting in a large leather chair by a fireplace in a dimly lit library, his uncle pouring drinks from a cart along the wall, counting the moments until he could go home to the two loves of his life.

His uncle handed him a glass that was heavier than he expected. He nearly dropped it. It was not only heavy because gravity was something he was still getting used to, but because it was heavy in its own right—thick crystal with only a little bit of liquor sitting in the bottom. Thankfully, he didn't drop it and only spilled a little. He sat back in his seat as his uncle took the seat opposite him and stared at him for quite a while, and Caleb began to wonder what his uncle wanted to talk about and why it was so urgent, and whether his uncle's silence was some strategy to wear him down before even knowing the topic of the evening.

"It's a 1770 Kummel Liqueur," said his uncle, finally breaking the silence. "Very rare."

"That's very old," said Caleb, nervously smiling as the sweet liquor burned all the way down.

"Yes. Many things in this home are very old. Our family, including you now, is invested in Earth's history."

Caleb took another sip and raised his eyebrows. And then, out of curiosity—legitimately and sincerely, he asked: "You're invested in history?" When his father warned him about his family, he assumed they were some kind of tech oligarch, or political lobbyist, or something like that, certainly not someone who dealt in something as benign as history.

"Yes, history. And rightly so, for it's only in history—and our ability to manage it—that we are able to ensure our future investments are intact," the uncle said, taking another sip from his glass. "What do you know about Earth's history?"

Caleb set the glass on the chair arm and began to think. He knew as much about Earth's history as anyone who grew up off-world. Earth had grown old. There had been a series of spiraling climate change events, consolidation of world powers, multiple great extinctions, more than one Exodus (which included the one his father snuck away on), but beyond the large brush strokes, he didn't know as much about Earth as he would want to. He had never lived here, but it did seem as good a place as any—maybe better than most—to put down roots and raise his daughter. And ultimately, that was all that mattered: having a quiet life with his family and being the best father possible.

"Not as much as I would like, sir."

"That's about to change, for you belong to a truly historic family. One might say that history is our primary business, and I'd like to tell you all about it, but first, would you be willing to sign an NDA?"

His uncle was doing exactly what his father had warned him about. He knew this was coming, and he planned to sign it. He had no desire to compete with, destroy, or otherwise engage in his uncle's business, no matter what it was, so an NDA was fine. He figured he'd be able to move on without anything holding up the sale. He signed, and his uncle folded the paper up and placed it into the inner pocket of his suit jacket. Caleb was planning to get up and leave, assuming that's all he wanted from him, when his uncle began to talk.

"By history, I mean time travel."

He was not expecting that. Time travel? Caleb would have spit out his drink from laughter if he hadn't just swallowed it.

"Don't laugh, my son. I'm being serious. Has your father told you nothing of us?"

"No, sir," he said, trying not to sneer.

"We have long sent signals back in time, not so difficult, for signals are small and able to traverse the timeline far more easily than humans. We used them to study our history, and with the same technology, we pointed them towards the future, which is less precise for all the logical reasons: it hasn't happened yet. But we have been able to estimate it. We can predict within a reasonable margin of error all major events— it's how we built our wealth, you see. There's good money to be had in telling people what will happen next."

"That is… unbelievable," and while he meant it literally, he let his tone sound impressed so as not offend him further.

"You don't believe me, do you? Of course not." He pulled out a series of papers from the drawer next to him and put on his reading glasses before passing them to Caleb. "To help convince you, I've commissioned some research on your family—the one on your mother's side." He laid a sheet of paper with a name and a photo of an old man sitting outside a wooden shack. "Your ancestor, who left the city for reasons I will never understand. Have you heard of him?" Before he could answer, his uncle placed another sheet on top: a photo of a young woman climbing a hill, then another of the same woman, older now, with someone who looked like her daughter standing beside her. "Another ancestor, Arya and Seren—grandmother and mother of Calvin and Emmanuel, who, if you knew Earth history, played a very important role in the collapse of AI." He looked up at him, peering over his glasses, "They are not very popular in my circles. A bit of an Icarus story if you ask me." Then he placed another, a young man standing in front of a farmhouse. "The last of your ancestors to live on Earth—Harper Profeta. From there, your family moved off-world, and our projection doesn't extend that far."

Caleb knew little about Earth, but he knew his family well. He had been raised by his mother, a Profeta through and through, and if they were anything, they were set on sharing the stories of their ancestors, as if those stories were the heart of their family's religion. And while he recognized them—as if he'd seen their photos in an old book—he wasn't about to trust his memory on such things.

"So, which would you like to meet?" his uncle asked. "I can put you in the same room, for a moment, to see them."

Caleb laughed again.

"Don't believe me? Just point to the photo, and I'll make it happen."

Caleb shrugged and reached out to touch the photo of Arya.

"Good choice," he said, "an interesting character in her own right."

His uncle turned towards the door and nodded, and Caleb got up to see whom he was nodding towards, but once he did, he turned right into a tree.

He was no longer in the library.

He was in a forest on a steep slope. The trees were old, and the greenery dense, and he knew he was either off-world, hallucinating, or somehow back in time. How else could there be such diversity of plant life?

He looked down at his body—his hands, legs, feet, clothes were all the same, but the sun was shining, and he could hear voices. He turned, and on the other ridge was a caravan of people hiking. He ducked so as not to be seen. That's when he saw Arya from the photo, just as she had appeared. She was walking a few paces behind the others.

"Arya!" said an older man, "Hurry, we should all stay together along this part."

"Yes, I'm trying, Ruben," she replied.

He stood up to hear what else they were saying, but when he blinked, he was back in the library by his chair, his uncle sitting across from him, laughing.

"A bit of a jolt, for the first time, but I knew you'd need some convincing." He handed him his drink again. "Drink, please. It will help."

Caleb did drink, and his head was fuzzy, and he wasn't sure who she was or whether she was whom his uncle claimed to be, or whether it mattered—whatever it was, he had clearly traveled somewhere, maybe somewhen, without ever leaving this room.

His uncle sat for a while, silent, as Caleb slowly felt the color return to his face.

"I hope that was enough to convince you."

It certainly had convinced him. His life would not be a very quiet, simple one if he stuck around here any longer. He had to leave. "I really should be going."

"Yes, soon, but first you must hear what I have to say."

"Ok. Fine. Get on with it. What's your big pitch? What do you want from me?"

"I want your help. I want you to work for the company."

"I'm not interested," and he set down his drink and got up.

"Will you not hear me out?"

"No." It was a lot easier to say "no" than he had imagined. Simple. Direct—exactly as he had planned. He was proud of himself. Caleb got up and headed toward the door. He grabbed the handle, when his Uncle continued.

"Go ahead, leave. It was always an 85% chance you would. But please, know that if you leave before you hear me out, the end of the world will be inevitable."

Caleb froze.

"You heard me. Inevitable. Walk through that door, and the world ends. I've seen it. So leave if you want, but if you love your wife and child, you'll stay and hear me out."

He turned. "What do you mean?"

"We've estimated that in five years' time, if nothing changes, there will be a nuclear war."

"How can you know for sure?" he asked, walking back to his seat.

"The same way I knew you'd move back. The same way I knew you'd try to leave just now. I'm telling you, our technology lets us predict the future with some assurance, and while most of it is information we can sell, there is one thing we'd never sell—the apocalypse. If we don't make any changes, in five years, there will be a nuclear war, and everything we know—everything we enjoy on Earth—will be destroyed. This house. This chair. This glass of liquor." He took his glass and threw it into the fireplace. It shattered, and the liquor went up in flames. "Poof. Boom. It will all be gone."

Caleb took a breath as he watched the fire burn back down. "What does your company plan to do about it?"

"It's not my company—but our company. Your father left more than just property; he's handed over his share in the holdings. It's a minority share, but nothing to laugh at. And because of our ability to project humans into the past, we've been looking for something we can change to prevent the inevitable. And we've been mildly successful."

"So you can stop it?" Caleb asked.

"Sort of. All we've been able to do so far is postpone it. Twenty years ago, when we first started working on the timeline and predicting the future, we found a point in history where our agents could make minor, surgical changes, pushing the apocalypse back five years without messing anything else up in the process. And we've done this year after year. Small, surgical, precise changes in history that push our projections further into the future. The oncoming apocalypse was originally scheduled to occur 10 years ago, but with our adjustments, we've pushed it back by 15 years already. What we're ultimately looking for is the one change that will remove it entirely." He got up, walked over to the bar, poured himself another drink, and came back. "It's called the Pivot, my son." He began to spin the globe that sat on a small wooden table by his chair. "The entire world turns on a single point. That's the power of the Pivot. We're looking for the singular change we can make, at some point in history, that will remove the apocalypse from the timeline without changing anything else. It will need to be very precise, and we must be careful not to change anything on a whim. You see, time travel is precarious like that. One wrong move, and none of us will be here." He sat back down. "We have hired hundreds of historians to go back in time very carefully—not to change anything unless properly approved—so that we can find the one thing that would prevent the nuclear war."

Caleb slouched in his seat.

"Your father was very uncomfortable with all this time-travel stuff, and that's why he wanted nothing to do with it. But you're not him. My question for you is this: If you could change the future, would you? If you knew our world would end at the whims of angry old men in power, and you could do something about it, would you?"

He thought about his daughter and his wife, and he knew he had to do whatever was necessary to keep them safe.

"Yes, of course, I would."

"Good, then unlike your father, we're on the same page."

The One Thing

3076 CE – Earth

The air in the Main Projection Chamber hummed faintly, warm with recycled heat and the static smell of charged metal. Hondo and two of his closest friends were in traditional outfits, handpicked by their handlers. Each held an antique technology representative of their destination: the twenty-first century in the States of America, in a province known as the Midwest, near the Atlantic Ocean. They were eager for their first trip, but they had to wait for final checks before they would be released, and it took much longer than any of them could bear. Hondo was the third in his family to travel through time. First, his grandfather, Caleb; then his mother, Iris, and now it was his turn, and he was tired of waiting.

"A few more checks and we'll be ready," said the attendant in the control room.

Hondo let out a sigh.

"All's set. Let's get into our positions."

"Yes, dears," said one of the old women in charge of young historians. "The time has come. Hondo, you're first. Then Aiden. Zeke, hop in after them, just as we showed you."

They squeezed in and held hands, typical among young cadets. Holding hands didn't assist the technology in any measurable way—

not technically, but it did make them feel safer, and that was worth something.

Then, with nothing but a blink, they were gone. Traveling through time was always less exciting than one would expect. You closed your eyes, and when you opened them, you were in a new world.

Since it was their first time, they traveled back to a period similar to their own. By the twenty-first century, the earth had already gotten as hot as hell, and the oceans engulfed much of the coastline. They were told they would find the technology outdated, but many other customs would be relatable. It was an easy first mission, but an exciting one: they were sent to the launch of the first human mission to Mars. Hondo had a few relatives who lived near Mars, and he had always hoped he could record a piece of that history. Yet, studying history was never as simple as showing up for the main event. It always included weeks of prep and undercover personas. They were more historical spies than traditional historians.

When they blinked, damp air rushed into Hondo's lungs, thick with pine sap and wet soil. They found themselves standing in a small, wooded area, and as their ears began to connect to the timeline, they heard leaves blowing overhead, then the sound of kids talking. As his senses adjusted to the new surroundings, Hondo looked up the hill. That's when Aiden pointed to the yellow bus they were told to look for. "Hurry, let's catch it," yelled Hondo. They ran towards it and joined the kids in line as they exited the bus. By the time they figured out how to turn on those handheld devices, a counselor was walking down the line of students to confiscate them.

Hondo never got to use one of those devices.

It didn't matter. He didn't need it.

It was the best week of his life.

They were fifteen, but they were expected to pass as twelve-year-olds—the oldest age allowed for the young astronauts' camp, located a short hike from the launch site of the Mars mission scheduled for later that year. Undercover as campers, they would be given a tour of the launch facilities. Attending the entire week was the easiest way to gain in-and-out access to scan the rudimentary launch equipment without unintentionally disrupting the timeline.

They played harder that week than any other. Hondo had been training to be a historian since he was twelve, born into a family of historians. He had forgotten how much fun being a kid was.

The night before they'd see the launch pad, the three of them snuck out of their dorm and down into the courtyard, where they found a growth of large trees and brush that made a thin path. The sheer amount of vegetation, trees, and plants was one of the highlights of traveling through the timeline.

They snuck between the trees and sat in the dirt, the soil cool and gritty against their palms. When possible, a team like theirs always met up to go over the details before the mission. They recited them to each other, like spies during the Cold War.

It was glorious.

They were about to get up and head back to their dorms when Zeke stopped them. He whispered, as if he didn't want the base to know what they were saying—as if they could hear.

"Can I ask you a question?"

"Too late—you already have!" laughed Aiden.

It took Hondo a second to get his joke, but he laughed once it came to him. Aiden had a joke for everything.

Zeke was always so serious, but even he'd laugh at Aiden's jokes—but not this time.

"Quick, look away, so they can't read our lips."

They all turned away from each other. Hondo had heard of kids doing this. It was a common way to keep the handlers from seeing what they were saying. With them all looking away from each other, Zeke asked, "If you were to go back and change something in history—one thing—what would it be?"

It was not only the most cliché question he could ask; it was also the most inappropriate one. It was not their past to change. Half of their training was about how to keep things as they were. Observe and report. Don't cause any ripples, because ripples can grow into waves, and waves into tsunamis, and that would be the end of them all. Hondo told Zeke as much, but only when looking away—he did not want to get them in trouble.

Aiden stopped laughing.

"The one thing?" asked Aiden, still looking away. He was serious, and it was one of the few times that week he didn't have a smile on his face.

"The one thing you would change," repeated Zeke.

"I'd kill Hitler—as a baby. That'd be the easiest way to do it, as a baby."—and he wasn't joking.

It was an unoriginal answer—kill a dictator? Ha. Given his half-German heritage, it made sense. He always seemed bothered by this part of German history, when fascism rose and caused so much pain. He was so bothered by it that he would often argue that it had to be the Pivot. People did this often; they'd hold onto the worst part of their ancestors' history and claim that if only this were different, the end wouldn't be so near.

But he was mistaken.

Killing Hitler could never be the Pivot. If the Pivot existed at all, it had to be surgical. History is not a sequence of isolated events; it is an ecosystem. Remove a foundational structure—however cruel—and the entire terrain reshapes itself. Languages shift. Borders dissolve before they are drawn. Economies never form. Migrations never happen. Families never meet. Children are never born. And somewhere along that chain, the line that leads to the observer breaks. If Aiden wanted to change history that much, he'd have to be willing to sacrifice his very existence—all of their existence—and no one wanted that. Killing Hitler wouldn't help Aiden; the moment he stuck the knife into Hitler's flesh, it would be as if he did the same to himself. Lower-level historians didn't understand the Pivot like Hondo. They couldn't.

This whole conversation annoyed him.

"Can we go back to the dorm now?" Hondo asked.

"What's your answer?" Aiden asked Zeke, ignoring Hondo, which annoyed him even more.

"I'd—"

They all froze as they heard someone walk by. They turned to look at each other and ducked under the bushes. If they got caught, there'd be a ripple for sure, and none of them wanted a low score on their first assignment.

Once they had passed, Hondo convinced them to come back with him. They snuck across the courtyard, up the lattice, and into the window back to their rooms.

The next morning, they toured the launch pad and held their gaze carefully, allowing the base to capture a full scan of this historic launch.

When camp was over, they headed to the bus stop, where they disappeared into the woods. From there, the agency brought them back home without anyone noticing.

Later that day, they questioned Hondo about the moment they turned and talked with no one seeing, and he could only imagine they asked the others, too. He told them they were saying nasty things about girls—it's what they had agreed to say, and in the end, with a little scolding and gazes of disapproval, they passed with no marks on their report.

His family made sure of that.

#

They celebrated at a restaurant overlooking the river, the kind of place that pretended it had always been there even though the building had been rebuilt twice in Hondo's lifetime. The windows were tall and curved, designed to mimic an older architectural style, and the lights inside were low enough to make everything feel important.

Hondo arrived with his parents early. His mother insisted on it— punctuality was respect, and respect was a currency she never spent lightly. His father ordered wine without looking at the menu. He already knew what he wanted. He always did.

By the time Aiden's family arrived, the table was already crowded with plates, folded napkins, and overlapping conversations. Aiden's parents entered first, moving through the room like they were still at a conference—hands clasped behind their backs, eyes scanning faces, nodding at people they recognized but couldn't immediately place. Aiden followed behind them, shoulders loose, smiling like this was a rehearsal dinner and not a celebration.

While the ultimate mission was to find the Pivot, two generations had come and gone, and the best they could do was postpone the inevitable a few years at a time. It remained the primary directive, but it wasn't at the top of most people's minds. Those who worked on the timeline did so for their love of history, just as those who built the nuclear bombs did so for their love of science. What upper management did with their discoveries was kept at arm's length.

As far as historians go, Aiden's family was among the most respected of their time.

Aiden's dad spent his career trekking through the Roman Empire, up through its ultimate fall. His mom spent her career witnessing Thailand's independence during the period of European colonization in that area. They met at the historical society's award ceremony, where the organizers asked them to co-present. The rest, as they say, is history.

The moment his parents kissed, their index jumped a whole point, triggering an automatic six-month suspension from work.

Spontaneity was the least desired quality for any respectable historian. His parents had worked long enough in the field to know how to get their score back down—repetition, predictability, and no rash actions. Aiden had learned from the best, and it showed.

His grandmother followed behind them, and Hondo noticed how Aiden tightened up.

She wore silk and the pattern was unmistakably Thai—bright, sharp lines that refused to fade into the muted tones of the restaurant. She took her seat slowly, gripping the back of the chair as if it were the last solid thing in a moving world.

They listened politely while the parents talked—about the launch pad, about the scan quality, about how clean the mission reports were— but when Aiden's mother mentioned that this would likely be the only time period Aiden would ever be cleared for fieldwork, something in his grandmother snapped.

She started speaking rapidly, her voice sharp and musical, cutting clean through the table's polite rhythm.

Hondo didn't understand a word of it.

Aiden stiffened beside him, then leaned over just enough to whisper, "She's upset that the agency won't let me travel far enough back to meet the Thai royal families."

It was sad that he'd be stuck in the modern era. A lot of people felt sorry for him, but it wasn't his fault he was a mixed kid, and nothing to be ashamed of either, as far as Hondo was concerned. His inability to travel through time before globalization was unfortunate but practical. That's just how things worked.

Zeke and his family arrived last.

He didn't sit right away. He stood at the edge of the table, as if he was taking everything in—the parents, the posture, the way Hondo's mother angled her chair so she could see everyone at once. When he finally pulled out his seat, he did it slowly, like he wasn't sure he belonged there.

The food came in waves. Plates were set down and taken away. Someone toasted "the next generation." Someone else joked that their first mission had been easy. Zeke barely touched his food.

When the noise grew too loud, when the adults leaned into their own stories, Zeke pushed his chair back.

"I need some air," he said.

Hondo followed him before he realized he'd stood up.

Outside, the night was cool and damp, the river dark and slow beneath the lights. The restaurant door swung shut behind them, sealing the laughter inside.

Zeke leaned against the railing, staring out at the water.

"You notice," he said, "how everyone talks about *access* like it's the same thing as *experience*?"

Hondo didn't respond.

"They call it safety," Zeke continued. "They call it practicality. But it always seems to mean the same people get to look and the same people get looked at."

"We're observers," Hondo said. "That's the job."

"Observers from *where*?" Zeke asked. "From whose side of the line?"

"What are you saying?" Hondo asked, sincerely confused.

And then, as if answering his question and also ignoring it, Zeke said, "I mean…When I grow up, I'm going to be the first to catalogue the African slave trade from the perspective of a person of color."

"As a slave?"

"Or something similar."

"Why would you do that?" asked Hondo. "There are far more comfortable ways to study that part of history, you know. Plenty of white people have already cataloged it."

"From the vantage of the oppressor?"

Hondo's face turned red, and he was hot, and he found himself angry for reasons he couldn't understand. None of this race stuff mattered; if the world ended, it would end for everyone. "No," he argued, "We're doing it from the vantage of the apocalypse! We're trying to stop the end of the world."

Zeke smiled. "For who?"

The restaurant door opened, spilling light onto the walkway. Someone called Zeke's name. He pushed off the railing and headed back inside, leaving the question behind.

Hondo stayed out a moment longer, watching the river slide past, carrying pieces of history no one would ever catalog.

#

The folder was thinner than Hondo expected. It had been ten years since his first mission, and he had been receiving threats from his family to be moved off the timeline. He worried this was the next step in their insistence. The folder was lying on the table between them, matte black, unmarked—no insignia, no seal, not even a label. That alone told him what it wasn't. It wasn't a mission. Missions came in thick packets, layered with contingencies and redundancies, all the ways things could go wrong cataloged in advance.

This was something else.

The handler sat across from him, his hands folded, posture neutral, eyes unreadable, as management had trained him.

"You're late," he said, though he wasn't.

"Traffic," Hondo replied automatically.

He nodded, as if that satisfied something on a checklist. "This won't take long." He slid the folder toward him with two fingers. It stopped just short of his hands.

Hondo didn't open it right away.

"Is this another extension?" he asked. "I just finished a clean run in Australia. No ripples. Zero."

"I know. That's why you're here."

He waited for the rest.

When it didn't come, he opened the folder.

One page. Just one. His name was at the top, his clearance code was beneath it, and a location was stamped in bold: Buenos Aires – Department of Timeline Preservation.

"This is a mistake! I asked to stay on the timeline. Just a few more cycles. I'm not—" He stopped himself. *Not ready* sounded childish. "I'm more useful out there."

"You've been useful," he said. "That's the problem."

Hondo flipped the page over, hoping for a second sheet. There wasn't one.

"Argentina," he said. "Why Argentina?"

"Distance. Perspective."

"From what?"

"I don't know. Your home?"

The door behind him opened. Hondo didn't have to turn around to know who it was.

His mother's footsteps were measured, the sound of someone who never hurried because the world always adjusted to her pace. She stopped beside him, close enough that he could smell her perfume—something sharp and clean, chosen for boardrooms.

She looked at the folder.

"So," she said. "They finally stopped indulging you."

Hondo closed it. "I wasn't done traveling."

She took the seat beside him without asking. "You were done years ago. You just didn't want to admit it."

"This is management. You said—"

"*I said* you would earn it," she interrupted. "This isn't an executive role. Don't flatter yourself."

The handler stood. That was his cue to disappear. "You'll receive your relocation details by morning," he added, already halfway to the door.

When it shut, the room felt smaller.

"You could've stopped this," Hondo said quietly.

His mother folded her hands in her lap. "I could've delayed it. That's not the same thing."

He stared at the folder again.

"I didn't want to end up like my cousins stuck in stuffy offices, unaware of what's really going on in the world."

"Good. Then don't. Go see the world, as you say, but this time, in the present."

His wrist buzzed. A message notification pulsed faintly against his skin. He glanced down before he could stop himself. It was a message from Aiden.

He didn't open it. His mother noticed anyway. She always did.

"Still hearing from him?"

"Sometimes."

"Part-time historian," she said. "In and out of rehab. Tragic, really."

It was tragic, and he wished he had done more to help him over the years.

Then he got another ping.

Another buzz. This time it was Zeke.

"Did you tell all of my friends about this?"

"I thought you'd need some encouragement. Go ahead, take the call. I'll leave you."

"I didn't ask for this."

His mother stood. "None of us do."

She paused at the door.

"Make me proud," she added. "Or at least don't embarrass us."

When she was gone, Hondo picked up the folder again and answered the call.

Zeke's voice came through thin and wind-worn, layered with distant surf and the low murmur of people nearby.

"Are you sitting down?" Zeke asked.

"I am now," Hondo said, lowering himself back into the chair.

"Good. Because I finally made it."

"Made it where?"

"The coast," Zeke said. "West Africa. Later today, I'll be walking the ports. Cataloging the markets, the ships—everything they'll let me get close to without asking too many questions."

Hondo pictured him squinting into the sun, skin dark against darker bodies, trying not to stand out in a place where standing out could get you killed.

"They actually cleared you for it?"

Zeke laughed. "*Cleared* is a strong word. More like they stopped finding excuses."

"You always said you'd get there."

"And you always said I shouldn't."

There was a pause. The surf grew louder.

"So," Zeke continued, "you sitting behind a desk yet?"

"She told you about my promotion?"

"Yeah, and should I say *congratulations* or *my condolences*?"

"I didn't ask for it."

"I know."

"I tried to stay out there," Hondo said. "On the timeline. I begged. But they're sending me to the Office of Timeline Preservation in Argentina. So much for finding the Pivot, now all I'll be doing is making sure nothing changes until we can."

"Still—it makes me feel better."

"Why?"

"Because if something goes wrong, at least it'll end up on your desk."

"You shouldn't be joking about that."

"I'm not joking," Zeke replied. "I'm relieved. Let's make this a tradition—every year on the anniversary of our promotions, let's chat."

Nothing about either of their roles felt like promotions, but Hondo agreed all the same.

"Sure."

"I've got to go. I'll be heading back to the 1600s soon. If you're curious, check my feed. You'll be able to do that in your new office, I'm sure."

"I will. And be careful."

"Always."

#

Hondo sat in his office, pretending to work—like most afternoons after he'd overeaten at lunch—his shirt faintly tight at the waist, when one of his analysts contacted him. He grabbed his leftover, cold morning coffee as his analyst told him about a stir in the timeline. He spit the coffee out, partly because it was disgustingly cold and partly because this was the last thing Hondo wanted to hear in moments like this. It fell in that slim line of time where it was too late in the afternoon to care, but not late enough to justify putting it off till tomorrow.

Hondo leaned into his desk, woke up his computer, and pulled up the data. The ripple had blipped in 1619, radiating out from the west coast of Africa. He didn't bother running the usual cross-references. He already knew. There was only one active historian on the West Coast of Africa working right now.

Hondo messaged his handlers, telling them he would confiscate their feed. They apologized for the blips and agreed to fill out the damage report immediately. They should have already filled it out. For him to catch this blip before their report was submitted didn't look good on the handlers.

It took a moment to connect.

The image came in blurry as the feed switched, and Hondo could tell Zeke was blinking to adjust to the transition. Switching feeds like this was evident to the person on the other end—it felt like a reboot of the brain, like falling asleep for a moment only to wake up in the same place.

The picture stabilized.

Hondo leaned into the screen, analyzing his feed.

He saw the ocean knocking against a wooden dock, and the waves drifting off towards the horizon. As the sun sat low in the sky, seagulls filled the air—it had been a while since Hondo had seen the ocean. Buenos Aires Metrorail had a route to the coast, but it was an hour's ride, and he was always busy. He had forgotten how beautiful the ocean was.

Then Zeke turned. The image stabilization kicked in, slowing the image down so Hondo could see a large ship in the harbor, the flag at the top of its mast flaring in the wind. When Zeke turned again, there were people who had dark skin like Zeke's, all bare-backed and standing in a line.

Hondo glanced at the ripple report on his second monitor. Zeke had stood out of line and spoken to the slave-holder in the slave-holder's language. There is no need to repeat what he said. It was brutal, using words the slave holders wouldn't understand, but had they, they would have done a lot more than chain him in line. It would have made Hondo laugh had he not been so concerned for Zeke's safety.

Zeke turned again, looking at his hands, which were chained together with thick, rough iron shackles, pitted and reddish with old rust, biting into his wrists each time the line pulled him forward. This continued for the length of the dock, a line of chained bodies, all the way to the ship bouncing in the harbor. He reached up and wiped his face, and when he brought his hand back down, there was blood on it. The slave-holder must have hit him, but he couldn't say for sure, since that would never cause a ripple.

Hondo called his analyst.

"I want everything you have on Zeke's current mission *now*."

Hondo had the ever-evolving ripple reports, but those only covered the details surrounding the incident that caused the ripple. He wanted everything.

Within a minute, he had Zeke's full mission report in front of him.

Zeke was cataloging the slave market near the Kwanza River. He was supposed to be a well-respected indentured servant of a prominent trader, which would have given him the freedom to roam the port without disrupting the timeline. This was when he had his first ripple. It went off when he found himself among the mob boarding the slave ship. Because of his dark skin, they had mistaken him for an enslaved person, and he was shackled and put into the line.

Hondo slammed his desk. This was precisely what he said would happen.

Hondo knew that by nightfall, Zeke would be on board the slave ship.

"We need to pull him out of there, first chance we get," Hondo yelled to his analyst through his office window.

"Can't right now, boss—too many ripples."

"I know we can't do it now, but as soon as possible."

Pulling a historian out in broad daylight went against everything they believed in. The last time that happened—when a guy just vanished into thin air—an entire religion was born. It took half a year of adjustments to get that religion worked out, but it could never really be wiped from the timeline altogether. A small group still gathers for worship in the hills of Switzerland—more of a cult now than anything.

Letting Zeke die on the ship would change the future less than saving him at the wrong time. If Hondo had understood this time period as well as he had hoped, they would soon load Zeke into the belly of the ship, crammed into a room only three feet tall, laid out on his back, like a drawer of socks neatly folded. If things went well, by morning the ship would head to sea, and the following night, in the darkness with the tossing of the waves as a distraction, they would grab him without anyone noticing him vanish. They could do it sooner, if it came to that, but Hondo had learned the value of patience, and he wasn't going to rush it.

Zeke stood on the dock, in the dead of day, for the next five hours, and Hondo watched. He had watched so intently that his office lights kept turning off, and he'd have to wave his hands like some flamboyant dancer just to get them to turn back on.

As the sun set, they carted Zeke onto the ship. Hondo kept a pulse on his vitals, and while his blood pressure was raised, it wasn't even close to registering shock, which was shocking. *Why wasn't Zeke freaking out?*

Zeke must have been resting, knowing that his incident had most likely landed on Hondo's desk. That even if Hondo was away from the office, this was the incident they would track him down for. He must have trusted him to do the right thing and get him out of there. They had prepared for this, in a way.

By midnight, Hondo nodded off a little on his couch as he watched the screen from his seat. Zeke had his eyes shut most of the time, and when he did, Hondo couldn't see in the darkness.

He thought about bringing him back twice in the night, but the ripple meter never got low enough to avoid a report. He could only assume those around him never got much sleep, either.

By morning, he sat with a fresh cup of coffee, too hot to drink, and watched as the sun shoot through the small cracks in the floor that sat inches from Zeke's face.

"I'm going to get you out of there soon!" he yelled at the screen.

He checked Zeke's health data to make sure he could wait until the evening. Zeke was experiencing mild stress, to be expected, but nothing dangerous. He had to give Zeke credit: they had plenty of footage of slave ships, but none from this vantage point. It would greatly expand their understanding of that era.

Later that morning, Hondo called his top analyst into the office—the one who had gone home last night. He explained his plan to him and asked for a full report on the ship. After he left, Hondo called in a different analyst and asked her for a full report on Zeke's ancestry, covering this segment on the timeline.

"Just to be safe, we're not crossing any lines," Hondo told her.

He smiled, hiding his fears. He had no reason—other than a gut feeling—to think this was anything but an unfortunate accident.

Within an hour, Hondo had both reports uploaded to his computer. He scanned the document himself. He could have run the diagnostic on the computer, but he preferred to do these kinds of studies manually.

Zeke's ancestors traced their lineage to the other side of Africa. Hondo figured that would be the case—they would never send him on a mission within walking distance of his ancestors, not given their low status in society. It was too risky. Had they been comfortable or wealthy, it would have been fine. But whenever a people group experiences oppression, the agency is careful not to place their descendants too close to the action. Even the best historians can be temperamental when pushed to their limits.

Hondo hoped that would be the end of the concerns, but by the time he finished comparing the two timelines, there was a crossline—hardly noticeable but detectable to those who knew what to look for.

The ship that carried Zeke would sail to the Americas, then back to Africa, docking on the eastern coast, where it would transport one of his direct ancestors to the island of Jamaica, where, if you traced his line, it led to Zeke.

Hondo pushed his chair back.

He tried to remind himself that these kinds of coincidences happen all the time. History is far more connected than most realize.

Then the ripple meter went off.

Hondo turned to his feed.

Zeke lifted his finger to the dark wood above him. The wood was damp and soft beneath his nail, leaving pale grooves that stood out against the blackened grain. In the ceiling's grime, he dragged his fingernail into the moist lumber, leaving clear marks in their modern dialect—and with each letter, the ripple meter beeped.

When Hondo realized his analyst had stepped away from their computer, he turned off the alerts and set Zeke's feed to private so no one else could see what he was doing.

"This is the one," it read.

This is the one?

A second later, Zeke wiped it with his hand, and the ripples subsided a little, but still too high to bring him back. Everyone was awake, and a few were watching him write on the lumber.

Hondo turned back to Zeke's feed on the monitor behind him.

He was writing on the ceiling again: "Hondo, trust me."

What was he doing using his name?

He couldn't move. Boy, was Zeke confident. How did he know no one else was watching? How could he be sure it would actually end up on Hondo's desk? He could only assume that was a test—had it been anyone else, they would have pulled him immediately.

Zeke wiped the ceiling again and wrote once more.

"I'll miss you, friend."

That was too much. He had to do something!

He reached for the black box on his desk with one hand and typed in Zeke's exit code with the other. He was about to pull him, but then Zeke wiped it clean and turned to the ceiling frame. Hondo's finger rested on the button, but he wanted to see what Zeke was doing first. He watched him pull back some of the frame and pull out a small piece of metal. Then he opened another piece of the floor and slid out a similar piece of metal, hidden within the wood. After that, he slid another to reveal a small compartment. He had to reach over the person next to him to get it, and they grumbled as he did.

With the two pieces of metal, Zeke hit them together, and on the first strike, a spark flew into the compartment and caught fire.

As soon as the spark flew, Hondo flipped the switch, but the code had expired, so he had to re-enter it. After he did, he slammed the button as fast as he could.

The screen flashed, and then Zeke's feed went dark.

The ripple meter turned red, blaring a siren, and before Hondo could figure out what had happened, his office was filled with every available analyst.

According to the recently updated logs, the ship exploded.

No one survived.

They pulled Zeke moments after the blast; his body was sent directly to the closest facility, but it was too late. He died before he ever made it to the table.

Less than a minute after the incident, Hondo was told to clear the room; the board was on the line. They all listened as his mother berated him about the end of the world and how accidents like this might hasten it.

They didn't ask him any questions.

And then, as if to punish him, in the only way that made sense, Hondo was promised an executive role outside of Time Preservation, but only after a cushy vacation, while they looked into the events.

A full review of the feed revealed that Zeke had been sneaking different parts of his rudimentary bomb into the ship piece by piece over twenty missions. Each had a small ripple, but so small that no one took notice. Through careful calculation, he determined the exact spot in line he needed to be laid by the compartment lined with gunpowder. It was brilliant—patient, brutal, and unmistakably Zeke.

#

Standing on the soil of West Africa, the ground was warm beneath Hondo's feet, fine red dust clinging to his shoes and the hem of his trousers. The air smelled of sun-baked earth and salt drifting in from the coast. It was a truly beautiful country, even after all that was lost.

It was unfortunate that it took a funeral to get him to visit.

He'd never been to a funeral with no family present.

Zeke's family didn't exist anymore, at least not in the way they had. They were still living in their homeland, and it was unlikely that Zeke would ever be born in that line. The ripple was too significant for that. The ship he blew up never made it back to the other side of Africa, and this disrupted the packaging of enslaved people enough for his family to be overlooked in their village.

Hondo wasn't the only person at the funeral. Aiden came, and it was so good to see him. His hair ran down his back, and his face was covered in a long beard. Hondo didn't recognize him at first.

Aiden was doing better—a year in recovery. And he had a kid; he showed Hondo some photos. He ended up marrying someone who was a family friend on his mother's side. She's 80% Thai, and her son looks just like her.

"He might grow up to meet the great Thai princes!"

Hondo was happy for him, but if he was honest, he'd met a few Thai princes before—as an assistant for a European explorer back in his early twenties. It wasn't as fun as you would think.

During the memorial, Hondo, Aiden, and several managers and handlers from the local office shared a few words. The company had convinced everyone it was an unfortunate accident, and their words at the funeral perpetuated this lie.

Hondo knew better.

Zeke never had the chance to tell them what he'd change that night on their first mission, but in the end, he showed them.

This was his one thing.

Zeke hadn't tried to save everyone. He hadn't shattered the system in one grand, impossible gesture. He certainly didn't bring an end to the apocalypse. All he really did was give his family a few hundred years of freedom.

And it cost him his life.

That was the part Hondo couldn't stop circling back to: not the brilliance of the plan, but the cost Zeke seemed to accept without hesitation. He would receive no medals. He would get zero bonuses or the opportunity to use them. He left no descendants to remember him. Just freedom for people he'd never know.

Thinking about Zeke and his final mission, an idea snuck past

Hondo's defenses, as if it came up from the ground itself, like a small vine breaking through the red soil into the light.

It was an idea that went against everything his family believed in.

What if they had misunderstood the Pivot?

Perhaps time was more complicated than a globe spinning on its axis, requiring not one great correction but countless smaller ones. Or worse, possibly real change demanded their inclusion in its cost. If that were true, it explained why the apocalypse had always remained just out of reach: no one had ever been willing to disappear with it.

Two Minutes Too Late

3132 CE - Earth

Linus had exactly 2 minutes to make it from the kitchen, where he had been eating a fine lunch of ham and cheese, with pickles, mustard, and mayonnaise, to the Main Projection Chamber before the nuclear bomb hit. He had zero time to explain to the security personnel why he needed access, or why it was wildly inappropriate to deny him access simply because his shift was over.

They never have before.

"Sir, that's because we're on lockdown. No going or coming."

"Yes, exactly. We're on lockdown *because* a nuclear bomb has been—"

"We have our orders," the guard interrupted, "and we have our superiors to report to, and we're not sacrificing our career for someone who forgot their wallet or some other stupid thing—happens all the time, you know."

"I did not forget my wallet! I'm trying to prevent something *worse* than a nuclear bomb!"

"What would be *worse* than a nuclear bomb?" the guard asked, now clearly confused.

"We are going to be hit with a nuclear bomb in a matter of minutes and when that happens, if the Projection Chamber is on, it could rattle through the ages—blow up the whole timeline—or worse, amplify the internal projection signal impacting the time and speed of development of our entire solar system—especially the Sun—which is very temperamental to such things as nuclear bombs when time manipulation is involved, you know."

They did not know.

They looked at him like anyone would when he rattled on about things they didn't understand. The company was far too invested in security and secrecy and not nearly invested in science. He had told his cousins this many times, but they had already moved off-world and couldn't care less what happened to Earth anymore. A sad remnant of their great, great-grandfather's legacy. At this point, he was no longer surprised they hadn't said anything about the bombs. They knew they were coming, surely—a year early, too. It was criminal, but he didn't have time to worry about himself or even these guards. There was a much bigger problem at hand.

"If a nuclear bomb were coming, we would have been notified," said one of the guards.

"You were! We're on lockdown, are we not?"

"Yes, sir, so please return to the break room."

"Call your superiors and ask them."

"We will call our superiors in the morning."

"We won't be here in the morning!"

He looked at his watch, and it was too late; there was no more time for debates or security or disbelief or heroic attempts to contain time in the midst of a nuclear war. Even if they let him in, he'd never make it. The hallway was too long, so long that he might not have made it, even if they had let him in to begin with, without any questions. He had run out of time, which made him half-laugh, for, according to his calculations, time would now explode with the bomb and run over, like water that drops into a pan of hot oil, splattering all over the kitchen. What a mess this bomb would make of time.

He slouched to the floor and leaned against the wall.

"Sir, there is no loitering here."

"Yes, I understand," he said, laying his head into his knees and then mainly to himself, "In a minute, it won't matter."

He had done his best, and that's all anyone could do. It wasn't his fault that no one listened. His only hope was that he was wrong—wrong about it all. That his calculations and hypotheses were nothing more than the musings of a young scientist. It would be the first time he was wrong, but there was always a first for everything.

Whatever happened, he had to remember that he was not designed to carry the full weight of the world; it was much too heavy in this gravity. And so, with his head bowed, the guards threatening to drag him away, and his hands clasped onto a small pebble he had pulled from his pocket, he surrendered—almost a prayer, but more like a feeling. It was out of his hands—time, the bomb, all of it—he should let things fall where they might.

The Ticket Taker

3133 CE - Earth

The military had shown up before the Arc was ready to board, and Kiln was glad they had. The last time he worked the ticket booth, there was a rush for the shuttle; more than one person died, and quite a few people were wounded. Not to mention the Arc took off before it was fully loaded—a standard safety precaution—which means there were even more waiting for this one.

Kiln didn't look up from his screen. As a volunteer, he'd been approved to run the scanners, and his only payment was a spot on the Arc—if there was room. Until his job was done, he'd measure who lived and who died, his price of admission.

The line stretched along the bay, with customers praying the computers were working as they should, the rain wouldn't mess up the facial recognition, there wouldn't be any riots, and a thousand other prayers and concerns, clearly visible on their rain-soaked faces.

Many claimed that space travel was their salvation, offering refuge on various colonies and space stations. But Kiln always wondered if Earth's governments would have been so aggressive without such an obvious escape route. Would officials make the same decisions from offices on the surface instead of in orbit? Would they have been as likely to blow up Earth if they were still there? Kiln had long agreed with the drunk rants he overheard in bars after work. Space travel led to Earth's downfall. Not its ultimate downfall, of course. Just the first of many. The end of the world happens more often than people like to admit, frequently overlooked by those at the top.

The privileged in orbit couldn't see the pain of ordinary people, even if they were right in front of their faces, which they no longer were, because the privileged were in orbit, and everyone else was stuck on a dying planet at the end of a war. Two nuclear bombs had already gone off, and more were expected soon. Everyone, with any connection, found their way off-world.

He knew that would be the case for Marylyn.

She was too important—too connected—to stay for the likes of someone like him.

He wasn't sure whether he was angry that she had left, sad he'd never see her again, glad she was safe, or all three at the same time. Love, the sincere kind, is complicated like that.

Marylyn and Kiln had met in school and had spent three glorious semesters wrapped in each other's arms, skipping classes, getting high, ordering late-night, fresh-baked cookies, and dreaming of their future together: A future off-world—maybe Primera or on a station. There was no future for Earth; everyone had already given up on things working out. That was before their school closed a semester early. The professors went on strike, and while they claimed it was for noble reasons, Kiln always assumed it was because they wanted their chance to catch an early flight.

Kiln and Marylyn should have left when things were calm, but they were too distracted by each other. The night they decided to go, the college green and all the surrounding streets were filled with protesters and looters. They got separated between the 7th and the 5th, when Kiln was knocked down and handcuffed by a police officer who thought he was with the crowds. He woke up at the hospital with a mild concussion, and Marylyn was nowhere to be found. He made a few calls, only to be told by her cousins that she was scheduled to head into orbit with her family.

It was within the final boarding of the final Arc, as his line stretched along the bay, the sun setting on the ocean's horizon, with the rain pouring down on the faces of those waiting to get on, that he saw her for the first time in two years.

She wasn't in line, but walking along the bay, as if she was looking for something.

He almost didn't recognize her, her face covered in a hood to keep back the rain. But she had looked towards the Arc, and he'd recognize those eyes anywhere.

What on Earth was she doing on Earth?

She was supposed to be in orbit!

Why would she be so stupid as to forsake her chance to leave? Seeing her wandering the launch pad, as the last line loaded onto the final Arc, and the crowds stuck at the gate, with the military holding them back, he was angry and disappointed—far more than when he had assumed she'd left. She shouldn't be here. She was supposed to be safe.

"Marylyn!" he yelled into the rain, his voice almost swallowed by the wind. She didn't hear him. He got up on his stool and shouted even louder, "Marylyn Profeta!"

She turned and looked at him. He waved her over.

Her eyes widened. "Kiln?" she asked, walking towards him.

He wasn't sure whether he should hug her or scold her! She walked up to him and answered the debate happening in his mind with the warmest hug he had felt in years.

"What are you doing here?"

"I'm one of the ticket-takers."

"Of course you are. And that means you qualify for passage, right?"

"Yeah, if there's room, which is unlikely, given…" he gestured to the line.

She lowered her hood, now that she was under the shelter that protected the ticket booth. Her smile grew. "There will be room. I've let them know there's room in my quarters."

Part IV: The End is the Beginning

Space Junk

3449 CE – Orbiting Mars

Abner had spent the ride over on the shuttle trying not to think about the ache in his back or the itch on his knees, and how no matter how often he prayed for relief, none seemed to come. This was only made worse by the fact that he had nothing to distract himself with. This flight, like most, had only a small selection of new releases to watch. He preferred the old movies—the ones about the pioneer days of space travel, back when there were heroes and outlaws, and everything was simple. He'd been on this route for 30 years, and space travel had become boring, and so had movies.

When the shuttle pulled into the station in Mars orbit, he was so annoyed and still in pain that he decided to go straight to the hotel before his meeting. After checking in, he locked his luggage to the magnetic strip next to the cabinet when his knee started itching again. With no one around to notice, he slid his fingers down into the space between the polypropylene pad and his bare skin, lifted his fingernails, and scratched. He scratched with the fury of someone who had just bought the last lottery ticket. He let out a loud sigh. When he pulled his fingers out, it was clear he had broken skin. Soon, he could see it bleeding through his pants.

"For Ammalee's sake!" he yelled—only to immediately regret taking her name in vain. He was not like others in the system. He did not take joy in disrespecting old-time religion.

He had to hurry and change if he didn't want to be late for his meeting. To save time, he tried taking his pants off over his boots, only to get them stuck. He scrambled to remove his boots, his pants wedged around them, and spent the next minute prying them apart. All the while, he wondered if he had remembered to bring the bandages and which bag he had put them in.

He missed the days when he could scratch his skin without it breaking open.

He would never let anyone see how bad it had gotten. He had to act ten years younger to get work. He had to act like those who grew up on a planet, away from the radiation of space travel. Or like those who could afford one of those fancy rejuvenation pods that littered Proximata's orbit.

With his knee bandaged and clean pants, he checked himself in the mirror. His white hair thinned more and more every day, and his thin arms and short legs came together at a torso that felt far rounder than he'd like. He turned from the mirror, refusing to dwell any longer than necessary. He knew it wasn't the looks that got a job. It was all about confidence. Faith, too—a kind of cousin to confidence. With his briefcase in hand, he went back to the hotel's main airlock and hitched a ride with a local shuttle, arriving at the office for his appointment with a minute to spare.

There was no one there to greet him, but the door opened on its own after he hit the doorbell. He grabbed the hatch handle, pulled himself into the entryway, and locked his magnetic boots to the floor, adjusting his pant legs to look natural before scanning the room.

It was a gracious hallway, with plastic green plants lining the wall and a long rug attached to the floor that ran the length of the hallway. His eyes followed this rug until they reached the door on the far end. He blinked, so his contact lenses would move to their proper place. He always felt glasses made him look older than he was. With the edges still blurry, he saw who was standing at the office door: Qaani Hillmore. She slowly closed the door behind her as she entered the office, then looked back into the room before fully closing it, and saw Abner. She smiled, as one does in those old movies, after two enemies face off in a duel and only one had time to pull the trigger.

He had arrived a minute too late.

The deal was as good as dead.

Qaani was the most popular broker in their solar system, and this was the biggest deal this side of Jupiter. Abner thought about calling the shuttle back. He'd seen it happen before. Younger brokers would skip meetings, call in late, leave halfway through, and in general had little respect for the profession—but that's not how he was raised. Plus, without this deal, he'd be brokering bits and pieces until he turned to dust.

He stood, fist clenched, legs straightened, and feet stuck to the floor with his magnetic boots. He stared at the office hatch so intently that he didn't notice the two attendants floating in the corner near a large potted plant with thick plastic leaves. One of the attendants sneezed, then apologized, and that's when he realized he wasn't alone in the hallway. Abner turned, and in doing so, relaxed his jaw, took a breath, released his fists, and took a few steps back. They both appeared to be men, with haircuts to make them look like boys, typical for attendants. Each held a large briefcase. Below them, where their legs would have been, sat two more cases snapped to the floor. One attendant still had some of his legs left, and he fit each stump with small canisters of pressurized air. A little air shot out every so often to keep him centered above the large case below him. The other didn't have any visible stumps and wore a pressurized cap at the bottom, keeping him perfectly centered above his case.

Abner worried he knew them from the refinery; he worried about this every time he saw an attendant. The mere thought that he'd run into an attendant he knew made beads of sweat run down his back, soaking through his shirt.

He tried to place them, but he couldn't. They must have come to be an attendant in some other way. He was considering this when he noticed what sat below them. Her luggage! She hadn't stopped at her room first. Abner should have known checking in was a bad idea. If he had gone here first, he would be the one in that office. He started to beat himself up, cursing his age and his knee and everything else. But he couldn't beat himself up for long, as his thoughts were interrupted by the muffled voices of Qaani yelling behind the office hatch. Abner couldn't make out what was being said, but it was clear Qaani was upset. He looked at the attendants, who now appeared worried. Nothing worse than being an attendant for someone who lost their temper.

Abner would never get involved with anyone's attendant, but he was a decent guy, and he did feel sorry for them, until he was distracted by the hope springing up for himself. This meant he'd have a chance. A moment later, the hatch opened, and Qaani stormed out and turned to her attendants. "Get my bags, and your halfselves, and get us back to the shuttle. We're leaving!"

Soon, the room was empty, the hatch was open, and it became quiet. Abner took a deep breath and picked up his briefcase.

Nile Ledger followed Quanni into the hallway. He stood tall, his shoes snapped to the floor just inside the round hatch. His hair was oiled and slick. He wore a dark blue suit with thin pants that stressed just how long his legs were. He looked at Abner and smiled.

"Abner Profeta, I presume?"

"Yes."

"Well, just as I was telling Qaani, I've read your proposal, and I'm intrigued by it."

"You—" he cleared his throat and straightened his legs as best he could. "You are?"

Nile leaned out of the door and looked around the airlock. "No attendants?"

"I travel alone, sir." He took a step and reached his arm out to shake Nile's. "Abner Profeta, with Profeta Brokerage, and my 30 years of exceptional service are now at your service, sir."

"Right, thank you. But you always travel alone?"

"Yes, sir. I'm old-fashioned like that, you might say." Abner smiled, hoping his lack of attendants wouldn't make him appear poor. "But you'll see I work twice as hard as anyone who has them, and you won't notice any difference in what I can offer—that's the Abner guarantee."

"Right. Come in, and we can talk about what you've got here."

#

Nile owned what was left of Earth—not Earth itself; that was public domain, but it still had 50 to 70 years before terraforming could make it ready for a colony again. Nile owned everything left in Earth's orbit, from the replica of the ISS to the 20,000 satellites and residents that danced around each other. Other than the habitations, most of it was space junk. Earth's orbit represented half a million metric tons of raw materials. By conservative estimates, that was more Kevlar and aluminum than the entire moon orbit combined. It would be enough to build two to three large ships. It was the most extensive collection of junk in this system, if only because it was the oldest. And after years of Nile's ancestors owning it, it was passed to Nile per the trust that had been set up when he was born. Rumor had it his uncle tried to challenge it, hoping to keep it in the family, but his pursuits were no match for Nile's legal team. As soon as the paperwork cleared and it was released from the trust, he put out a call for brokers to facilitate a sale.

Nile owned the satellites, but most of them had leases tied to families that went all the way back to when Earth was populated, and these leases required antiquated provisions for relocation, making it impossible to complete a sale without meeting the demands of every individual lease, all grandfathered in from the old days. In other parts of the systems, the provisions are much easier to work around.

This project was larger than all of Abner's other jobs combined.

"Abner, I like what I see here—I think you make an interesting case—specifically your handling of some of the historical artifacts, something that others haven't considered. But explain this to me: why would you sell the ISS separately from the rest of the junk? It's got to be worth more in raw materials than anything else."

Abner had snapped his feet to the floor and adjusted the straps on his pants. He stood back up, holding his briefcase. "That's an excellent question, Mr. Ledger." He took a breath. "In this solar system, the ISS isn't worth anything but parts. But that's a simple problem of supply and demand. As you know, the Refinery runs the show around here, and they want all the Kevlar and aluminum they can get their hands on. But if we take the ISS to the next system over, where there are resources to spare, and everyone has the luxury of nostalgia, its value increases. Even as a replica, it's older than anything else in orbit and the only replica of its kind. It will go for quite a bit to the right collector."

"But we've run the numbers. By the time we transport it and sell it, we will have lost money on it."

"I've seen your numbers too, and let me guess? The Refinery provided them to you?"

Nile didn't respond, but his smile confirmed the suspicion.

"I've run my own numbers, and they are in the proposal as well, as I'm sure you are aware. When it's all said and done, there's a profit to be made on the ISS—not to mention, you will get a lot closer to a majority of residents signing this deal when they know they are taking a piece of history with them."

"I saw your profit margin—it's slim, compared to others."

"It's the only way to win over the more stubborn residents. They are a unique problem and one I'm uniquely suited to deal with." While Abner had no claims to family (other than his sister, whom he hadn't seen in years) or close friends, he was good at winning people over. He found it easier to win people over if he didn't have any real expectations of them. He preferred relationships like this: short, friendly, and to the point, free of the baggage of oversharing.

Nile smiled. "I'll tell you what, the job is yours, but under one condition."

"Thank you, sir; anything you ask."

"There's an old man. He lives a quarter turn from the ISS, in an old space lab. I've gotten enough people to sign off on relocation, and we've arranged resettlement for all of the residents, except for this old man—he won't budge, and the few holding out are waiting to see what he does. The commission is yours, but only if you get him to sign."

"You only have one holdout? I figured it'd be a lot worse. Consider it done."

"I love your confidence—Now, sign here, and we will get this started."

To get to Earth meant a layover at the Refinery, a place he had done his best to avoid for the past 30 years. He hoped to remain anonymous, and it would be much easier if he didn't leave the shuttle.

The attendants tried to escort him out so they could clean the seats, but he assured them he wouldn't be in the way. It took every bit of his charm to convince them to let him stay. The attendants continued their checks, with Abner sitting in his seat, buckled, his head resting against the window, looking out at the shipyard.

He didn't hate everything about the Refinery. On the other side of the orbit, he opened a garden in an old space station a half turn from the shipyard. With a small team of volunteers, he had grown quite a collection of plants. He spent hundreds of orbits tending plants and reading horticulture magazines in his free time. It was the only fond memory he had at the Refinery, and he would love to see the garden again. But it would require a shuttle to get there, and who knows if he'd get back in time—not to mention running into someone who might recognize him.

After he left, he spent what little money he wasn't saving on a subscription to that same magazine. He had the most recent issue with him. He pulled the blind shut, and he spent the rest of the layover reading about the future of hydroponics, until the first passengers boarded.

Two guys came in together. Abner could tell they didn't work for the Refinery. They were from the next system over, where people had grown up free from radiation, wrapped in clothes made of authentic cotton.

"I've never seen so many halves in my life!" said the tall man.

"I don't think that's the proper term for them," said the other guy, smiling.

It wasn't proper—it was very derogatory, and it made Abner squirm in his seat, just listening to it. They might as well have called them an *other*. To many, they were thought of similarly. He had been raised better than that, going to temple every week as a child, and learned there were no halves when created in God's image.

"Whatever you call them, I've never seen so many in my life. I couldn't do it. I couldn't work there—not even if they paid me."

"I think getting paid was the idea."

He laughed.

They got close to Abner's seat, and he adjusted his pants, so they fit more naturally over his prosthetics. They passed Abner and found their seat, right behind him.

"I just—why are there so many? I mean, I know more than a few back home who have attendants at their residence in orbit, but nothing like this."

"I think they get paid to give up their legs."

"Who's paying?"

"I think they sell the meat to a ranch, for cattle feed or something. They use the rest for compost—but I really don't want to think about it."

Abner almost interrupted, but the fear of follow-up questions kept him from engaging. He had worked in the Refinery's human consolidation department for his last five years of his time there, and he knew for a fact they weren't selling the parts for cattle food. The mere idea made him want to throw up. They were right about the compost, but that's what happened to all human remains.

"The real savings come in the fact that they take up a lot less space, I guess—the smaller dorm rooms and everything else. I've seen the numbers on some stations. We're talking fifty percent less room per person. That's twice the bodies—twice the hands, for the same cost. It works for the bottom line."

They were right about that. It did work for the bottom line. Abner had helped provide those numbers to the higher-ups. And there wasn't a day he didn't regret his part in it all. Listening to these guys go on and on didn't help. He had to listen to them talk the rest of the trip. And talk they did. They went on while everyone else took their seats. They spoke during the pre-flight instructions. They talked over the in-flight movie and the baby that cried in the back row. They talked until they landed at the low-orbit docking bay for Earth, and over the last eight hours, Abner had heard them refer to attendants and Refinery workers as "halves" 152 times. He had counted.

Once docked, the two got up—it was supposed to be Abner's turn to exit, but they had talked through the instructions as well. The tall one got up first, and then the shuttle got hit with a piece of space junk, knocking him into Abner's lap. His hand smashed his cup, and the lid fell off, knocking a glob of water into his magazine, bouncing off it.

"Sorry!" he said. "My bad, sir, I didn't mean to spill your drink." He turned towards the shuttle attendant, who was helping people exit. "Hey, one of you halfers—Yeah, you. Get over here, will you? We got a spill."

"He's an attendant," inserted Abner, shaking his magazine dry.

"What?" asked the man.

"The correct term is attendant. Or Sir. Or Madam."

"Struck a nerve, huh?"

"No nerve, just prefer you use proper titles."

The guy looked back towards the front. "Attendant, he decided he wanted to clean it up himself." And with a laugh, he hopped into the aisle and headed towards the exit. His friend paused on his way, and handed him a towel from the back of his seat.

"Sorry. He doesn't mean anything by it."

As if *not meaning anything by it* wasn't the problem; most problems in the world came from people who *didn't mean anything by it.* Abner said nothing in return, but he took the towel and used it to fan the floating globs of water towards a nearby vent, where they would be sucked up.

#

The old man named Enor lived a half orbit away from the docking bay. Abner figured he'd start by making an introduction and letting him know he's in orbit. He didn't expect to convince him of anything at the first meeting, but if he could build a little trust, he might get a second meeting, and from there, he would do his best to win him over. This meant an additional, single-person shuttle ride to the far side of orbit before arriving at Enor's airlock. He decided he'd skip checking in at the hotel until after his meeting. He wasn't about to make that mistake again.

On the ride over, his left boot kept malfunctioning. This meant walking from the shuttle to the front hatch with only one boot locking to the ground. It was only after he had used Enor's doorbell that the other boot glitched. Without either, he started to float—and he'd never heard of a pitch going well with someone floating. How could you take an offer seriously when you're standing at such awkward angles? He tried to straighten back up—impossible with malfunctioning boots. He was at an awkward 135 degrees when the hatch opened. He grabbed the ceiling and used it to tilt his head towards the hatch. A pale, bearded man, at least ten years Abner's elder, floated in the hatch, upside down. For a second, Abner thought of adjusting his stance, for he feared he had read the cues wrong and arrived at this person's door upside down. A quick scan of the airlock and it was clear that he hadn't. It was the old man who was upside down.

Enor wore round glasses as thick as a finger. He didn't have a shirt on, but loose-fitting pants, and no shoes. He floated in the room as freely as his pants floated up his white legs. He pulled his head into the airlock, looking around.

"You alone?"

"Yes." Abner extended his hand to shake, but Enor didn't meet it. "I am Abner and I wanted to—"

"Yes, I know who you are. And I know what you're here for. And I'm not interested."

With that, he slammed the hatch and latched it.

Abner took a breath, and rang the doorbell again.

The hatch opened. Enor squinted his eyes, this time right-side up, and stared at Abner, who smiled back, awkwardly moving from 135 to 145 degrees—making it hard to make eye contact. At that point, it made sense to just swing all the way around, which he did, but only in a way that found himself face to face with Enor.

"I'm not interested."

"I understand you're not interested. But I've traveled a long way to get here, and the shuttle is a full orbit away. Do you mind if I wait inside?"

"Hmm." He adjusted his glasses. "I'll let you in, under one condition."

"Name it."

"No talk of acquisitions. Period. No exceptions or excuses. And no other deals. Take it or leave it."

Enor started to close the hatch, assuming the answer.

"It's a deal," said Abner, grabbing the door. "No talk of acquisitions today."

#

The blue planet, spattered with white clouds, filled the large window framed by vines of the greenest greens. It was a marvelous view of Earth, low enough in orbit to be free from the clutter of space junk. Yet, Abner didn't even notice the view. He was immediately taken by the plants that filled the home. Plants lined every wall and ceiling, with pots attached to every flat surface, and branches growing out in every direction, so much so that he had to push a few leaves out of the way to get to the seat that Enor offered him. There was even a small, prickly plant that grew on the table next to his chair where he sat. He stared at it for an entire minute before turning to the others. He was familiar with quite a few of them, but there were far too many species for him to know them all. Abner had never seen as many plants as this—more than all the plots back on the moon combined. It was like he had walked into the Garden of Eden. It took his breath away, which, given his health, was something he needed to be careful about.

"You have a beautiful place. Do you entertain often?" asked Abner.

"I have a lot of visitors," said Enor. He worked in the kitchen on the far side of the room, behind a wall of vines, prepping some drinks. He attached a drink pouch to the teapot's hose. A dark, bubbly liquid filled the pouch. "I'd say I've had most of the citizens over for tea, at one point or another—everyone except for the Claimer Family." He paused with the tea and turned to look at Abner. "You wouldn't want them over either, if you knew them." He laughed. Then he got serious. "But don't want to give you the wrong impression. I like my solitude. I get along with most people, but there is nothing better than when they leave—no offense to you, of course."

"No, I get it. I couldn't agree more. I've preferred my friends this way."

"Yes, friends are always better when they are acquaintances—and a friend is nothing more than a needy acquaintance."

"Yes, yes, they are!" laughed Abner. "So no chance of us becoming friends then?"

Enor poked his head through the vines, his glasses hanging low on his nose, and his eyes looking over them. "As if you came here to make friends." He adjusted his frames. "How do you take your tea?"

"However you recommend."

"I'll give it to you as Ammalee intended, with cream."

Abner wondered if Enor, too, was an Ammalean, and, even more so, whether She had a preference for how tea was served. To Abner, that seemed like a very trivial thing to concern Herself with.

Enor carried two small pouches to where Abner was sitting and handed him one. The pouch was hot, and the liquid inside was dark, with white clouds working into the darkness, like the blue planet behind him. He took a sip. The bitter drink melded with the cool cream as it touched his tongue. It tasted as good as it looked. It was far better than any tea he'd ever had, which wasn't saying much. He had only had fresh tea once before. It was on Proximata. While he couldn't afford to go down to the surface, he stayed in a hotel in orbit, which claimed to have all the same benefits, including fresh, planet-grown produce. The tea was lovely there, but not as good as this. He sipped it slowly and carefully.

"Good, isn't it?" asked Enor.

"Yes. Easily the best I've had."

"That is very nice of you to say."

He took another sip. "I sense a little cinnamon. But what is that other flavor—I'm not as familiar with it?"

"That's correct. Well done. Yes, cinnamon is part of it. But the trick is the tea leaves themselves, dried right here in my cabin."

"You grow your own tea?"

"Of course! And if you want, I'll gladly show you. Would you like to see?"

"I'd love that." And he had never been more honest.

Enor led him to the next room. It was humid in this room, and inside, hundreds of plants filled the walls and shelves, creating narrow hallways. "I've got the largest collection of native Earthen plants in the whole… well, anywhere, I guess. People have tried to grow more; some have even tried it back on Primera or even as far as Proximata, but it doesn't work the way they want. Want to know why?"

"Why?"

"Everyone has theories, but legend has it, these plants like to be close to home." He pointed out the window at Earth. "They don't want to be relocated."

Abner smiled, his hands holding the pouch, sipping. "I thought we agreed not to talk about the acquisition."

Enor paused, looked at him, and matched his smile. "Very clever. But no, I said you couldn't talk about it. That rule doesn't apply to me or the plants. Oh, here it is." He reached for a small plant behind a large leaf. He plucked one. "Camellia sinensis—that's the base, and it's part of what you're tasting—imitation tea can't capture it. But I add a little of…" he reached for a plant with a bright white flower and pulled from it a long green seed.

"Vanilla?" asked Abner.

"Well done!" Enor tore the pod open and lifted it to Abner's nose. "It's great in a lot of things. But the trick is to cook it in boiling water, then let it dry for about 3000 orbits, and it will turn dark. Then, and here's the trick, and you've got to make the sacrifice, plain and simple: soak it in some spirits."

"Alcohol?"

"That's the trick. And you will have the best vanilla you can imagine."

"Well, I'm sure imitation vanilla can't compare."

"It doesn't!"

"Seems like a lot of work though."

"Well, of course it's a lot of work," pulling the seed back to his chest. He looked at Abner, his eyes crossed through his thick glasses, and his neck stretched. "You think I should spend my time doing something else?"

"Not at all. What I mean is: I wish I had that kind of time."

"All work and no play. And for someone your age?" he asked, grabbing Abner's left arm, shaking them lightly, the skin flapping. "You've got the bones of a traveler."

Abner pulled his arm back.

"Sorry, didn't mean to impose—senescents like us forget our boundaries. But we need our rest, and I'm guessing you're living without any. You hide it well."

"You could say that."

"I did say that, and I'll say this too. I'd tell anyone who asked: it ain't right." He drifted to the wall. "They should improve shuttle walls—no one can live a full life exposed to that much radiation." He reached and tapped the outer shell of the room. "These walls are some of the best, no expense spared, back when they knew how to build satellites." He flexed his muscles, which looked the same as Abner's, even though he clearly felt they were impressive. "That's why I'm so strong." He laughed.

Abner adjusted his sleeve. "How did you afford all this dirt? It couldn't come cheap. Must be worth a ton."

"Ah, yes, to me, it's priceless." Enor turned towards the window facing the blue planet. "Wasn't easy getting it up here either. Didn't happen all at once." Abner turned to join him, looking out the large window as they passed over a continent, the blues turning to browns and whites. "If you look here," he said, pointing, "You can see the remnant of one of the great rivers that ran north and south, considered by many the origins of humanity—and my family can trace my line back to the people who used to live there. Now it's no more than a dried basin, like the rest of Earth." He turned to one of the pots and pinched the dirt. "I'm often hit by the fact that this dirt is some of the last clean dirt left from Earth."

"Oh!" said Abner, "It's from Earth? That has to be some pre-radiation dirt then. I've never seen any, myself. May I?"

"Please."

Abner stuck his fingers into the dirt—smoother and darker than what he was used to. "This has to be priceless."

"My ancestors got rich off terraforming—building Earth out of rock. I bet when they started their research, they didn't imagine we'd need that same technology back at home."

Abner watched the planet run past him. The green in the room against the browns down below contrasted in a way he hadn't ever considered.

Enor pushed off and headed back to the front room, and went to the entrance of the airlock, and called back to Abner, who was still looking out the window. "Come, sir, your ride is here, and I'm getting tired. But you can come by tomorrow if you want to try out some of my other teas, but only if you commit to the same rules."

#

For the next week, Abner stayed at the local hotel, the only one still in operation. It had been a five-star hotel in its day, but with Earth closing years ago, it was only a glimpse of what it had been. Yet, some benefits didn't decay over time. The walls of the hotel were thicker than most, the thickness of any five-star hotel, with the kind of radiation protection only the wealthy usually enjoyed. He noticed the difference after only one night.

Every day, Abner visited Enor, drank tea, and talked about plants. Once, they even spent the afternoon watching a few short films from the golden age of space, out of Enor's impressive movie collection. And every day, he felt a little better, and he wasn't sure if it was the hotel or the organic tea or the good company. By the end of the week, he had slept the whole night. He couldn't believe it! He couldn't remember the last time he'd slept the whole night. Usually, he'd wake up, tossing and turning from a sore on his knee or an ache in his back or coughing up mucus.

In between their visits, Abner used his free time to explore the orbit. He stopped at the ISS and, while he appreciated the history, found the displays and gift shop outdated and dusty. He wondered if it would catch the price he had initially suggested in the report—it would be a complex sale, for sure. After that, he toured the satellite graveyard. Each stop meant another history lesson about a company he had never heard of. Even after ten years in the refinery, he was surprised that any of this junk was worth what he had proposed.

All in all, he was enjoying himself, except that he wasn't any closer to getting him to sign than the day he had arrived. In fact, most days he forgot all about the acquisition.

He spent his evenings at the canteen, and there was no keeping a secret about who he was or what he was trying to do. Most had signed on and were waiting for their relocation bonuses. And even though he was told enough residents were holding back, he hadn't met any. Those who had signed seemed hesitant to show their frustration with Enor, but whispered their opinions in snide comments that always ended in something like "be sure to keep that between us" and "I'd never want the old man to hear me say that."

One night, he even ran into Devon Profeta, who claimed to be his distant relative—a second or third cousin, or something—although he'd never heard of him before. He went on about his plans for a new kind of AI, the first of its kind since the age of AI, and how he was throwing away everything people thought they knew about AI and starting from scratch, and was already well-funded. He went on for half an hour more with similar details that Abner mostly ignored, but kindly nodded and smiled. It was clear this so-called relative was very smart, very connected—he knew Nile Ledger, for example—very wealthy, and a tad unhinged. Thankfully, he was rushed to catch a flight for Proximata, so the conversation didn't last longer than 40 minutes, which was just long enough for Abner to nod a dozen times, pretending to pay attention, smile long enough to make his jaw tire, and sneak out two yawns when Devon wasn't looking.

There weren't many who lived in orbit—fewer than two hundred. By the end of the week, Abner reckoned he had seen at least half of them. But not a single attendant. He couldn't stop thinking about it. Once he had noticed it, he couldn't stop noticing it. The attendant who cleaned his room wasn't an attendant—not in the traditional sense. She had her legs. The same thing at the canteen: the service staff all had their legs. And now that he thought about it, the same for the terminal where he first arrived. No attendants. Later that day, after sipping a hot blend of chamomile and lemon, he interrupted Enor's lecture on the herbal benefits of chamomile and how difficult it is to grow.

"Does Earth have something against attendants?" he asked, sipping his tea.

"Attendants." Enor raised his eyebrow, as if he was trying to decide whether the conversation was even worth his time. "Against attendants, you ask?"

"Do you?"

"Hmm. Yes, as a matter of fact, I do. We all do, here. They are illegal in this orbit, and if you don't mind me saying so, I think they should be everywhere else too." He set his tea pouch down, clearly frustrated.

"Illegal? What's so wrong with people without legs?"

Enor spit his tea out. "Oh!" He wiped his mouth. "Oh, no. Not at all. You are confused, old man. You think those are the same thing?"

"They aren't?"

"You think people without legs can only ever be attendants?"

"Well—then—what I mean is—are people without legs welcome here?"

"Of course they are! Who do you think we are? Everyone is welcome, except for attendants, at least while serving as one—nor should they be anywhere. This is Earth or what's left of it. It's been illegal to own another human on Earth for generations."

"Attendants aren't owned by anyone. They're hired men, an honorable profession."

"Sure, you keep telling yourself that. But can they leave their contract before it's up?"

"Not exactly."

"How likely are they to get any other job outside the refinery?"

"It's tricky, to be honest."

"Ha! Then what's the difference? Call it what you want, but they aren't allowed here."

"How? Isn't this under the same laws as anywhere else?"

"No. As long as there are citizens from Earth still in orbit, our old laws are grandfathered in." Enor finished his tea and went to the window, looking down at Earth. "Don't get me wrong, we aren't better than Proximata or Primera; we're just older. We've had time to learn. Thousands of years' worth of lessons, and we've had a fair share of people like attendants in our history. More than I'd like to mention." He turned back to face Abner. "But I'd like to think we've learned our lesson and are still paying for the crimes—in here," he said, tapping his chest, "And down there," he pointed towards the blue and brown planet. "It didn't turn brown on its own, you know." He went back to his seat after squeezing more tea into his pouch. "You won't find anyone but free people traveling in this belt. And it's quite fun to watch," he said with a chuckle. "If you stay long enough, you'll get to see what I mean. Just watch the brokers come, the ones who use two or three attendants to do anything. Without their attendants, I swear, they barely know how to wipe their own asses. It's embarrassing," he chuckled. "I have to laugh to stop from crying." He looked at Abner and stopped laughing. "But that's not you. I knew it the moment you arrived. That's the only reason I let you in to begin with."

"Why?"

"Because you hit my doorbell like you'd done it before. I had one guy show up here and sit in that airlock for 30 minutes waiting for me to open the door—didn't even try to find the doorbell. Another tried to shoot himself into space, and I nearly let him! No, you keep your eyes open, and stop looking for the masters, and you'll see a few able-bodied fellows here. They will stand on their own, so to speak. Now, can I ask you a question?"

"Of course."

"That paperwork you've got in your briefcase, that you've promised not to talk to me about… if I sign that, there will be no more citizens of Earth, and if we go, so do our ways. And when Earth gets terraformed— and it will, I promise—after we've all left, it will be just like the other systems, as if we've learned nothing. So my question is: what does that paperwork mean to you? I've told you what it means to me, but what does it mean to you?"

Abner took a breath and sat back in the seat. "If I'm honest, it means I'd have enough to retire. Find a nice place like this, behind thick walls, somewhere safe, if I can afford it. It means I'd be done with traveling. I could rest."

Abner tried not to oversell it. The truth was far more dire. He needed to retire—his doctor hadn't given him many years if he didn't do something to reduce the radiation exposure. He'd never live on the surface—his body had long passed the point where that would be an option. He was a zero-gravity lifer, and he'd accepted it. But with this job, he could afford a nice place somewhere safe, with proper radiation shielding.

Enor smiled. "With nothing to do but grow plants and herbs and drink their tea and eat their fruit and let your bones heal?"

"Yeah. I guess. That was the plan."

"Well, if I'm honest, it's not a bad plan. Not a bad plan at all—and if it didn't cost us so much, I'd want to support it."

#

That night, Abner noticed a young man, his legs clearly missing, at the canteen table with a few other wealthy-looking men. Had it not been for Enor, he wouldn't have noticed. He would never have imagined a guy like that seated at the table with people like them. It's possible he had seen him a dozen times and never noticed him until that night.

How did he go his whole life and not know this about Earth's orbit? His mind started to race. Could it be possible for an attendant to stroll into the canteen, short of any legs, and actually get service? Would anyone even notice? Would anyone care? They'd be able to order a drink without someone trying to order a drink from them, or ask them to clean up a spill, or ask them to carry their bag, or require them to show identification before ordering.

He noticed four more people like the young man pass through the canteen, and it was true: they got the service they requested —a seat and a drink—no questions asked.

He had never seen anything like it before.

His hands got cold, and he felt a shiver go down his spine all the way to his knees. This was the one place in the whole system where attendants had legitimate respect and dignity, not to mention actual rights, and it was his job—the entire reason he came here—to make sure it all went away. A wave of nausea rolled through him.

He stared at the floor, unable to move.

That's when he saw someone walk up, a pair of expensive boots locked to the floor a few feet from his table. He followed the boots all the way to their eyes, which were staring right back at him. It was Nile Ledger.

"There you are," said Nile. "I've been looking everywhere on this goddamn orbit for you." He pulled himself down to Abner's table, latched himself to the seat, and called for the server to order a drink.

"So, how's old man Enor doing? Get him to sign?"

"Not yet," said Abner, still trying to catch his breath.

"Of course not. Would I be here if you had?"

"I—I—I guess not."

"But you're close, right?"

"I think I'm making excellent progress."

"Excellent progress?" Nile looked into Abner's eyes and then laughed. "He's got you wrapped right around his frail, little fingers, doesn't he? Well, that will be the end of this deal, I promise you."

"I'll get him to sign."

"You better—you only got a few orbits left before it won't matter."

"What do you mean?"

"I've given you—I've given him—a chance. But eventually I need to move forward, one way or the other." With that, he got up, went to the bar, and ordered a drink, chatting with the bartender for a few minutes before bringing it back to the table. He swallowed it in two gulps, slamming it down.

"Six orbits, Abner. Six—that's it." He lifted his hand to get the bartender's attention again, who smiled in return.

What Abner couldn't understand was why Nile would give him any time at all. He had been there long enough to know that Enor was the only one fighting the acquisition, and sure, some people wanted to honor him on that, but most were eager to get their cut. He didn't have to wait to convince Enor. And if that was true, why go through the trouble?

The bartender came over and placed the liquor on the table, and patted Nile on the back, as if he was just anybody, and not the judge and jury for this patch of space junk. "Now don't you listen to anything Nile says," the bartender said, addressing Abner. "If he gives you any trouble, I'll pull out some of the old photos of him running around here half naked, like he owned the place."

"Don't you have other customers you can bother?" asked Nile.

He looked around the room, which was now empty. "Nope." He smiled.

"You grew up here?" Abner asked Nile.

"Hardly. Only when I was visiting family. A few weeks here and there."

"Don't listen to him talk like that," added the bartender, patting Nile on the back again, a little harder this time, in a way that clearly made Nile uncomfortable. "He loved coming here. I was just talking to Enor the other day about your visits—all the trouble you'd get into. Do you remember—" but before he could continue, one of the servers ran into a table, knocking the drinks from her tray into the air, drifting through the room in a dozen different directions. "Oh, come on, I told you to be careful!" and he jumped over to help. Nile and Abner sat and watched them scurry through the room, grabbing the flying liquor pouches when Abner finally figured it out. He didn't need Enor's vote. He wanted it. He turned to Nile. "Enor's your family, isn't he?"

"Yep," said Nile, leaning in to speak more quietly. "He's my uncle—my dad's brother—, and he's the last of my family to still live in this god-forsaken place. And because he's my uncle, he has earned a little extra attention, but only a little—that's why you're here: You don't use attendants, and your plan preserves more of this space junk than any other. I've made room for as many of his complaints as I can afford. If he won't sign your deal, then there's no getting him to sign any. So you listen here. You get him to sign—you convince him—or in a half dozen orbits, I'll go with Qaani and her better profits." Just then, Qaani entered the canteen, but with no attendants. She looked around, saw Nile, and waved.

"Speak of the devil." He got up to greet her, but first leaned in towards Abner. "Six orbits. Six."

#

Abner stood outside Enor's door without moving. He stood for so long that the leaves would have already been picked and sorted, the water warmed, and the tea brewing—he was missing all the best parts. But he couldn't hit the doorbell. He couldn't face him, not until he decided what he would do. On the one hand, he certainly wasn't going to ask him to sign. How could he? He'd never forgive his part in bringing the end to these old ways. But on the other hand, he had to convince him to sign. His body wasn't going to survive in open space any longer.

These two positions pulled on him from both sides, leaving him stuck, quite literally, in the airlock, for longer than he realized.

He didn't notice Enor open the hatch.

"Are you coming in?"

Abner took a breath. "I can't."

"You can't come in? I hardly believe that. Something wrong with your legs?"

"Yes—I mean, no." He put his briefcase down, used his other hand to wipe his sweaty brow, and took a step back. "I'm going to go."

"Don't be foolish. You're not leaving, not without first drinking your tea—I've already made it, and I'm not going to waste it. Now come in. I insist."

They sat down, distributed the pouches, and drank a unique mix of mint and basil tea. It was more bitter than the other teas, but Abner couldn't tell if it was the tea or the tension in the room. He looked around at all the plants, the way their leaves cast shadows and their vines weaved through every possible nook. He remembered the canteen, the attendants, and everything this orbit had to offer. It was only then that he realized he had already made up his mind. He set his tea down. "I can't let you sign."

"Oh, not so eager to make your fortune anymore?"

"It's a bad deal—for you—and for this place."

"Well, isn't that interesting?" He laughed. "You come here trying to get me to sign, and I won't. Now, you don't want me to sign, and I plan to. We've done a regular old reversal on each other, haven't we?"

"You shouldn't sign."

"Oh, I shouldn't? Nonsense. I've read it—I had a copy before you arrived. And I've put off the inevitable as long as I can. It's the best deal that I can expect to get at this point."

"You don't understand."

"I don't understand? How so?"

"It's the only place I've seen attendants treated as equals, and you can't give that up. We have to try and fight it."

Enor tilted his head, surprised. "Well, that's interesting. Are you ready to start a revolution? In our old age? Revolutions are for the young."

"I'm not joking."

"I thought you wanted this deal? No, from what I'd say, you need this deal."

"I did—I do—but I can't. I—" Abner couldn't think straight, and his head started to feel fuzzy.

Enor's eyes got wide. "Oh, I see what's bothering you." He took another sip of the tea.

Abner looked up.

"Don't get me wrong, you've hidden it well. You really have." Enor took a breath and whistled a sigh. "Few things get past me, old man. But you've hidden it well. And for that, I'm sorry." He reached over and patted Abner's lap.

Abner felt the room spin. One of Abner's greatest fears awakened, as if it was going to sneak up and slap him from behind. But instead of sneaking up on him, Enor blurted it out right to his face.

"Your legs!" Enor pointed. "Your prosthetics are showing, old man," with a big laugh, which seemed to echo in Abner's ears like comet debris hitting a shuttle. Enor continued, but Abner couldn't hear him. He looked down to find his pant leg straps had loosened, exposing his prosthetic leg, just above his boots. He stared at it as Enor went on, almost yelling at this point. It took every bit of energy for Abner to reach down and cover his prosthetics back up, reattaching the strap to his boot.

He felt as if he was watching it happen outside his body.

Enor kept talking, except now he was flinging a piece of paper, but Abner wasn't listening. All he could hear was that laugh, that old man's jolly laugh, like a knife that cut through a space suit, with all the breathable air escaping out the slit.

"I need to be going," Abner said, trying to catch his breath.

The next thing he remembered, he was in the airlock, waiting for a shuttle, with Enor's muffled apology behind the door.

#

This wasn't the first time someone had noticed his prosthetics. It had happened before, and every time it was embarrassing. But this one felt worse somehow. He blamed it on the laugh, but he was old enough to know something else was going on that bothered him. He wished he still believed the Ammalean teaching that wounds reveal truth. Right now, they haven't revealed anything other than an upset stomach and the overwhelming desire to run away. He stayed up all night thinking about this. By morning, he had decided to move on.

Space was big, and it was easy to disappear from embarrassment.

By morning, he had booked a flight out of that orbit. He packed his bags and sat on his bed waiting for the time to head to the shuttle. He was on his way to the main terminal when he realized he was short of one piece of luggage: his briefcase.

He had left it at Enor's.

He paused, locking his luggage to the floor while deciding whether his briefcase was worth going back for. He decided he wasn't going to mess with it and turned to grab his luggage when he saw Enor standing a few feet down the terminal holding it. He almost didn't recognize him. He was wearing large magnetic boots and a nice button-up shirt, instead of being barefoot and bare-chested.

Abner froze, and Enor drew closer, handing him his briefcase.

"I've never been known for being gentle, and I tend to laugh when I'm nervous—I'm sorry. I'd never be able to live with myself thinking I'd made someone feel small for who they are."

Abner grabbed the briefcase.

"Thanks."

"Can I make it up to you?" asked Enor. He lifted a thermos in his other hand and pulled out two pouches from his pocket. "Freshly brewed and ready to be enjoyed—a brand new recipe too."

"I've got the next flight out of here. Leaves in half an orbit."

"Plenty of time for a cup of tea, then. Come, let me make it up to you." He placed his hand on Abner's shoulder, but he pushed it aside. "Please."

Abner could smell the tea lofting from the thermos.

A younger man would have stormed off and never talked to Enor again. But Abner wasn't raised that way. He'd give him a chance to make his peace, and then he could go on with his life without any more regrets.

They sat near a window overlooking Earth, with two full tea pouches, a necessary distraction from his thoughts. Abner could taste the sage and hibiscus, but he couldn't pin down the third flavor.

"Dandelion," said Enor as if answering his thoughts. He said it in a tone far softer than Abner was used to, so much so that he looked up. "That's the new ingredient, inspired by an ancient folk tea I read about recently."

Abner took another sip. "Never heard of it."

"Easy to grow—hard to keep from spreading. Got to keep it isolated."

"Like us?"

"Ha!" Enor nearly spat his tea out, and with that, his voice rose to his standard pitch. "Like us, that's right. Isolated lonely old senescents — that's us!" He laughed.

Abner took another sip and then set down the pouch. With all things considered, he liked that Enor laughed as he did. He enjoyed it as much as the tea itself. But how could one laugh bring him such joy and another such pain?

They sat there for a few minutes until Enor interrupted the silence.

"Can I ask you a question?"

"Sure."

"Were you an attendant? Or did you work at the Refinery?"

"The Refinery."

"Excuse my ignorance, but do they require amputations?"

He shook his head and brushed his arm across his forehead. "No, they don't require it, but the bonuses are nice if you sell them."

"So, why do you use prosthetics? Why cover them up? Are you ashamed?"

"It's bad for business. You can't lead a meeting when everyone thinks you're an attendant."

"So you're not ashamed? Good for you."

"Ha! I didn't say that. Of course, I'm ashamed! I'm half the person I used to be."

"Now, you hear me, Abner Profeta, you're not half anything, and I'd prefer you not use that language here. You're you and no one else. Nothing you do changes that. No matter how much you sell of yourself or anything else you do. I certainly don't think any less of you, and if I had known how hard this was for you, I wouldn't have laughed."

Abner wasn't one to use the half language on himself, and he wasn't sure why he had just then. He blamed it on the fact that he spent most days counting how many times he had heard others use it. But it was more than that. He knew he was just mad at himself. There was more he wanted to share—more to the story—but it was a part of himself he had kept covered up for the last 30 years.

He worried he had missed his chance.

Just then, he noticed Quanni, reflected in the window behind him, carrying her suitcase. He turned, and her two attendants were waiting for her by the shuttle, stuck on the other side of the line separating Earth's jurisdiction and the rest of space. He stared at them as his words started to fall out of his mouth.

"I'd be wrong to make you think this is about me. I didn't just sell my legs. I worked in sales, which meant I got a commission every time I convinced someone else to." He turned back to the terminal and watched as Quanni passed her luggage off to her attendants. "And now every time I see an attendant my age, I wonder: Was I the one who convinced them to do it?" He turned to look around the terminal. "But then I came here, and for once, I thought I might have a way to make it right."

Enor sighed. "Oh, if only it were that simple. As much as I've wanted it, this place could never be the solution. It'd be like wrapping a bandage around a sore as large as the galaxy itself."

"Yeah, this is more than I can fix by myself."

"More than anyone can fix. Plus, you're not the only one with regrets." Abner turned and looked at Enor. "Before my brother died, he reached out. He tried to contact me a few times—even came to this very terminal, but I wouldn't see him. We had fallen out years ago, one disagreement after another, until I vowed never to talk to him again. I only found out after his passing that he was trying to hand this bit of orbit over to me in the will." He looked at Abner, his glasses hanging off his face. "Don't you see? I could just as easily blame myself for all of this. And some days, I do." Enor sipped up the last of his tea, placed the pouch in his pocket and pulled out a piece of paper. He handed it to Abner.

"What's this?"

"My nephew dropped it off yesterday. I was trying to show it to you when you left. My appeal has been denied. I'd been waiting—keeping you here, buying time—holding out hope, but there's nothing I can do now. I have no better options other than the one you're offering." He grabbed the paper back from Abner, folded it up carefully, and placed it in his pocket. "So you have your regrets, but so do I. That makes us equal, right?"

He took a deep breath. "Yeah, I suppose so."

"Good. Now, are we going to sign, or do I need to go grab that other broker before she gets on the shuttle?" Abner didn't want to imagine how much worse Quanni's deal would be for Earth's orbit or for Enor. He'd close the deal, and he'd never have to worry about closing another for the rest of his life.

The Trials

3553 CE - New Earth

Her last three friends had their applications denied, even though they had done precisely what they were asked to do. Lira had every reason to expect the same. Everyone knew the trials were nothing more than a way to show humans what they'd never be allowed to enjoy.

She wasn't even sure she wanted to live on New Earth. She was very content with the temperature-controlled quarters, diverse ration options, and the ability to fly to Primera or Proximata without taking a shuttle to orbit. Not to mention, she was a little old for the trials. Her body hadn't handled real, authentic, Earth-bound gravity in… well, ever. If the time in the centrifuge were any indication, this trial would be nothing short of hell on earth, with hurting legs and bleeding lungs, only to be told she'd be stuck in orbit.

They should have terraformed Earth the old-fashioned way, with sweat and blood and hard work, and not by contracting it out to these soulless entities. They claimed they could not only terraform the planet much faster but also establish a civilization composed of those who have honestly shown their willingness to care. The last Earth had been based on principles of suffering and exploitation. No one wanted the same for this one, if only because they had more than enough places for that elsewhere, and if people were ever going to live up to their best intentions, it was with places that held such nostalgia as Earth. Orbit children like Lira were taught early: *You do not inherit Earth. You earn the right to tend it.*

And now Earth was ready for the trials.

Little was known about the trials, but from what she had heard, they included a few days of trekking the New Earth, ultimately cataloging one of its natural wonders. Her friend Julie showed her a few photos she had taken on her trip, photos of the vista from the top of the mountain. She had hiked for three days to the peak, snapped photos—just as the Devos had suggested—and she was denied. Her other friend, Lori, had shown her some rather beautiful images of a waterfall, and it was gorgeous. All of the photos she saw from people's trials were beautiful. In fact, she'd even seen some truly professional-looking pictures hanging in a museum exhibit from one of the first trials. They were breathtaking—yet even they were denied. The Devos were that picky. Lira was crap at taking photos—or doing anything artistic—so she had no hope of making it.

The final decision was left to the Devos, per the multi-system agreement made three years ago before terraforming began. They were AI, in a sense, if AI could be projected into the world as energy and tasked with caring for creation. The first AI since the age of AI had come and gone. *Spirits*, some would call them, but only the obnoxiously devout. Most people her age called them annoying, including Lira—even though it was her great, great-uncle who built the Devos system. She had met that side of the family, and they were not the kind of people she'd want to invite over to hang out with her friends. The same could be said for the Devos… and Earth, for that matter.

Still, the invitation came only once in a lifetime. Her friends would laugh if she didn't even try. She'd take the trial, visit Earth, in all of its so-called glory, and have even more reasons to be happy when the Devos rejected her application. At the very least, she would be eligible for a tourist visa, and she'd hate to miss hanging out with her friends if they got theirs.

#

The first thing she noticed out of the shuttle wasn't the green grass or the blue sky or even the overwhelming warmth of the Sun, but the gravity. The oppressive, knock-you-on-your-butt gravity. The only thing worse than the four painful weeks in the centrifuge was the idea that it hadn't half-prepared her for the real thing. It was like she had become a toddler and had to learn to walk all over again. Or like she was so hopped up on painkillers she couldn't walk and likely wouldn't remember anything in the morning, except she'd remember this. It hurt and was nauseating, and after trying to walk a few feet, she slumped to the ground and thought about giving up.

She would have, too, but that's when she saw the pack with her destination and supplies. She could at least see what they had assigned her. Crawling on all fours, she made it to the center of the small clearing where her pack sat. They didn't let her bring anything with her except what she could wear. They said they would provide everything she needed. She opened it to find an extra pair of clothes, clearly old and out of style and not anything she'd wear while in public (or in photos), some rations, and a large water bottle with the filter that would allow her to fill up from a stream. (The idea of water flowing along the ground! The mere amount of water it would take to keep a stream flowing was the stuff of luxury space yachts and one of the things she hoped to see for herself.) Finally, there was a small handheld with a touchscreen and a camera. The moment she pulled it from the tablet, it unlocked, and her instructions loaded.

"Your device will guide you in your trial. Experience your appointed site with attention. Your attempts to capture or categorize your site may significantly influence your final eligibility."

"*Attempts to capture,*" she said to herself, "as if taking a photo or geo-tagging the site was complicated." The Devos had built the surface; they knew every river and forest. Why did they need humans to catalog it? She could only assume it was for her benefit, somehow.

The introduction went on for a few more page scrolls, which she skipped over—small print about how if she were hurt, they'd not be held responsible, and while every attempt would be made to get her, no promises of a safe retrieval could be made. She had been warned about all of this before she was sent down. She signed at the bottom and hit the "continue" button, hoping to see where it would send her and how long it would take. The trial lasted 6 days, 5 camps, and 11 Kilometers a day.

She dropped the handheld onto the grass. 11 Kilometers a day! That was like walking the centrifuge almost 30 times in a single day, but with *real* gravity! And she only had 6 hours to reach the next waypoint, before it got dark. That is, if she could get up and walk.

#

That night, she woke up at her campsite. Her fire had gone out, and she meant that in every sense. Her legs were sore; the roots in the ground left bruises on her back—she was sure of it. Her blanket was far too thin for the cool air, which meant she was shivering, and now she was soaking wet from the morning dew. There were a hundred other things she'd love to complain about, but she neither had the energy to find the words nor anyone to complain about them to. She could assume there were a few Devos nearby watching, judging her, really, and complaining to them would only hurt her chances.

She rolled over and stared at the coals.

Why in the world had she agreed to do this at all?

The only thing that got her up was the promise of rations and something warm to drink. She started the fire again, and soon she was enjoying a cup of tea and a full stomach. The tea gave her a lot of warmth, and soon she was looking at the handheld, trying to decide whether she could spend another day hiking.

She did, and every step hurt.

While no one had been approved yet, everyone had completed the trials. She'd quit if she had to, but not without a good fight. She wasn't going to be the first to leave before she reached her destination.

The second night was the same. Hardly any sleep and completely drenched by morning. But then she remembered the change of clothes and put them on. They were dry and stayed much cooler as she walked. They also kept her warm at night, and she wished she had changed into them the moment she was given them. At that point, she couldn't care less how she looked for while she was in "public" in every sense of the word, completely exposed, it was also the most alone she had ever been—

other than the trees, and birds above, and snails she'd seen on the log near where she slept, and they didn't care what she wore. And while she didn't have the words to explain it, it was nice being around living things that didn't care how she looked.

That night, she fell asleep without even starting a fire and slept the entire night, waking up dry as a bone and well rested. The clothes they gave her were rather impressive, and she thought with a few adjustments, she could try and make a style out of them back on the station.

Over the next two days, her legs grew stronger, and she began to enjoy herself. She was lonely and talked to herself more than she'd like people to know, but the sights around every bend, valley, and crest were better than any movie, story, or friendship she had ever had. She wondered if this was what the old women felt when they sat in prayer at the temple, lost in thought for hours. It was in every way a religious experience.

On the sixth morning, as she climbed what she hoped would be the final hill to the top of the mountain and her "designated site," a Devos passed close. She didn't see it with her eyes—no more than a blur against the trees—but she felt it—like warm water poured over tea, or a hot shower after a long day. Oh! How she would have died to have a shower. She could barely handle smelling herself; the stains on her knuckles looked permanent, the bags under her eyes would take the nicest spa to undo, and the dirt under her fingernails was determined. Yet all of this fell to the back of her mind with each new wonder, and only amplified when the Devos passed by. She felt as if it were speaking to her, even though it did not use words. It was a question that brushed against her mind: *will you dare to capture it?*

She instinctually said "yes," even though the question didn't feel like encouragement. It felt stronger than that. More like a warning. What was it warning her about? She would do her best, and that was all she could do. If it wanted to help, it'd come behind her and help push her up this Ammalee-forsaken hill. "You've made this so difficult, it's like you don't even want us here!" she yelled. She was mad about it, now. Not like when she started, for unlike then, she now felt as if Earth had left an impression on her that she could never remove—a stain of sorts, but one that was so beautiful she'd want to frame it and hang it in a museum. She had spent the last six days walking in woods no one had ever seen before; trees and sights and birds no one had ever cataloged or captured in photos. She had seen the entire known galaxy, if only through a screen in movies and books, but how could one capture *this*? The trees stood too tall. The moss was far too soft. The light and shadows of the morning sun, as it cut through the morning mist, would take her breath away. She was thankful that the sun looked best in the morning, for it was only in the morning that she had breath to spare. And that surprised her as much as anything, for it was the exertion that she loved: the rush of doing something she never thought she could.

She took another step up the cliff, grabbing a branch to help her, and paused to look at the hill she had climbed. Even if the galaxy's best photographer had taken the trial, how could they capture it? In fact, she decided right there, as she climbed the final hill, that they shouldn't. If people wanted to see this, they should come to see it for themselves. Maybe that's why it rejected every application—for as soon as one person settled on this world, it would, in time, stop being the world that people would go to for trials. Keep it closed off and locked down! Preserve it. And for Ammalee's sake, don't ruin it with a few measly photographs. She had seen the ones her friends had taken, and they were beautiful, yet they did not do it justice!

No, someone must encounter for themselves, undisturbed by the pollution of human civilization. In fact, she was beginning to feel that humans were the ones who were uncivilized, no matter how hard they tried, compared to this.

That's when she reached the top of the hill. It was her destination. She didn't need to reference the handheld to confirm. The grass had been cut, with a path lined with rocks, the entire valley below them as the backdrop of a stage set for her alone. At the end of the path, at the very top of the hill, was a small flower bed with a small log set upright as a seat.

As she sat, petals unfurled in impossible colors—white into violet, into gold, into something that felt more like memory than hue. Bioluminescent spores lifted from its center, drifting skyward like a prayer dissolving into dusk. The entire miracle lasted less than a minute.

She thought about grabbing her handheld, but she couldn't. She had made up her mind. She would not let them judge her on how well she captured this, for she had already judged herself. This was not the thing to be captured or cataloged. Instead, she watched and then sat. If she were never to return to Earth again, not even as a tourist, this would have been worth it—not because she had earned a place, but because she would carry this with her. And there was no greater duty in life than carrying one's lessons to the next generation.

That's when she felt a Devos press against her from behind. It didn't seem angry—the energy was warm and kind—and she felt as if it said something to her—not in words, but in feelings. Like the feeling when someone does something they thought was impossible, or the feeling a kid gets when their parents are proud of them. And somehow, she knew—even before checking her tablet, she knew. Her citizenship on Earth had been approved without as much as a simple photo of the entire trip.

That's when she pulled out her tablet, for an idea was forming in her mind that almost made her laugh. And on that hill, before a recently blooming flower, surrounded by the world's best painting, she re-read the instructions.

"Your device will guide you in your trial. Experience your appointed site with attention. Your attempts to capture or categorize your site may significantly influence your final eligibility."

Her almost-laugh turned into a full burst of chuckles and tears when she read it. Of course! She understood it now—as clear as the streams she passed along the way! Those who had gone before her had read it with the wrong intent. They had misunderstood. They had missed the whole point. The Devos were not instructing people to capture and catalog, but warning them not to! Clearly, the Devos were looking for people who would focus more on what was in front of them than on what they might share on a screen with others. So, she did as her conclusions suggested, and set her screen down, and looked out over the horizon one last time. Soon, her shuttle would arrive, and she'd have to decide if she'd tell people what she'd discovered or be like the Devos and let them discover it on their own.

The Banquet

3607 CE – New Earth

The forty-first anniversary of New Earth arrives without announcement, and the air feels no different for it. There is no scaffolding, no last-minute corrections, and that, more than anything, pleases me.

I arrive early—not because I must, but because I want to see it empty one last time. The tables, the best I've ever built, stretch exactly as designed, branching outward like the spindles of a great wheel upon which the New Earth spins. Light hits the wood the way I had hoped it would, catching the muted finish of the grain. They are placing the food on the table, and I look for any wobbles or misalignments. They stand strong.

There is nothing to fix.

That is how it feels when the world is complete: nothing asks me to fix it—only to receive it, and pass it on to future generations unchanged.

I hear people mutter from the scriptures, "Come and gather for God's great supper."

The air carries layers of sound—wind moving through high leaves, water folding over itself somewhere beyond sight. And with the sound comes smells: loaves with torn edges, fruit split exposing their inner colors, bowls of grain that smell faintly of earth and fire. There is enough. No one reaches, and no one hoards.

People arrive, wearing linen—white, not blinding, but soft, like the way the moon is bright, and yet dim compared to the Sun. More come each year, children and travelers. Today, I sit by both, knees brushing a child who swings her legs on my left and a traveler who smells of exotic spices and oils on my right. I am happy for them. I wish I could experience the banquet for the first time.

The Poet sits in front of me, and I ask him about the liturgy, and then our Priest sits next to him, and I greet her. I always appreciate her prayers and blessings, and she will offer both today.

Everyone takes their seat.

They wait.

I wait.

The anticipation is the loudest of all silence, the way a conductor feels before the first note. There is a moment that matters. Everything must be timed perfectly, for our spotters have already told us they are on their way, first seen flying over the mountains to the east.

It is time.

The Banquet is beginning.

#

I ask if it's the biggest meal we've ever set because I don't know what else to ask. It's the first time I've ever been to the New Earth Banquet, and my parents have told me very little about it. "You must experience it for yourself," they said as we walked the path to the clearing where the tables sit.

I do not know why they made me wear this white dress, or why it looks like everyone agreed to do the same, but I do not like it. It is uncomfortable and makes me feel old.

Everyone's quiet in that way adults get when they're trying to force someone to feel like something is meaningful when it's just dull.

The tables go on forever, like paths you could follow until you forget where you started. I swing my legs under the bench and look up, wondering why there's a table set, but we're not seated at it. The man sitting next to me looks down at me, and my parents whisper, "That's the one who designed the tables."

They are nice-looking tables, if only I could get a little closer to see them.

The food smells good. Not scary-good. Just…good, like something I would eat without complaining too much, but would never ask for on my birthday. Not that it matters—it isn't my birthday.

If I'm honest, I don't know why this day matters so much. I'd ask, but my parents have already told me to be quiet—everyone is quiet, a lot longer than I feel is necessary.

The leader of our village breaks the silence with a simple prayer. He speaks in Ammalee's words. The words land wrong in my ears, like a song I almost know. I look at my parents, and I fear they are embarrassed that they haven't tried harder to teach me.

#

The prayer is nice, but the leader's accent is distracting. They do not speak here as they did on the ship where I grew up. I only arrived two weeks ago, and I am still getting used to the density of the gravity and the absolute beauty of New Earth. I am hungry too, so when someone asked if I'd come to the banquet, I said "yes" immediately.

I grew up in deep space, where food was stale and limited. It took every bit of my family's money to get here, much more than the quality of the ship we took would suggest. I always wondered if we couldn't have bought our own—not that we'd want to own something as broken as that one. I'm surprised we survived.

I don't understand why they have us sit so far from the table. I can only imagine it's part of the procession. That's the thing about people on New Earth—they like their liturgies and prayers and processions. They call it slowing down. I call it waiting while my stomach aches.

A bell rings.

Now it is silent.

I hope to eat after the prayer and the ringing of the bells, but we do not.

A man, the one I heard the guy next to me call "the poet," stands up from the seat behind me and walks to the center. I nod at the right moments, but my eyes keep returning to the bread and the fruit, to determine whether there will be enough for everyone. I'd have to rush the table when it's time if I want my portion. I know it.

#

I have practiced the final lines until they feel inevitable.

The words are meant to shape gratitude. Naming a moment completes it.

I do not want to give the wrong impression. My poem is far more liturgy than poetry, for this moment deserves nothing else.

I read it, and I look at people receiving my words. They close their eyes. They nod. They smile, and some shed tears, and I join them.

I reach my favorite part and trust it will be all that I hoped it would be. But I am unable to read it, for wings interrupt the poem. The birds arrive early, and the people gasp around me, as they fly like synchronized swimmers, performing choreographed routines to music they alone can hear. They descend and eat.

I try not to be bothered by the interruption. I know it isn't about me.

Those new to the feast are surprised—they are always surprised as if this feast was for us.

There are more birds this year. They must have told their friends. And I smile as I think about the idea of birds having friends. I *hope* they have friends. What is life without people? Or poetry without those to hear it read?

Hundreds descend upon the table, devouring the food, tearing grapes and bread like soldiers would tear limbs from their enemies. Grapes burst under beaks. Bread disappears in seconds. It is a sacred massacre—glorious and generous. It is a holy moment.

I want my words to matter. But holiness arrives without waiting for them. A truth I still struggle to accept, even after all these years on New Earth.

I fold the poem and pocket it.

The birds finish, and everyone breaks into applause, and I feel jealousy awaken in my heart. I knew they would not applaud me, even if the birds had given them time, but in all the ways New Earth has changed me, I still have much room to grow. And in a way, this makes me grateful. What fun would it be to have arrived?

#

The work is done.
The mountains no longer bruise the sky.
The seas have learned their edges.
The soil remembers every name that was taken from it.

We give thanks.
For the world has been made new.
Blessed are those who were invited here,
 who crossed the winepress,
 who learned to lay down the sword,
 who learned restraint when abundance returned.

See how the tables stretch outward.
See how the feast is prepared.
This is the wedding of heaven and earth,
 the joining of breath and dust.
The moment when history exhales
 and says *enough*.

We are learning,
 now and always,
 to live without treading the winepress
 of the world until it bleeds,
 only to get drunk
 on its fermenting fruit.

We give thanks.
Let us receive what has been given.
        As we give what has been received.
Let us take our place at the table.
        As we set a seat for others.
Let us eat and remember.

As we will one day be remembered.
Let us know
    As we are known,
—that this abundance has been prepared
not for us,
but for all.

#

They want a blessing, but I fear they are stuffed full of blessings, more blessings than they can handle. They speak of this world as finished—*complete*—and I know this is not the case. Even if it is, it cannot remain this way forever. Things do not stay perfect forever.

They smile as if things could not be any better, but comfort is often a distraction. I worry. Do I say something? No, this is not the time for critiques or hard words. It's a celebration.

But I was never very good at joy, and this is what bothers me the most. Are my concerns real or just the fears of someone who struggles with pleasure?

Is this revelation from God, or fear, long buried, breaking the surface? I pause. I must be careful, for history reminds us: those in power have often baptized their fear and called it holy.

The birds are done, and I stand before my people. Beautiful people, and that much is not in question.

I bless them with words that give the appearance of joy, even as my heart worries that the joy is insincere.

We head to the lodge and eat our own meal, a feast in its own right. My plate is full.

I don't remember when it was empty.

Everyone is generous, and that is no surprise. It's easy to be gracious when there is more than enough. I hope the same is true if my plate ever becomes empty, or my fears become real.

The Day the Sun Died

3614 CE – New Earth

Alexis stood at the edge of the cliff, overlooking the city, as the Sun began to kiss the sky goodnight. Many others had gathered on the cliff to see the Sun, for it looked like it hadn't fully woken up, or had shown up to work without a proper night's sleep and shower. It looked hungover, or worse, on its deathbed—and everyone noticed.

Hundreds now stood along the edge, watching the Sun like a child would watch their grandmother on their deathbed, too young to understand that death was not the same as falling asleep, and that with her passing, they would also lose her stories and all the warmth they brought.

Then an older woman muttered to herself, words that sounded old, words that, in all her time in church, Alexis should know the source of, but she couldn't remember. The old woman goes on about how they will "no longer need candles" (as if they still used them) or the "light of the sun," because God will become the light they need. It didn't make any sense. They certainly would need the Sun, that's for sure.

They had first tracked the dimming of the Sun years ago, but their people—not all of them, just the majority—refused to listen. The Sun wasn't scheduled to die for a trillion years, so why would anyone believe what the scientists said?

Not that she or her people understood the science behind it. What did they know about how to split the sun's rays into its individual wavelengths, to see which bands were dimming? What did her people know about such things? Then the orbital scientists said it was all because people were messing with time, as if that were possible. As if we were just supposed to accept that the Sun had jumped ahead a trillion years and was done. She had generally accepted scientists' theories—even those in orbit—but even this required more faith than she was used to.

She had her doubts until the Sun started to dim. Anyone could now see the Sun growing darker. After all they had done to terraform and prepare the new Earth, after all the trials, after all her ancestors had invested in making sure New Earth was taken care of, it would simply go dark, and at no fault of their own? It was a cruel joke.

She worried it was too late. The scientists and those who had listened had long since immigrated from Earth, from their entire system, and were now living in Primera or even as far as Proximata. They were kind enough to leave behind the plans needed to survive, if only those in charge would take action. And surely the Devos were pledged to support the efforts, whose energy was unrelated to the sun and wouldn't be affected by its death. Even with their help, it would take a miracle. Her people would have to accept plans that would fundamentally change how humans on New Earth lived. The plans were so radical that they had long been considered "heretical."

But the Sun's dying was considered heretical too, and yet it had.

If it meant surviving, it did not seem heretical to her. Yet, in their resistance, she watched her faith leaders grow harsher and unbending, as if resisting the inevitable were a poison that turned her faith into something she could no longer recognize.

She stood, pondering these things, alongside a crowd of others, stuck in the silence as they watched the dying sun from the city's best vantage point. That's when someone tried to connect to her through the local network; she could see the message pop up. She entered the virtual just long enough to see it was from her mother, who was worried about her and wanted her to come home immediately. She was about to reply when she heard the crowd gasp simultaneously. She looked up, and the sun flickered and then noticeably dimmed.

It looked more like the moon than its true self.

She could feel the panic in the crowd overlooking the cliff, and people began to shuffle in fear. A few standing behind her pushed her closer to the edge, as the mobs moved about. She pressed back and wondered what she could do to calm everyone, if only for her own protection.

A small girl, her neighbor Jenique, ended up next to her, and she grabbed her just as someone accidentally shoved her, and she tumbled to the edge.

She looked for a Devos—surely there was one nearby. Weren't they designed to prevent mobs like this? Or did all the disrespect from her people leave them not caring—were they capable of not caring? She looked for their blurred shadows against the wall but couldn't find any.

Her foot was dug into the crumbling rock as people shoved into each other. She held Jenique to keep her from falling off the ledge. Her ancestors would never become this violent. Had they forgotten their ways? Or were their kindness only a matter of convenience? That's when she did the only thing she knew to do—the one thing that would calm her nerves when she was afraid, and the one thing she hoped would calm the chaos of her people.

She lifted her voice as loud as she could.

"Do you go on, to be made whole?"

The crowd slowed for a second, but no response. This time, she sang the words to the melody her mother had taught her in the back pews of her church.

"Do you go on, to be made whole?"

A few in the crowd responded this time, "I go on, though I know not the end," singing it.

She sang it again, louder, as the crowd had settled and everyone could hear her. This time, the crowd joined her in the chorus and continued through the entire song, all three verses, in a call and response that echoed off the back of the mountain and into the valley where they lived. Her mother would have been proud.

That's when the sun flickered again—as if it was encouraged by the song, as if their voices had given it the strength it needed to shine just a little brighter.

The crowd broke into applause and cheers.

The sun set moments later, shining like it had earlier that day, and everyone headed back to the transport with hope that it would rise again—their songs would make sure of that.

On the way back, Jenique walked up to Alexis to thank her. Her mother nodded in appreciation from a distance, and she sat down, holding onto her arm. She sat there for most of the way, the car filled with joyful, religious chatter.

"If the sky gives nothing, how can we live?" asked the young girl, finally.

Alexis didn't know what to say. She couldn't tell her that their parents had made a mistake—they should have left Earth years ago. They shouldn't be here. She pushed these thoughts from her mind and smiled, "We live because we believe," she said, and as the words came out, she realized how much of that belief had been borrowed from those who taught her how to sing. Faith was as much their salvation as it was the bind that held her family—including all those who had gone before her—together. Their faith was all they had left, for better or worse. Their faith, and the plans the scientists had left behind, if her people were humble enough to accept them.

In the morning, the sun didn't rise—what snuck over the horizon was a shadow of what it once was, cold and dark. She was glad she wasn't standing on a cliff when it rose. She could hear the panic coming from the streets. They'd have to listen to the scientists now. Hopefully, it wouldn't be too late.

In the Name of Ammalee

3666 CE – Eaetth (Dark Earth)

The preacher's voice hijacked Kold's audio interface, knocking him and everyone within range back into reality. Kold had been sitting under an ancient tree, in soft grass, with a light breeze, minding his own business, in a world where the sun still shone, and his suit could mimic the warmth of its rays on his face. Now the jagged walls of the cave stared at him through the augmented lens of his suit's helmet. The line of others, all in similar exoskeletons, their faces lit by the light of their screens, all waking up, looking for the preacher who had disturbed their slumber.

They had been standing in line for a year, moving forward each day, getting lower and lower into the cave, and this was the last place Kold expected to see a preacher. There were plenty of preachers protesting at the cave's entrance. And there was even more lining the roads that brought him and his sister there. More than once, they had to ditch the road entirely. But they were in the cave's second-lowest room, and the only way to get this deep was to wait in line like everyone else. There was nothing more dependable than the stubbornness of preachers.

A nicer suit could have blocked the frequency, but they couldn't afford anything like that. Based on the reaction of everyone else in line, none of them could either. He scanned the line, ending at the old man behind him, who was too old and frail and likely starving to death to be annoyed by a preacher.

Unlike this old man, Kold had planned; he had enough supplements for himself and his sister for a year and four months, and while his sister had begged him to hand some over to the old man, Kold knew they couldn't risk it. What if the Devos pushed them to the back of the line? They would run out. He promised her the old man would be alright— that the Devos would make sure he had what he needed.

Kold turned from looking at the half-dead man to his sister, Dejah. He checked her logs. She hadn't logged into the virtual all morning. She had been listening to the preacher before he hijacked the frequency. The preachers weren't allowed in the virtual. In there, Kold could control every part of the experience, silencing those he wanted. Reality wasn't so kind. Kold paired his suit to Dejah's comm. "Ignore him. Just ignore him," he said. "He doesn't know what he's saying."

She turned and looked up at him.

"I know." She said it as calmly and unassuming as anyone could. She said it like a true believer. It was embarrassing.

"Why are you listening to him anyway?" asked Kold.

"I don't know," said Dejah. "But I like listening to him."

The preacher started to speak in the tongue of the ancestors. If there was anything worse than a hijacked frequency, it was hearing someone preach in a language they butchered. Kold might not believe in God anymore, but he knew enough about this historic tongue to know when someone was butchering it.

"What's he saying?" Dejah asked.

"He's trying to quote one of our prayers, but he's got the inflection all wrong. "*t'áá altsoni,* which means *all the things* will be revealed in the *'adinidíín,'* or *light* —that's the quote, but even you could do better than him, if you had the text in front of you."

Kold turned to watch him struggle with the translation. He could see the pack on the left shoulder of his suit, which was used to broadcast. Kold imagined what it would be like to leave the line, run over to him, knock him to the ground, and … well, he wouldn't hurt him. But he'd knock that antenna off his shoulder. Then everyone could enjoy waiting in line without being forced to listen to him. But he knew he couldn't do that; a few Devos were close by, only visible from the blur they cast against the walls of the cave. They had been increasing their patrols as they approached the void.

Dejah knocked his arm.

"Do you miss Dad?" she asked, pairing to his comms.

Kold turned to her. "Of course, I miss Dad."

"Do you miss his preaching?"

Kold paused. He looked down at her as she looked up through her tinted helmet, the glow of her computer system lighting her face in the otherwise pitch-black cave.

"I miss a lot of things about dad," said Kold.

He wasn't lying. He missed a lot of things about Dad. But he didn't miss the preaching. Or sitting on the corner of the street watching him pray, which he was far more likely to do. He didn't miss watching him get harassed, beaten, or tossed out of places because of his prayers, even though it was what his dad deserved, which is precisely what he would do to this preacher if it weren't for the line.

He felt their faith had become less about faith and more about proving they had faith to others, a reaction of sorts to a world that had gone dark and forgotten God.

A few moments later, the line moved forward, and their suits gestured for them to do the same, nudging them, but forcing them to do most of the work themselves, a testament to how close they were to the void. Kold dragged his feet, his muscles aching, and once in his new spot, he turned to look behind him. The old man hadn't moved with the line. His eyes were glassy and rolled to the side.

He shifted his suit to block Dejah's view of the man. He didn't need her to throw a fit. Slowly, the line repositioned, winding around the old man, and a new person walked up to Kold. It was another old man, who looked very similar to the first—similar enough that Dejah might not even notice. Kold smiled and nodded to him. He hoped this man had enough supplements to make it through the end.

#

For almost a year, Kold and his sister waited in line, slowly progressing down a long, narrow shaft, deeper into a cave, waiting for this very moment. When they entered the last room of the cave system, they left the range of the preacher and a Devos connected to their suits to give instructions, which were repeated every hour for the next two days, each time knocking everyone from their dreams. The Devos explained that it was for the best—that it would prepare them for where they were going. But it gave Kold a headache and made him sick to his stomach. He forgot about his pain and queasiness when they stood before the void.

Kold hadn't expected the void to look like this. He anticipated something bright. Maybe it would spin, twisting reality into a swirl of colors. Or perhaps it would be loud—or some kind of presence that he could sense. He expected it to be noticeable. It wasn't any of these things. It was dark, as if they were looking at it without their suits' augmented vision.

"We're going to do it!" said Dejah.

"We made it," said Kold.

"And once we get back there, we will find Ammalee!"

He checked to make sure her comms were set to private. He didn't need any trouble this close to the void. She had become convinced that Ammalee lay on the other side of the void, and, from what he understood of the timing, it was possible that the historical Ammalee, the founder of their faith, would be alive at the time of the void's exit. But he had little hope she would be anything like what they had come to believe about her, if she was real at all. "Just focus on the instructions."

"But we will find her, right?"

"If you pay attention and do as you're told, we will search for her, but you must prepare. When these suits get removed, I won't be able to see you or talk to you directly. Understand?"

"Yes. I'm ready." She knocked his suit. "Do you go on, to be made whole?" "I go on, though I know not the end." He recited the response as he had been taught his entire life. But he didn't mean it. Not anymore, and hadn't for years.

Dejah slipped a prayer pebble from her pouch and pressed it into his mecahnical palm, like their father used to do when words weren't enough.

He held it, looking at it.

The faithfuls gave God credit for everything. But Kold knew better. It was Devos who discovered the void, and they had nothing to do with Ammalee. They were the ones who gave us these suits. The same science that built the towers that powered the suits and Devos, the energy that sustained them, projected into the world, much in the same way as they had projected people into the past, that ancient old Earth technology that made the void possible. Science—not faith—saved them. But that didn't mean he couldn't recite the response. It was a habit he hadn't broken. It was nine ancient words that helped his sister calm down—and if he ever needed her to be calm, it was now. He placed the pebble in his pocket.

The Devos explained the process one more time and then began the countdown. There had never been an easier way to travel back in time—two steps towards darkness and 1600 years would rewind in the blink of an eye.

It was a rebirth.

Back to a time when suits were no longer needed, where they no longer worked.

Kold would have done anything to keep his suit, but Dejah would go through the void without him, if given the choice, and he wouldn't let her travel alone. Kold took in a deep breath right before it opened. The helmet lifted off his headfirst, and without it and his screen, the darkness of the void engulfed the entire room. He tried to breathe, but choked.

The life support tubes were removed from his body next. He squirmed from the sensation, but tried not to cry. Mostly, he worried about how Dejah was handling it, but without the suit, he couldn't see her. He knew she'd be praying to Ammalee, and he would pray too—if he thought it would help. Thinking of her prayers, he reached for the pocket in his suit she had given him earlier. It was the first time he had ever held it without a suit. This one had been passed down in their family for generations, so far back that no one even knew how old it was. He had never thought much of it, but now, holding it in the darkness, he could feel the years and all the stories it held, as if they seeped out of the rock like water. He held it tight and focused on the Devos' instructions, growing lightheaded from the lack of air. Without the suit, he realized how cold it was in the cave—and moist.

He stepped out of the rest of his suit as it opened. Tubes hissed as they disconnected, and the joints cracked as they detached. Then the innermost layer peeled off of him, exposing his body. He found it hard to lift his leg without support. Every day, the suit would force them to move in place, strengthening their muscles. They claimed his muscles would be ready to stand on their own by the time they reached the void. But when he lifted his leg, it was a lot harder than he expected.

Tripping, he fell to the ground. After he got back up, he stood for the first time free of his suit. Then a moment passed where he wasn't sure if he was still in the cave or on the journey into the dark. He couldn't see, but he could hear his sister crying. He reached for her, but couldn't find her in the darkness. He reached for her again, and then he felt it. A Devo brushed up against him. He had never felt one against his flesh before. It was soft and warm, like a summer breeze against bare skin in a world where the sun still shone. Then it passed through him, and he could feel his skin waking up. Then a Devo shoved him into the darkness.

#

"Welcome to the year 2066" was the first thing Kold heard when he woke up.

He was on his back and couldn't move. It felt like he was in a stalled exoskeleton, but he was certain that he had taken his suit off.

He tried to open his eyes, but all he could see was white. Blinking, he hoped the whiteness would wipe away. He tried to lift his arms again, but couldn't tell if they were tied down or if he was too weak. He blinked again, and this time it worked. The white gave way to shapes and blurs, as if the room was filled with Devos, all surrounding him—their projections against the white walls.

"Your eyesight should return fully in the next four hours," said the voice in the room. It spoke with a thick accent.

"Where am I?" His attempt to talk forced him to cough up phlegm. He spit it out towards the ground.

"You are in room 102 of the C-Block of the Immigration Intake Hospital in Sector 4."

"Where's my sis—?" His voice cracked again, loosening more phlegm, which he hacked out.

"You need to strengthen your vocal cords—your body isn't used to operating without support."

"Where's my sister?" he asked again, straining his throat.

"One of the members of your group was a DNA match and thus is located in the bed next to you. She is awake but refuses to communicate with us."

"Dejah! Where are you? Are you there?" he asked as loudly as he could. He tried to move again, but couldn't. He was certain now that he wasn't just weak. He was tied down. "You need to let me go. I need to see my sister." He pushed, but he couldn't break free. All he could see were blurs, one next to him that looked as if it might be her. "Let me out of this!"

"She is awake and is looking at you, but refuses to communicate," repeated the voice. "You will be reunited with her soon. For now, it is unwise to yell. It will make the recovery longer."

Kold turned towards the noise of a door opening. The shape was of a human, tall and dark, but still out of focus.

"Who is that?" he asked.

The figure spoke for a minute in the tongue of the ancestors, before going back to the language he couldn't understand. Kold caught fragments—familiar syllables from half-remembered prayers—but not enough to follow their meaning. What startled him most was that strangers were speaking it at all. The prayer language had always felt like a ritual, a relic. Yet here it was, alive on foreign lips used in casual conversation, something he had never experienced before. A hand seized his arm. He jolted, tried to wrench free, but could not.

"Don't move," said the voice.

The person poked his skin with a needle. It hurt. Then he heard Dejah cry.

"Let me see my sister!"

"Your eyesight will return shortly, at which time you will be able to see her," said the voice.

"No. I want to be with her. And who was that? Where am I?"

"This is your doctor," said the voice. "He's just discharged you."

"Discharged? Was that the poke you put in my arm?"

"That was a needle, with the last of your prescriptions—they will help your body adjust to life outside the suit and your mind to life outside the dream. It will take time to experience the effects. Either way, you've been released. I will show you to the door." With that, the straps holding him released. He shot up and went in the direction of Dejah's cry. She met his arms, and they held each other on the bed.

"I'm here, Dejah. I'm here," said Kold.

"It is time to leave. Follow me, please," said the voice.

An arm, like that of a person in an exoskeleton, lifted him from the bed. Dejah followed, and they walked to the door, hand in hand. His legs were tired, and he breathed heavily, which is what he noticed first. He breathed freely and without support from a suit. With each step, his thin legs slid along the floor, and his sight started to return. He looked at the person helping him, only to realize it wasn't a person at all. It had arms, but no legs. It moved with a set of tracks that ran along the floor like wheels. In place of a head, it had a screen.

"What are you?" asked Kold.

"I am bot PRZ4745, but you can refer to me as P45."

"What is a bot?" asked Dejah.

"It's like a Devos—sort of," said Kold.

"Yes, I am told I am similar to your Devos—if they were confined to a machine, instead of projected as energy—but I have never met one myself, so I cannot confirm ."

It was dark outside, and it made it easier for Kold and Dejah to see each other. They turned to notice the sky. This was the first time Kold had seen the stars outside their dreams, and the two didn't compare. The sky was darker, the lights looked brighter, and the sky—the same sky they had lived under their whole lives—felt bigger.

Behind them, a steep cliff sat above the entrance of the cave, now blocked by fences. In front of them, two-story buildings lined a long dirt road that P45 led them down. To the right, the buildings sat next to a tall rock wall, with a fence that ran along the top ridge. To the left, more buildings stretched on towards the night sky. And behind them, they could see the cliff above the entrance to the cave. They had been here before, but at a time when there were no such structures. As they walked, P45 explained what they saw.

"In each dorm, there are one hundred rooms, and in each room, there are 1-4 visitors."

"Visitors?" asked Kold.

"That is what we call you. For you are not a resident here," said P45.

They passed hundreds of others like them on their way, all sitting out on the steps of the buildings and leaning against walls, their white skin glowing in the dark. A few residents were walking around as well, accompanied by similar bots. The residents stood out for having hair on their heads, being shorter, and having thicker arms and bodies overall. But visitors and residents both wore thin, body-hugging exoskeletons that rarely included helmets. Kold noticed he had a loose-fitting exoskeleton on as well. He touched it. It was non-metallic and didn't provide any added strength or apparent protection, and only covered his chest, legs, and parts of his arms. The rest of his arms and head were exposed. His feet were covered too, but separately from the rest. All of this reminded him of the stories of his grandparents, before the suits, back when the sun still shone.

He looked at Dejah; she wore a similar suit, and neither had a mask or any air support.

While they walked, P45 continued to give them instructions, but he spoke fast and with such an accent that it was hard to understand.

At one point, they stopped, and P45 spoke more directly. They stood outside of a large building, with a black door that butted up to the dirt street and a long awning that stretched out like a stick hanging from the face of a rock. Kold looked up and read the heading above the door: "Building for Immigration #5."

"According to the Time Preservation Act of 2056," P45 explained, "you are permitted to live your final days here, in this time displacement camp," he said, gesturing with his metallic arms, "but during your time, you are not allowed to contaminate the outside world. You have been assigned to Dorm 367, which I will take you to directly. Tomorrow, at 0800, you will have your intake interview here with an immigration officer and me. If you miss this meeting, marks will be added to your profile, and it will affect your future work release. Now this way."

They walked again. Most visitors ignored them, but a few would pause and point as they walked alongside P45. Then, after passing a few more buildings, P45 stopped again.

"This is where you will find body supplements. Your clothes will no longer feed you—this is very important for you to comprehend. In the back of this building, they will teach you how to consume properly." He pointed towards the building.

Visitors were lined up. Kold watched as they waited patiently to get in. Then, one person left the line, walked a few feet, turned towards the moon shining in the night sky, and knelt to pray. Without his suit and its reminders, Kold only realized then that it was time for evening prayer. The visitor began to raise his voice, praying loudly in the tongue of the ancestors, jumping between speech and song, with a voice that could raise the dead.

Kold looked around and noticed no one else had joined him in prayer. The man started to bend up and down, his arms loose in the air, waving back and forth, his voice getting louder and more beautiful. It was the first time he'd seen someone pray without a suit, and it was captivating. He noticed Dejah let go of his hand and started to kneel when he grabbed her.

"No. Not now."

He went back to watch the man when someone left the line and walked up to him with a tray. He swung and smacked the man across the face. Then a few others ran up and started to kick him.

Dejah clung to Kold's arm, and he pulled her behind him to block her view of the incident. The hope that life on the other side of the void might be different died for Kold in that moment.

"Oh, please disregard him," said P45, "The visitor received a bad match on his housing, and this creates tension in his unit. His transfer is being processed." P45 continued to give them instructions as if nothing had happened. "You will get famished tonight, but your next meal will be with the return of the Sun. You must remember the location of this building in relation to your dorm. Your guide will meet you at your dorm and will assist you. Now this way."

A few more buildings later, Kold and Dejah entered their dorm, and P45 escorted them to their room. "After a week's time—after your body has had time to adjust—you will be assigned work. It will be in your best interest to do all you can to get yourself to a place where you can accomplish the work required of you. Do you understand?"

"Work?" asked Kold.

"Yes, everyone here has a job. In a week's time, you will be required to work. Now, one final piece of advice. You can not sleep standing up anymore. It is recommended that you lie down on these." He gestured to two beds, one on top of the other. "Surely, you are tired. Please sleep."

#

Kold and Dejah were left in a small room by themselves, with nothing but a dresser, a window, and two beds stacked on top of each other. They sat down on the lower bunk. Kold's legs were burning from the walk—the longest walk of his life without a suit. Kold turned to Dejah to talk when the door opened.

Three older men stood at the entrance.

"A paley, huh?" asked the old man in the front. He had thin, white skin, old but free of wrinkles, and covered in red burn marks on the tip of his nose and forehead.

His hands were stained black.

"Paley?" asked Kold. He tried to stand up, but his legs were too tired. He sat back down.

"Yeah—pale as the sun!" The old man in the back laughed. "Not just palies, but young ones too. And no parents?" He shook his head.

"Let me give you some advice: I'd keep to myself if I were you. Little ones like you don't fare well here."

"Oh, give them a break," said the man in the middle. He looked similar to the other two, but was shorter, and his hands weren't stained.

"I'm just being honest with them, Whitt—it's in their best interest. And I'll be honest about this too: We sleep when the sun returns, and you palies are so excited to see it, you're always up. But we don't want any noise, you hear?"

"We want silence—"

"You will regret it if you don't. Now, welcome to the year 2066. Just what you always wanted, huh? Paradise! Yeah, dry, hot, paradise!" With that, he slammed the door closed, but the man in the middle caught it before it latched.

He waited for the other two to leave before talking.

"Don't mind them." He pushed the door all the way open and latched it against the wall. "They aren't as bad as they seem—well, Frill can be a pain sometimes—what I mean is, they work in the mines—like most of the guys here, and it always puts them in a mood." He extended his hand towards Kold. "I'm Whitt and I'll be your guide this week." Kold flinched at the gesture. "Oh, yea. Sorry. It's called a 'shaking hand.' I learned it from the residents. It's a way to greet someone. Like this." He reached for Kold's hand. "I've learned lots from the residents, you know. Got a job in their offices. Some judge me for it, but they don't judge me when I bring home extra supplements. And that's not the best of it."

He entered the room and looked behind him. "Want to hear more?" He didn't wait for a response. He unlatched the door and let it swing closed. "The world you see outside isn't all of it—that's what I like to tell new visitors, because I don't want you to get the wrong impression.

"I've seen pictures in the office. I wasn't supposed to, but I've seen it. There are places where the plants grow as tall as buildings. Where the ground lifts out of the dirt, a green carpet soft to the touch—I've seen it myself. It's better than the dreams—doesn't even compare. I've heard the residents talk about it, too! Snow in places. Not around here, of course. Have you ever dreamed of snow? Of course you haven't! You can't dream of things you haven't seen. Some places got lots of it. Not like this dirt bowl."

Dejah leaned towards Kold and whispered, "Is this the waiting place Ammalee spoke of?"

"Shhh," returned Kold, pushing her back.

Whitt straightened up at her remark and he smiled big, showing off his mouth of missing teeth. "Oh, little girl, you need to be quieter if you don't want anyone to hear you. You ain't got a suit to change the frequency on," he said, tapping his head, as if he was still wearing a helmet. He leaned back down and got close to them. "Now, I knew the moment I saw you two: I bet those were a couple of faithfuls, holdovers from before the days our system went dark and did most of those with faith—I knew it, and I was right—and I ain't got anything wrong with it either. I don't, and there's nothing anyone can tell me to change my mind. But it'd be unfortunate if the wrong person found out, especially for someone as small as you. It seems many brought their anger with them, and they are still upset about getting left behind." He stood back up. "If you want to stay safe, I'd tell your sister to keep that private."

"We're not like other people of faith," said Kold.

"Oh, I'm sure you're not, and I'm not either. But unless you want to transfer to one of their dorms, I don't recommend talking about it here. You can trust me on that. It's a promise—and worth your attention. But you don't have to worry about anything tonight—Old Whitt is going to take care of both of you. I've been asked by your immigration officer herself, so you can be sure it's 100% guaranteed. And as a sign of appreciation, take this." He handed them a bar, wrapped in cloth. "You're going to wake up hungry—and by the looks of it, you won't even know what it means to be hungry, until you wake up with it. This will help. You chew it and swallow. It'll hurt at first, but it's the only way." He reached down and grabbed Kold's cheeks, squeezing them. "You got your teeth too, so that helps." Kold shoved him away. "Now, what you two need is sleep. I'll make sure no one bothers you."

He left without giving them time to respond.

Dejah hopped off the bed and looked Kold right in the eyes.

"We have to find Ammalee!" Her eyes were bright, and she spoke with the stubborn tone of a child who got whatever they wanted if they asked long enough.

He grabbed her and had her sit back down, and then, more quietly, "You heard the man, we can't talk about that here."

"But you promised! You promised you'd help me find her."

"Shh. Be quiet! Dejah, we're here. We've made it into the past. We can breathe the air. Tomorrow, we will see the sun for the first time. We have everything we need, and we need to make sure we keep it that way. We don't need to stir up trouble talking about our faith."

"But you promised!"

"We're not talking about it—not here."

Dejah got quiet. She sat back down on the bed, but this time on the far side, away from Kold. She whispered, "I wish Dad were here."

If only she knew the truth about their dad—a person of faith, sure, but he was far from perfect. She should be glad he wasn't there.

That night, Kold dreamed about his dad, and unlike the dreams in the suit, he couldn't control them. His dad was praying and talking to him, and none of it made any sense, but it made him want to cry, and he couldn't get him to stop. He woke up covered in sweat, struggling to breathe.

He was afraid to fall asleep again after that.

#

Kold and Dejah sat on the front steps of the dorm. The sun was returning, and they wanted to be there to watch it sneak past the buildings. With each inch it went up, their eyes squinted to adjust. Soon, it was so bright that they could only see white. It was warm, like the embrace of a Devos, but a hundred times better. He felt his bad dreams and uneasy fears burn away. He took a deep breath.

"We made it," said Kold. And he had done it without his dad, and while he would never say that to Dejah, he couldn't help but wish she appreciated it. He was all she had anymore.

"Yes, we made it," said Dejah, smiling.

Kold turned to her, and his eyes adjusted.

"Look, I'm sorry about last night. I know I promised we'd look for Ammalee." He put his arms around Dejah. "But you know that there's no reason to believe that we will find her. If she lived during this time, she lived a very private life, and what are the odds she'd be close by? This part of the world is massive, and we don't have suits to help us walk it."

"I know," said Dejah. "But we are going to look for her, right? We have to keep looking."

"Sure—I doubt I'll be able to stop you."

Her frustration turned to a smile, and she hugged him.

Kold turned back to the sun, and his stomach growled. He took out the last of the bar Whitt had given them. It was hard to swallow, but he got a few more pieces down and handed some to Dejah. He leaned on his arms, turning his head up towards the sun, and, with his eyes closed, let the warmth embrace him.

"I'd be careful if I were you," said Whitt.

They turned and let their eyes adjust to the hallway's darkness behind them.

"You're gonna burn if you don't get out of the sun."

"What?" asked Kold.

"It's going to burn you. Your skin isn't used to it, not like the residents, and even the lighter ones have to be careful. And if you're in the sun too long, it'll burn you. Likely to reach 310 Kelvins today."

Dejah leaned in and whispered into Kold's ear again, "tongues of fire above their heads..."

"Shh. Not here."

"But it's just like we were told—tongues of fire!"

"Be quiet, Dej."

"You two need to practice it a little more on your whispering," said Whitt.

They turned again. Whitt looked around and then leaned down towards them. "But there are a lot of things that Ammaleans will say are true: Sun burns. I've heard it—tongues of fire. I heard a lot of other things too. That's not the worst of it. Look around: notice anything?"

They looked around. The dirt road stretched on with buildings lining it as far as they could see. There were only a few visitors out walking—not nearly as many as last night. And they were all draped, from head to toe, in white cloth.

"You don't notice? There are no babies! The only children we get come through the void—like you. Now, I know what you're thinking: We don't have our suits, so how would we incubate one? Well, I'll tell you how! The old-fashioned way! Did they teach you that in your dreams?"

"Of course," said Kold. Except that he didn't learn it from his dreams. He learned about it from the older man behind him in the line. Before he ran out of supplements, he liked to use the comms, talking to Kold as often as Kold would allow.

"Well, that part works—with enough practice, and once your bodies are done waking up—and it's great; something you're gonna need to figure out, both of you, eventually. But still no children… Why, you ask? Well, the residents won't tell us anything. But we got our theories. Some say it's because our bodies evolved too much. But others say it's…" He looked around again, then bent down and started whispering. "They say…. It's for the same reason they keep us locked up in this compound. They don't want us mixing with society, or we will mess everything up. Of course, we all know that isn't how time works. The present is the one responsible for the future, not the other way around! But the residents don't listen to reason. What I'm saying is they don't want us leaving here, or living here more than we must." He stretched his neck back into the dorm to make sure no one was coming down the hall before continuing. He lowered his voice. "So, it would make sense that back in the hospital, they made sure we couldn't give birth. Maybe it's in the medicine they gave us. Or maybe it was some operation—oh, don't look surprised! They are so worried we will impact the way things are; it's only logical. They wouldn't want to keep us here forever—for generations, I mean. But, as a faithful, that's where you say, 'They are cutting off our children' and well, depending on how you look at it, I'd have to agree with you. But, you didn't hear that from Whitt, did you? You didn't hear that from me! Not any of it." He held his hands up to his mouth to keep him from talking anymore. "Ain't gonna say anything else," he said, through his fingers. "And just in time, too." He pointed towards the road. "Looks like you've got to get yourself ready for intake."

Rolling up to their dorm was P45. Whitt leaned in. "I wouldn't say anything like this around P45, but you're gonna love your immigration officer—she's good people." And with that, he disappeared into the building.

#

Kold and Dejah were escorted to the immigration building after a brief breakfast and ended up in a room with a row of chairs, where they waited for their appointment. Their throats hurt from eating, and to make it worse, they were still hungry as if the pain was for nothing.

The sun had shone on them the entire walk, leaving their white skin bright red. Kold watched Dejah press the sunburnt parts of her forearm. With each impression, her skin turned white, and then red again when she lifted her finger.

P45 entered the waiting room. "She will see you now."

He escorted them into a small room with a table in the center. At the table, a woman sat behind a stack of white, leaf-like material, and then a small screen with a pad of buttons. Kold looked at the buttons and recognized the letters on them as the ancestors' alphabet.

The woman started talking in the ancestors' language, and Kold thought he could understand what she was saying, but P45 interpreted her before he could piece it together. "I will be translating for Officer Maya," explained P45. "She said, 'Please come in, and have a seat. I will be with you in a moment.'"

This was the first resident they got to see up close. Her skin was dark—far darker than most of the residents he had seen. She had long black hair, as well as the little patches above her eyes. She even had hair on her eyes! And when he looked closer, he saw other places as well.

"I love her hair," whispered Dejah to Kold. She had practiced controlling her volume, but not enough to be successful in an otherwise quiet room. Officer Maya looked up at the comment and at P45, who started to translate, but then she lifted a finger to stop him.

She brushed her hair behind her, tied it back, and put on a hat.

As she talked, P45 translated, often overlapping her words.

"Sorry, I know the hair can be a distraction. Please don't let it be."

She closed her computer.

"It is nice to meet you, Dejah and Kold. Welcome to the year 2066. I see you found your dorm last night and made it to the cafeteria this morning. I hope Whitt was of assistance—he is a bit to handle at times, but he means well. I know eating can be difficult at first, but I'd encourage you to take your time and let your throat heal. Do you understand?"

Kold was sure he could understand a lot of the words she was saying, but her accent was thick and nothing like the pronunciation he had learned from his dad. But it was similar enough if only P45 stopped translating over her, and he had time to listen.

"Now, I'm told by your guide that you are faithfuls." She shuffled through her papers and found their housing form. "If that's the case, we need to get you moved immediately. You won't be safe where you are. Faithfuls don't do well in the general population." She turned to P45, speaking in her native tongue, and Kold tried to listen. It seemed Maya was worried about their safety in the current dorm, but P45 said the transfer process would take longer than the officer wanted. Then they argued and talked too quickly for Kold to understand. He was so set on translating them that he was startled when Dejah grabbed his arm and nearly knocked him out of his chair.

"Is she alright?" asked Officer Maya.

Dejah pulled Kold close and whispered into his ear again.

"Look!" she pointed to one of the white, leaf-like sheets on her desk. Written in the top corner, it read "name" or more accurately translated "in the name of" and next to it, written in an almost indistinguishable scribble—"Ammalee," said Dejah, in a forced whisper.

"Yes, Ammalee—your religion," said the Officer. "But it'd be wise not to say that outside of this room."

Right in front of him was a sheet of paper with the name he had recited a thousand times. It read, "In the name of Ammalee." He swallowed and reached for the desk, running his finger across the paper. He could only assume it was a list of inmates, possibly even those in his block.

They knew very little about the original Ammalee, for her life was shrouded in secrecy. She was honored for saving thousands, but the stories were written down only many years later, and they were unreliable at best, especially in any historical sense. Most reputable scholars abandoned attempts to find the historical Ammalee. She was more likely a metaphor or a combination of different leaders all woven into a single story.

"We need to get you transferred," said the officer, "And until we do, you need to keep your faith to yourself."

He touched the name and couldn't make sense of it. She might be here, of all places, right here. Everything he had pushed down inside of him began to crawl back to the surface, and he began to speak.

"This name." The words stumbled out in the language of the ancestors, "Ammalee," pointing to the paper. "Do you know it? *Adiists'a*?"

"What did you say?" asked the officer, surprised to hear him speak in words she could understand.

"This name: Ammalee. *adiists'a*?" he asked again.

She grabbed the paper, looked at it, then at P45, and hid it under her stack of papers. "Never mind that. Do you speak my language?"

P45 started to translate, but she waved her hand again to stop him.

"*Adiists'a*'. Yes," Kold said. "Can you introduce us to Ammalee? *Bik'is* Ammalee?"

"No. Absolutely not. And you really shouldn't discuss such things here." She smiled, but it wasn't a warm smile, more like a polite one that hid the judgment behind it. She was annoyed. Across the barriers of time and language, he could tell. She was as annoyed as everyone else who was forced to interact with his people. Kold felt his cheeks turn red.

"Ammalee—we must find her!" yelled Dejah.

"Quiet Dejah."

"This meeting is over. 45, please escort them out."

With that, she left the room.

#

Dejah was standing against the small window while Kold kicked his bed. He looked for something to throw, but the room was sparse. So he kicked the bed again before slumping to the ground and resting his head against the bed frame. Dejah walked up and placed her hand on his back. Then she sat down and rested her head against him.

"That was so stupid. What got into me?"

"She has to help us," said Dejah. "She has to introduce us to Ammalee—she has to."

He turned around and grabbed hold of her.

"No, she doesn't. How stupid do you have to be? That could have been anyone! Anyone today could have that name. We know nothing about the real Ammalee, and we will never find her. All we have are made-up stories designed to make people feel good—and they can't help us now! This is our life now. All of this, with everyone else. We have to accept it, Dejah. We have to accept it." He shook her while he talked, and she started to cry.

When he let go, she went back to the window and slouched under it. "We have to move on," he said.

Kold crawled into bed and pulled the sheet up over his head.

His stomach ached. His arms and legs were sore. His head felt fuzzy, and there was nowhere to escape to. He wanted to cry.

He didn't know he had fallen asleep. His dreams felt similar to his time in the virtual when he sat under a tree, except in his dreams, he was unable to make the sun shine. He failed to make anything different. So he slept in a dream as dark as the world he had just left. When he woke up, he turned over and lifted the sheet to look for his sister. He assumed to find Dejah under the window. But she wasn't there.

He threw the sheets off and got out of bed.

She wasn't in the top bunk either.

He ran down to the public bath and then out to the front door of the dorm.

She wasn't anywhere. She had run away—again.

#

This wasn't the first time she'd run away. He remembered when she tried to do it back in the colony. He couldn't convince her to stay—she insisted on making it to the cave, and traveling the void, even though their dad wasn't around to take her. In the end, he left only because he knew he couldn't let her go alone.

He ran to the immigration building, hoping to find her there. She would seek out information about Ammalee, which means she wouldn't leave the immigration officer alone until she agreed to help. He peered around every corner of every building but didn't see her—or many other visitors. The sun was directly overhead, and he could feel it burning his skin.

When he arrived, Dejah wasn't there, and what made matters worse, their officer wasn't at her desk either. She had just left and wouldn't return until the following day. A bot at the front desk scheduled him for a meeting and explained he could file the paperwork for a missing child with her then.

He went back to his dorm and looked for Whitt, but couldn't find him. He knocked on Frill's door to see if he knew where Whitt was, but he threw him out into the hall so hard that Kold hit his head against the corner of the hallway, cutting his head open. He felt the blood drip down the back of his neck.

He got up, went to his room, shut the door, grabbed the sheet from his bed, threw it over himself, and wished to be back home, in his suit, where things made sense. He wished he could disappear. He wished he could find a place to sit, free from all of this. He didn't know what to do. He didn't know who to ask for help. He didn't know how to make things right. So he sat up on his knees, the sheet still covering him, as if to hide his posture from the world. With the sheet forming a tent draped over his head, and blood bleeding through it, he grabbed the pebble Dejah had given him in the cave, and placed it carefully in front of him. He bent his head to the floor and spread out his arms, waving them slowly. Against all that he believed, he threw out a prayer in the direction where the sun returned each day. "To the God of Ammalee…" and began to sing quietly. For a short moment, he felt himself disappear, like a dream, as peace began to wash over him. But then he was jolted into the present when he heard his door creak open.

"Well, what do we have here?" asked Frill.

Kold threw the sheet off and turned to the door.

"I come in here to apologize for tossing you earlier, only to find out that you're one of them?"

Kold sat up and turned around. The other man from earlier walked up and stood behind Frill in the doorway.

"I'm not like other faithfuls," said Kold.

"So you are one of them!" said the other man. "What are we going to do with him, Frill?"

"I'd say he requires a little history lesson." Frill pulled out the cord that wrapped around his waist.

"Well, I've always loved teaching a little history," said the other man, laughing.

Kold jumped back against the wall. He knew this would happen eventually, and at this point, was glad to welcome it. He deserved to be punished—for believing, for scaring his sister, for all of it. "Just do whatever you need to do and get it over with!" said Kold, turning his head away to protect himself from what would come next.

But Frill paused.

"You want to know what pisses us off so much about the faithfuls?" asked Frill.

Kold stared at his feet, teeth clenched, waiting.

It wouldn't be the first time he was beaten because of his family's faith.

"It's not the fact that you people ran the government in the end, or even the fact that your leaders used the false promises of heaven on Earth to keep us from leaving this rock when everyone else had—no, that's just the tip of the mountain peak. What really pisses us off is the fact that you think you are so special." He whipped the cord, snapping it inches from Kold's face. "That everything you see belongs to you, as if the world were made for you, as if you were perfect, no matter what terrible things you did."

Kold looked up and locked eyes with him, relaxing his stance. He let out a sigh. He agreed with Frill. He had never been able to put it into words until now. This is what he hated about his family. That's why he hated his dad—no matter how much he did to hurt Kold, he always asked for forgiveness and would go on as if he had never done anything wrong. It was sick.

"You ain't perfect," continued Frill, "And that's the difference between you and me: I know what kind of animal I am." Frill took a few more steps into the room, and the other man followed, closing the door behind them. It nearly latched when a small metal rod poked through the narrowing crack. It pushed the door open.

"Kold?" asked P45. His screen turned to the men standing over him. "Do I detect a problem?"

They backed away and lowered their arms. "No problem, bot. Just checking in with our friend here."

"I think it's wise to check in on someone else, if possible," said P45, his taser now ready.

Frill and the other man left.

"Your officer has returned early. She will see you now. Please come with me."

#

Kold sat at the table, and across from him was an empty chair. Next to the chair stood P45. The Officer entered with her handheld screen and placed it on the table. She didn't make eye contact with Kold until she had sat down and adjusted the papers on her desk. "Kold, I understand your sister has gone missing? I'm sorry. Let me explain how this will work." She reached for her stack of papers and then shuffled through them. She turned to P45. Kold tried his best to translate their conversation, but it was brief. All he could make out was that she needed something that was left somewhere else, and she wanted P45 to get it. P45 disagreed, for he wasn't supposed to leave the room during a session, but in the end, she insisted, and he left.

She turned to Kold. She reached across the table and took his hands.

"We have a few moments alone, so listen. Do you understand? *Adiists'a'*?"

He thought for a second, translating her words, and then responded, "Yes, I adiists'a'."

"You can find your sister at the Immigration Building 457. Go there tonight. This evening, when the sun runs away, and the moon is here." She pointed to the ceiling above her. "When the moon is here, go to the back of building 457. *Adiists'a'*?"

"Yes. Adiists'a'."

"Exactly 4-5-7. Be there. Don't tell anyone. Especially 45."

He nodded.

At that, P45 entered the room, and she straightened up and stopped talking. They filed the paperwork for a missing person and then escorted him outside. He couldn't go back to his dorm. He sat in the shade of a nearby building until evening. The moments passed like days.

He prayed again, not by kneeling this time, but in his mind, like he had taught his sister.

He prayed she was safe.

#

The air was crisp, and Kold's clothes were too thin for the light breeze. He held his arms around his chest as he stood behind Building 457. A few yards from the building, a cliff towered over him, and above that, the compound's fence was visible only as a dark silhouette against the midnight sky.

In the stillness, he heard his name.

"Kold," said someone. He turned towards the rock wall. "Over here," they said again.

Kold ran up to the voice. It was Whitt, from his dorm. "Do you have Dejah? Give her back, Whitt! Give her back!"

"Calm down. Calm down. She's right here." From behind Whitt, Dejah ran to Kold.

"Dejah!"

"Quiet, quiet—we don't want to draw attention."

"Where have you been?" he asked her.

"I didn't come back—I told them I couldn't. I was afraid you wouldn't leave with me if I did."

"Leave?" he turned to Whitt, "What have you been doing with Dejah?"

"Me? I was doing nothing, and I don't appreciate your tone. Now, are you ready?"

"Ready for what?"

Whitt laughed. "You don't know what's going on, do you? Did she not tell you?"

"She hasn't told me anything!"

"Your time has come, my friend—much sooner than most, but it's for the best, I promise you. Transfers are tricky, and you won't survive praying back at your dorm—not someone as young as you two. Now come!" Whitt grabbed him and pulled him to the rock wall, with Dejah in tow. Near the crevice of the rock, a small cave opened up. A few meters into the cave, a metal grate blocked a cement pipe.

"What is this?" asked Kold.

Dejah pulled on his shirt, and Kold bent down to her. "Ammalee— she's real. She sent me to Whitt and then sent for you—we're leaving,

Kold. She's delivering us, just as the stories said."

"You met Ammalee?"

She didn't have time to respond, for Whitt pushed them towards the gate, unlocked it, explained what to do and which turns to make, but not much else. His urgency kept them moving forward with no time to talk.

"I don't understand," said Kold.

"It's not my job to make you understand. It's my job to get you out." With that, he shoved Kold into the tunnel and closed the gate behind them. "Or at least that's my understanding of it," continued Whitt, "I don't understand half of what she says—not without the help of a translator—and that wouldn't do us any good. Those bots aren't any help to us, not without the right paperwork signed and stamped. No, I don't know the ancient language as well as you. It's rather impressive, I hear."

"What do you mean?"

"Oh, you think you're the first to come who had been trained in the prayers of Ammalee? You think you're the first to see her name on the paper, as if it were placed in front of you by accident? You would be foolish to think so. You aren't the first, and you won't be the last. One day, when my service is complete, it will be my turn! Now get!" And with that, he locked the gate and ran off into the darkness, and Kold and Dejah had no option but to head down the tunnel.

#

The tunnel wound down and soon filled with water. Kold waded through it and carried Dejah into the deep parts. They felt the cool walls and the thick water beneath their feet, and there was no way to escape the darkness. There was no way except forward. Kold prayed, hoping it would distract him enough to keep going into the darkness, until they turned a corner and saw a light. When they arrived at the end, there was a similar gate, and on the other side, someone stood waiting. She unlocked the gate, and she moved into a nearby lamp that lit her face.

It was their immigration officer.

"Officer Maya?" asked Kold.

"Yes," she said, with a big smile. "But there's no need for the use of such titles here." She reached out to shake his hand, and he received it, as

Whitt had taught him. "Just call me Maya," she said.

"What is going on?"

"I'll explain everything when we get out of here. But for now, hurry and get in."

She gestured to a large metal-and-glass box on wheels. The back of the box had a latch, and she opened it. Then she lifted the box's floor to reveal a compartment.

They climbed into cramped quarters, and for a moment, he felt he was back in his suit—cramped and comfortable. But this time, squeezed in with his sister, his arms around her, and another old man squeezed behind him, much like the cave, except hot as hell, and their skin touching through their thin clothes in ways he found unpleasant.

He looked up at the Officer.

"Why are you doing this?" he asked again. He sat up, letting go of his sister. "Do you know Ammalee? Is she real? Was that her name on the paper?"

She paused and then leaned in. "Yes, it was. You read it very well—and I'm sorry for lying to you back then, but I had to—at least with P45 in the room."

"When will we meet her?" asked Kold, somehow still embarrassed even to ask.

She began to talk but paused. She shook her head, looked at the watch on her wrist, and back at them. "Soon, but first we need to get you out of here. You're not safe—and you haven't seen the worst of it. We have to hurry." Dejah looked like she was trying to hold back a smile. Kold couldn't figure out what was funny about any of this.

Maya gestured for him to lie back down and leaned in to close the fake floor, and when she did, her name tag, which was attached to her waist on a long retractable cord, got within a few inches of Kold's face. Under her title, it had her full name, which he hadn't noticed before. It read "Officer Amaya Leah Nez."

"Amaya Leah?" asked Kold, sitting back up.

Maya smiled again. "Yes, and I'll explain everything when we have time. Now, you must be quiet." Dejah let out a big laugh, as if she had always known, and Kold was foolish for not realizing it sooner. She didn't laugh long, though, for Maya gave her a stern look, and she got quiet. A second later, she closed the floor and latched the hatch.

They sat in the darkness, a feeling they knew all too well, as the car bounced along a dirt road. Soon they stopped while official-sounding voices chatted on all sides of the vehicle, but eventually started moving again. They sat in silence for most of it, until Kold finally spoke up.

"I'm sorry, Dejah." He reached into his pocket and handed her the pebble.

She pushed it back. "You keep it. You need it more than I."

He smiled and looked at it before placing it back in his pocket, wiping the tears forming in his eyes. "I'm sorry for everything."

"I know."

She said it like she always said, "I know"—the way she responds when she knew she was right all along. All he ever wanted to do was to keep Dejah safe, but in the end, it was her faith that got them out of the camp, not his.

#

Maya lived on a farm two hours north of the compound and a short walk from her parents' ranch. A few trees grew along the road that led to her garage. One large tree grew next to her house. Its branches reached out towards the horizon and cast a deep shadow on hot summer days. Thin patches of grass grew under the tree, and sharp, thick stalks of green leaves grew out of the ground like tongues coming out of the dirt. Many other plants grew nearby, many of them sharp to the touch.

Dejah and Kold never adjusted to the sun and spent many days under the large tree. Other visitors would come, but over time, they would leave, sneaking to a network of safe houses. Most were children, the elderly, or the sick—visitors who would not survive in the compound. Many of them were faithfuls, but not all. She saved anyone she could figure out how to, without getting caught. Oh, if only some of them knew it was *Ammalee* who was keeping them, they would have been so mad!

All in all, Maya smuggled 5,000 visitors out of that compound.

Ten years after their escape, visitors stopped arriving from the void. Everyone assumed it was a sign of the end. That the future finally collapsed, maybe the towers failed, and the last of the humans died, frozen in their suits. They couldn't know for sure, but over time, the compound grew smaller and smaller until it was closed down for good.

Maya had three small children with her husband. Her kids became friends with Kold and Dejah and learned the stories of their mother. Eventually, Maya's children shared these stories with their children, grandchildren, and great-grandchildren. For generations, this faith traversed the known solar systems, until one day, hundreds of years in the future, it returned to Earth, and a little boy named Kold heard the stories for himself.

Epilogue

You might have guessed how I fit into all of this. I'd consider you a fool if you haven't—or at least accuse you of not paying attention. I was born after the Sun died, and I was among the first to navigate the void. At the time, it was nothing but a rumor whispered among families. It was only later that the line formed.

I arrived before the construction of that dreadful camp.

In time, I found a place to settle, and—much to my own bewilderment—I found someone with whom to share the rest of my life. I married Maya, yes, *that* Maya—my beloved Amaya Leah, who first saw me lying in the dirt outside the cave and nursed me back to life. You could say I was the first person she saved, and you wouldn't be wrong.

It was only years later that we rescued Kold and Dejah, second cousins, whom I had never met but knew about. I offer these stories to them, and to all my other ancestors, who, in the strange twist of time, are also my descendants.

Our family's pendulum is less a swing and more the hand of a clock spinning in continuous circles. When the world ended, I was cast back to this time. That is Ammalee's gift: survival through repetition, lives folded back upon themselves. As Emmanuel always taught, when we leave one world, we are welcomed into another, not on identical paths, but in spirals.

Yet in all those loops, the world keeps ending, as far as I can tell. I fear our ancestors are neither equipped nor concerned enough to prevent it. It's not for lack of information. We all could see it coming, but the present needs always outweighed the future, and investors needed their profit margins, in the same way as children need their ice cream—which is to say, they'd be better off without. That's the cost of comfort; it's so very addicting.

If left to us, I worry that the circle of time cannot be shifted, that we will always be far too much like our ancestor Hondo and not enough like his friend Zeke, unwilling to risk our comforts for real change. I don't say this to discourage you. I say this so that you are challenged to prove me wrong. *Oh, how I wish you would prove me wrong!*

My wife often speaks of the four worlds her people traveled through, each a threshold that must be crossed to enter the next. Now, with us together, our children joining the great line of ancestors, and you carrying more than enough stories to give you pause and concern, I can't help but wonder how it might be different.

We might change the world.

As long as it's not too uncomfortable, of course.

Appendix

Our Genealogy

The Chronicle of the Generations of the Profetas begins with John "Proff" Profeta, who was both the First and the Last, for in the year 3656, he traveled to 2055 and became the root and the fruit of his own line. Amaya took to herself John "Proff" Profeta, the traveler through time, and they had a child, Thomiel (2059), a quiet man of the desert plains of New Mexico. Thomiel fathered Ronan (2094), who fathered Asher (2135), who fathered Ellen (2169), whose ancestors carried the Profeta name down 10 more generations: Tenis (2207), Joplin (2239), Afil (2284), Kelp (2315), Trinity (2355), Pneuma (2392), Hold (2425), Gilt (2455), and Hope (2495), until Gavriel (2530) is born, a shepherd of machines and simple bots. Gavriel fathered the one known only as *The Man* (estimated birth: 2565), whose name was forgotten in the records, for in the year 2605, he fled the ordered cities and made his dwelling in a Disconnected Village. *The Man* fathered Mara (2610), who mothered Trillian (2635), who mothered Hamlet (2661), who fathered Isabell "Birdie" Pinkert in the year 2693. Birdie lived after the manner of the people of the Village, but in her youth, she fled outward to join the great Network in the year 2713.

Birdie mothered Seren (2718), and Seren mothered Emmanuel and Calvin Profeta in the year 2743. They grew up and went to college along the Western Coast for programming, but Emmanuel went on to

Seminary, becoming a person of faith like his grandmother. His twin, Calvin, became a robotics specialist and founder of Lossless Technology. From the vantage of the autonomous bots, he was considered their "Creator." Calvin died with his brother alongside the bots he created, but not before his greatest achievement, designing the largest ship ever to leave Earth's orbit—Star City—whose destination was hundreds of years away, and it may still be traveling through space, looking for a home. Calvin's son, Zander (2771), became its first Commander. What became of Zander and his Profeta line is far beyond this narrator's scope, but I can only imagine it would make for quite a spectacular story. In the year 2790, Emmanuel and Calvin died alongside the persecuted sentient machines.

Emmanuel and his partner fathered Joan (2785) and Ron (2787) through the same surrogate. Joan left the coast before the final evacuation to the Midwest, where her first husband was from. Dean came with her, and she cared for him until his death. And soon her brother Ron moved nearby as well. Joan mothered Harper in 2812, who followed his dad, from Earth to the Asteroid Belt in 2831, where miners sought rare ores and the sentient bots were outlawed. Through Harper, Rehe, the Clone, gave birth to Arya in 2831, but was forced to give her up as she was considered a minor, even though she had the body of a 23-year-old.

Arya moved to Primara in 2852, at the age of 21, after being granted adulthood. Arya mothered Maisie, who, when grown, departed for Proximata in 2897. She bore two children, her son, Huxley Jr. (2899), and her daughter, Sera (2898).

Sera bore Elsbeth (2935), who bore Primrose (2960), who married into a wealthy family and, with her husband, traveled the Three Systems until he died in 3035. Primrose mothered Caleb (2995), the first to travel the timeline. Caleb fathered Iris (3023) the first to be born on Earth, who mothered Hondo in the year 3051. Their research and detailed notes contributed significantly to this collection.

Hondo fathered Marylyn in 3109 and Linus in 3106. Linus worked at the Projection Control Chamber in Buenos Aires, where all timeline projections originated, but died in the early years of the nuclear wars. Marylyn lived to see the Arcs rise in 3133. Marylyn rescued Kiln from the atomic fallout, and together they became the ancestors of a long line that would stretch across centuries: Astrell (3154), a child of the Arc Era, Junel (3187), Calyx (3215), Theron (3240), a scholar of the Second Migration, Liora (3264), Sennetin (3290) as people began to migrate back into Earth's solar system in preparation for its eventual terraforming.

Sennetin fathered Vara (3325), and Vara, nearing the end of her travels around Mars, mothered Maelin (3346). Maelin mothered Abner (3378), a man who grew up around the orbit of Mars. Abner took no spouse and sired no children. The line followed Abner's sister, Mary (3371). After her years among the Martian rings, she mothered Ruthen in 3401. He fathered Selith (3428), who fathered Ion (3460), who fathered Merev (3483), who mothered Tallis in 3508, who fathered Lira (3529), the first citizen of New Earth. Lira mothered Aramon, the Poet, (3557), who read his works at the Great Banquet, prophesied in Revelations 19:17.

Aramon fathered Alexis (3592) when nuclear wars and the volatile chemistry of time travel had altered the solar reaction, like a chemistry experiment gone wrong, and without anyone knowing until it was almost too late, the Sun leapt ahead of its appointed age and went dark. Alexis mothered Kora (3628) in the dimming years, and Kora mothered Kold (3649) and his sister Dejah (3654), where humanity survived only in exoskeletons, and no star system welcomed them. In that dark generation, when all other worlds sealed their gates, Kold and Dejah discovered the path of the black void, long foretold by the prayers of Ammalee. In their youth, in the year 3666, they stepped backward through the ages, seeking the one from whom all their line began.

It was eleven years earlier that Kold's second uncle, John "Proff" Profeta also journeyed backward through the black void. He married Amaya Leah, who would later be known as Ammalee. She was a native— in time and space—to the past. She would become the mother of them all, the beginning and the end of this genealogy, the first and the last, the ancestor who is also a descendant, the root who is also the branch.

Acknowledgments

This collection would not exist without a handful of people who believed in my writing long before it learned to behave itself.

First, to Emily Jones from The Worlds Within, who was brave (or reckless) enough to be the first to publish my fiction in the Ohio Writers' Association's *Outcasts*. The short story *"The Priest and the Robot"* appears in that Anthology first, because she said yes when saying no would have been safer. For that early confidence—and for opening a door I didn't know how to knock on yet—I am deeply grateful.

To the Ohio Writers' Association, which has become a wonderfully diverse and generous community of writers. I would not be the writer I am today without OWA.

To James Graves, my brother and phenomenal graphic designer. His support in not only designing the cover, but in helping me think strategically about the marketing, has made a world of difference. This book would not be what it is without his support and generosity. As a thanks, go follow him on Instagram. You won't regret it. @visualjams

To Finn, my nine-year-old son, who read some of these stories and offered the most honest literary critique I've ever received: *"I don't like your cooking, but I do like your writing."* For the record, I am not a bad cook. He simply lacks a fully developed palate. Still, praise is praise, and I'll take it.

To my wife, Allyssa, who has encouraged and supported my writing in a thousand quiet ways, served as my copyeditor, and gave up countless hours together so I could write.

And finally, to everyone who has ever read my work, including you, right now. There is no greater joy for a writer than knowing their words have been read. Thank you for taking the time to read these stories.